Changeling Eleven Changeling Eleven Chang

Series editor: Allan Cameron

www.vagabondvoices.co.uk/think-in-translation

Memoirs of a Young Man

by Ričardas Gavelis

translated by Jayde Will

Vagabond Voices
Glasgow

First published in 1989 as *Jauno žmogaus memuarai* © the heirs of
Ričardas Gavelis

Translation copyright © Vagabond Voices 2018
This edition published in April 2018 by
Vagabond Voices Publishing Ltd.,
Glasgow,
Scotland

ISBN 978-1-908251-81-7

Printed and bound in Poland

Cover design by Mark Mechan

Typeset by Park Productions

The publisher acknowledges subsidy towards
this publication from Creative Scotland

The publisher acknowledges subsidy
towards the translation from the
Lithuanian Culture Institute

For further information on Vagabond Voices, see the website,
www.vagabondvoices.co.uk

In memoriam L.C.

Contents

Introduction

Memoirs of a Life Cut Short, which was written in 1987–88, is narrated through letters sent from beyond the grave by Levas Ciparis to his estranged friend, Tomas Kelertas. The idea was suggested to the author, Ričardas Gavelis, by an unhappy event: his friend Leon died in Moscow in November 1982 at the age of thirty. The tragedy was compounded for Gavelis by their lack of contact over the previous five years and for Leon's family by the coincidental death that same day of Leonid Brezhnev, whose corrupt and stultifying reign is the object of Gavelis's satire. The potentate's funeral lasted for five days, preventing Leon's family from commencing their own more modest bereavement. According to Gavelis's widow, Nijolė Gavelienė, the novel is full of Leon's life, thoughts and experiences, as he had always been very sincere and frank with the author, who in turn considered him a good and genuine person. We should not of course confuse the inspiration with the finished work; a novel is not written solely for those who understand its genesis.

When the author started on *Memoirs*, his manuscript for *Vilnius Poker* had already been relegated to a shelf at home, awaiting "better times" – more liberal times when such works could be published.* Both works were in fact published in 1989, a couple of years before the fall of the Soviet Union, and established Gavelis as an important and influential figure on Lithuanian literary scene, although behind him he already had a successful career as a writer, playwright and journalist spanning a quarter century.

* An English translation of *Vilnius Poker* was published Open Letter, Rochester, in 2009.

Memoirs was actually published a few months earlier than *Vilnius Poker*.

Some may think that there's little to be added to fiction's take on the Soviet Union, ranging from the classic Russian authors, starting very early with Yevgeny Zamyatin through to Bulgakov, Platonov, Pasternak, Solzhenitsyn, Trifonov and Grossman (the last two critical of the regime rather than fiercely against it), to foreign authors starting early with the Franco-Russian writer Victor Serge (actually a Belgian citizen of the world), Koestler, and of course our own George Orwell, who was motivated by his experience of Stalinist treachery in the Spanish Civil War. But they were writing of the brutal Stalin years; in *Memoirs*, Gavelis is the devastating critic of the stupidity and stasis of the Brezhnev ones. But this book is much more than that.

Placing *Memoirs* in the late period of anti-Soviet literature is quite logical for anglophone readers, but it risks understating the originality and scope of this work (though much of the genre was innovative and varied, partly because of the difficulties writers had to encounter and partly because it was their society and not the distant reality it would have been for the English-speaking reader). *Memoirs* could just as easily be seen as a highly evolved version of those European classics going back to the early twentieth century that initiated the tradition of the "inept" protagonist who cannot find a place for himself in the modern world. Inept protagonists can, like Charlie Chaplin, get into all kinds of scrapes resulting from their ineptitude, but come out on top following a series of absurdly luck-laden coincidences. Italo Svevo's *Confessions of Zeno* is the finest example of the more humorous take on the alienation of modern life, and Gavelis's protagonist, Levas Ciparis, does have some lucky breaks in the snakes and ladders of an absurd regime, which also produce the novel's more light-hearted but still mordantly satirical moments. Closer to this dark work, however, is Sartre's *Nausea*, in which an isolated intellectual has to confront the dull stupidity of a dull provincial town where all human feeling appears to be atrophied. But *Memoirs* is still some distance from that.

I would place this novel closer to a "minor" classic, Giuseppe Borgese's *Rubè*, in which the inept's ineptitude is overwhelming and unremitting, and the novel's concerns extend to the specific reality of a society and its regime, and conversely to a moral statement on the limitations of the human condition in all societies.

But Gavelis is very different even from the closest examples on one essential point: while in other works, the inept appears to be unique in his ineptitude although he very probably is a metaphor for widespread alienation in modern society, our writer is explicit in demonstrating that all his characters are alienated and can at best achieve a useful compromise with a regime which is to some extent a prisoner itself to its own twisted logic, and "twisted" is a word that recurs.

Tomas Kelertas, the man to whom these letters from beyond the grave are addressed, is a case in point. He, more than anyone, appears to be the master of nonchalance and manipulation who could find his way under any regime, and the early letters appear to confirm this interpretation. I don't want to write a spoiler on this central character (central because he and Levas, the dead letter-writer, are each other's foils, though he is absent from a good part of the narration), so I'll restrict myself to asserting that the reader's assessment of Tomas will evolve and in one particular moment undergo dramatic change, after which Levas's emotional dependency on him only appears to grow.

It becomes clear, particularly in the second half of the novel, that Levas represents feeling, naivety and perhaps innocence, whilst Tomas represents intellect and reason. Levas starts the book in accusatory mode, questioning Tomas's failure to engage with the regime and attempt to improve it. He despises the other's intellectual aloofness and perhaps envies his nonchalance. The characters are perfectly realistic and probably recognisable to most readers, but they are also symbolic of two approaches to tyranny, both valid in their own ways and both inevitably flawed. They can also coexist in the same person, perhaps they were both experienced by the author himself, and perhaps they could exist in all of us. There is certainly evidence in the text that this could be the case: Levas reveals towards the end of the book that he can only see those who think about him, or in other words life beyond death is conditional on being remembered and thought about, which is bad news for Levas, as it appears that Tomas has almost completely wiped him from his memory, having found him deficient and contemptible, whilst Levas obsesses about Tomas. Yet, if Levas can still observe Tomas and write him letters, Tomas must still think about Levas to some degree, and in fact the intellect must always be aware of the emotional dimension to us all, anything less would be irrational, and Tomas is extremely rational. Unlike the quixotic Levas, he knows how far he can go and he knows the limitations imposed by the regime that governs him. What Levas takes for aloofness in Tomas is in fact his friend's ability to create the highest degree of autonomy within an authoritarian state (or perhaps any human society, given the ubiquitous mechanisms of power). In the end, Levas admits two important discoveries: reason is the only route to inner freedom, and Tomas's aloofness is virtuous, because Tomas was never interested in power, only in ideas and the intellect.

Nijolė Gavelienė has provided us with the interesting information that associates Leon with Levas and therefore by extension Gavelis with his creation Tomas Kelertas. This has to be part of how we interpret the text, and yet Levas is not Leon, because Leon had family desperate to find out what had happened to him, while Levas had no one when he died. No one. The last person to give him some assistance – always provided on the basis of omniscient self-interest – was Father-in-Law. Levas was both something less and something more than Leon: something less because he was an invention of the author's imagination rather than a real person like Leon who had suffered and died young, and something more because he represents the suffering of all good men and women who, with the best intentions, self-criticism and a desire to belong, find their way continually blocked off.

If Levas and Tomas were the only archetypes in this world, it would probably be a fine place to live in, but there has to be another entity, another corner to make the triangle: the Nietzschean will to power, which for Gavelis is always a Faustian pact whereby the powerful lose their souls and create the machinery of oppression. This is represented by the character always referred to as Father-in-Law. All three of these characters are complex and full of surprises, but this is even truer of Father-in-Law who is definitely not a caricature of the archetypal bureaucrat (a word that Gavelis finds very unsatisfactory); he is intelligent, cunning and totally self-aware with only one emotional "flaw", his love for his daughter. At one point he expresses his disdain for Levas when Levas takes to reading subversive literature. Father-in-Law is not shocked, but disdainful of Levas's clichéd choice of texts: *1984* and *Yawning Heights*, which most readers of English certainly wouldn't consider a cliché and few would have heard of. It is imaginable that the second one, Alexander Zinoviev's Swiftian satire of the Soviet Union, was well known to those of dissident inclinations, and its author was certainly an eternal dissident: no sooner was he in the United States than he turned his critical eye on the West and when the Soviet Union fell, he returned to Russia to add to Yeltsin's problems. But Father-in-Law dismisses Orwell and Zinoviev not for their opinions, as he is above opinions, but because he considers those books "popular crap". He suggests that Levas pass by his home so that he can introduce him to the real stuff. Poor Levas feels a failure even when it comes to his foray into dissident literature.

Father-in-Law is something worse than the Soviet Union of the Brezhnev era, something more atavistic in that state's history. He is both cleverer and more evil, and his power feels omnipotent at least in Lithuania, in which nearly all the narrative unfolds (the two exceptions being Levas's trips to Leningrad). He is the third element of the triad on which Gavelis structures this novel. His soulless but lively intellect is probably the most unforgivable typology in the author's universe, but he is not alone in his thirst for power. The other example, a lesser character, is the Great Li, the Korean leader of a strange, "semi-underground sect". The distinction between Father-in-Law and the Great Li is similar to the one between Tomas and Levas. Father-in-Law is reason and the Great Li is emotion and feeling. Father-in-Law, one feels, was always corrupt, but the Great Li is corrupted by his success. Father-in-Law and Tomas survive in this "phantasmagorical" nation because they are rational, whilst the Great Li and Levas fail as they cannot fathom the unpredictability and relentlessness of the regime. Levas and Tomas, on the other hand, are incorruptible because they are not attracted to power, though both understand to differing levels of perception that they have to live with it. Power is the problem.

I have already suggested that the characters evolve through reality as Levas describes it, and they do so as the carefully calibrated narration intends. This leads us to another startling aspect of this work: the skill with which Gavelis dresses up a structured critique of all levels of a society as the random and perhaps inchoate ramblings of a lonely and mediocre intellect. The deceased letter-writer is an honest man, partly because of his self-confessed naivety, but he is also a confused and indeed unreliable narrator. This is what allows the other characters to evolve so credibly and so powerfully, as Levas discovers new things about them and indeed himself.

The final word on *Memoirs* must go to the author's widow: "The novel, *Memoirs of a Life Cut Short*, was written in a single breath, simple, clear and concise. You could find resonances of this one novel in all his future works, themes and metaphors. This novel is Ričardas's manifesto. Even today many people find this novel so daring, shocking and provocative that it disturbs and calls for deep reflection."

Allan Cameron, Glasgow, January 2018

Memoirs of a Young Man

The First: on teachers and students, on ecological niches and being yourself

Metals are united by their malleability,
beasts and birds by an aim, fools by fear
and greed, and honest people by a viewpoint

I always wanted to write you letters. In these tumultuous times, as everyone chatters over one another, failing to listen to when others speak, perhaps the only way to tell your story is by writing letters. No one can interrupt a letter, and they won't start arguing with it; they'll have to listen to your thoughts through to the end, whether they like it or not. I've thought that for a long time. I always wanted to write you letters, but I didn't send you even one. I started probably a hundred. I would write at night once my family were asleep, sometimes into the early morning. Then I would collapse for an hour or so to nap, overwhelmed by a strange elation, and yet the morning would unfortunately and unfailingly be wiser than the evening and have me tear up that letter, the fruit of so much mental anguish. I would throw it away, and only rarely would it survive until the afternoon, when the dustbin lorry passes. Sometimes I would burn it for greater effect. The paper would coil and become charred, and an unbearable stench would spread throughout the room. The paste ink from my ballpoint pen would smell horribly as it was burning

On more than one occasion, just after writing a letter, I colluded with the night to toss it in the postbox and then let happen what may. But as it turned out I didn't post a single one: I would see your thin, sceptical face before me, and I would sense the smoke of the smouldering cigarette in the corner of your mouth, almost knowing what you were going to answer. I destroyed those letters, I killed my thoughts, because you would have responded to them immediately.

I ached to write you letters, but I didn't want to get your replies.

Even if I had begged you not to reply, you wouldn't have held back. As you had a distressing lack of listeners, you would have spoken sooner or later. Which is why I didn't send you any. If I had sent one, I would have lurked around your postbox afterwards until they brought it so that I could take it out and tear it up. And that would have been totally laughable. You yourself liked to say that the worst thing in life is to be the object of other people's laughter. You can be proud – your pupil took note of this lesson well. Along with many of the others.

Along with many others!

You were my Teacher – could I have ever said that to you any earlier? To admit that to you, and then once again chat and argue with you like nothing happened? I didn't have the courage, I was uncomfortable, and perhaps I didn't even want to believe it myself: what kind of Teacher could a sullen man full of irony be, one almost the same age? I have come to believe it only now, after all that has been said and done.

In these sceptical times, it's a rare person who has a real live Teacher. The young don't want to listen to the old – and they're right in doing that. It's precisely the old that created this whole phantasmagoria, today modestly called the "period of stagnation" – only the mad or the suicidal would genuinely listen to them and learn from them. However, the young don't want to listen to other young people either – except perhaps to rock musicians. No rock musician could be a Teacher. He could be a megaphone or he could be a noticeboard – but never a Teacher.

They say that a true Teacher has to be like God. There

has to be a radiance emanating from him. No radiance even thought of emanating from you. You could be angry and unkind. You did bad things to a lot of people. And to me as well. What can we do? What is dear to us is dear, even if it brings affliction. After all, who doesn't value their body, even when beset by all kinds of ailments? You can dislike your body, you can even hate it now and again, but you have to value it. In this way you can fail to love your Teacher, even hate him now and again, but you always believe in him. I believed in you, which is why I perished. But a destructive faith is better than none at all.

No, I didn't pray to you, and I never listened to you unquestioningly. There were times I didn't agree with you, desired to argue with you, was enraged at you, or wouldn't listen to you, but you were still my Teacher. Now and again I would hate you, wanted to do bad things to you, and even kill you, but still you remained my Teacher. I doubt you knew that. I doubt you wanted to be one. You brought my ruin, though perhaps I should be thankful for that – at least I didn't turn into a living corpse.

You pushed me towards the Path, and what came of that – you know yourself.

I was always astonished by your ability to push other people towards an ideal, towards a resolute fight, to destruction, and remain the same as you were before: imperfect, sometimes abominable, sometimes appalling. Even now I don't understand what forced me to believe in you. I met any number of intellectuals in my life: quite a few madmen in the good sense too. I mingled with parapsychologists and hypnotists, but even they didn't manage to influence me in quite the same way.

You have a gift from God – you are a born Teacher. A Teacher without students – perhaps that's the only way one could exist during these catastrophically godless times. Perhaps that's best for you as well, and your possible students. I understand that this idea of mine is horrifying, however, it's probably right. You remained there, and I ended up here. We're both the same. We both killed our godly spark, both of us rose to flight and spattered on the ground far, far from our goals.

Teacher, your one and only student sends you greetings from the beyond.

I don't know when it all started. "It all", it seems, is none other than me myself. So I don't know when I started, was born, created myself. I don't know when a creature of the human race, having my first and last name, turned into the true "me". I remember one peaceful summer evening we both sat in our dormitory room and spoke precisely about that. I complained (or perhaps was surprised) that even up till then I didn't understand whether I really was me. It always appeared to me that some of my actions were controlled by another person who was distrustful, angry and dishonest. That alter ego was not just my dark side, my dark shadow. Sometimes he would appear to have been smarter than I was, sometimes more tender or jollier. He would often act better than I would have.

You seemed to be listening carefully, but then you shamelessly started picking your teeth. You felt my mortification at once and made a crooked smile. You always saw right through other people with relish, but most of the time you didn't heed them.

"Slowly the seedling of a new person is sprouting within you," you said tenderly. "Now and then it does something for you."

"I don't want any new person," I shot back angrily. "It's bad enough that I'm not able to deal with it by myself. That's all I need is another person to make it even worse."

"And how do you know that the 'other' is not your real you?" you uttered in a profound manner and, it seemed, immediately forgot what you had just said.

But I made a note of those words. More than once I

stubbornly interrogated you as to whether you ever felt some sort of effect from an outside creature.

"For fuck's sake!" you shot back, "I was always me." I took note of those words of yours too. My greatest misfortune was that I didn't become myself right away. No one taught us to be ourselves. We were taught to be this or that, and model ourselves on some sort of squalid or unearthly ideal model which we didn't think up ourselves. They taught us to change ourselves, break ourselves. They taught us to adapt.

However, they never taught us how to be ourselves.

It's by no means easy to be ourselves: we need great talent do that. Now I often think that all genius is simply the perfect ability to stay firmly, stubbornly true to ourselves until the very end.

"The biggest mistake people make," you once reluctantly explained, "is to stop at an ecological niche of the noosphere and try to establish themselves there at all costs, breaking themselves, befouling themselves, adapting themselves right to this very niche, the closest ecological niche. Especially if there is some sort of esteemed, reputable sign hanging above it. Energetic men sometimes start to reorder that very niche according to themselves. That's nonsense, a destructive intoxication. Patient and thorough people plod slowly through life, trying out ever more niches – perhaps one will appear suitable to them. Sometimes they find refuge this way, other times they remain without shelter.

"So what's the solution?" I asked naively.

"You need to create an individual niche for yourself," you retorted somewhat irritably.

"It's that simple?"

"My stubborn little goat," you grumbled without anger. "Simple? Don't forget that you will always be all alone in such a niche. Alone as can be. That's the deal."

I hastily rushed to explain that such an ecological niche is indecent, that it's shameful to occupy a place only for yourself, knowing full well that you can't invite anyone to come along... You interrupted me and suggested we listen to some music. It was probably '72. You put on the fourth album by Led Zeppelin.

Now I can write and write, and you won't interrupt me. You'd definitely interrupt if I was alive. You never knew how to listen to people. Well no, what was worse – you knew how, but too often you didn't want to listen to them. Writing letters definitely has advantages. Now I can say everything I want without being disturbed.

After all, it's very important who you talk to. I don't want to speak to just anyone. I don't want to talk to the void. I want to write letters precisely to you, because you were my Teacher.

By the way, I don't want to write just to you; I'm planning on writing to Lenin and Stalin, Nietzsche and Russell, Jesus Christ and Prince Myshkin. Most likely there have been more than a few that have written to them, but I'll try not to repeat other people's thoughts. Perhaps I will write to them someday. For the time being it hasn't gone particularly well. For the time being I'm still sharpening my quill.

As it must already be clear, I don't have a quill of any kind. So you can imagine how difficult it is to sharpen a non-existent quill.

You really can't answer me. That's not so good. I can't ask you if you want to read my letters.

So I'm not asking.

You have to read these letters. That's your duty. Who else will do it if not you? Who else, if not you, who deliberately or by accident taught me something, but who never taught me anything completely? Who else, if not you, who destroyed me, who casually expelled me to the other side? Who else if not you, the present-day opponent of Father-in-Law, the author of the famous opus *Perestroika in Albania*?

You will have to listen to me – whether you want to or not.

Otherwise I will start to haunt you. Even now you sense me, you should sense me. Even now you remember me often. You cannot fail to remember me. I'm haunting you ever so slightly even now. You recognise me in the figure of a lonely passer-by. You stop, irritated, and want to call me by name, though you know very well that it's not me, that I can't walk the streets of Vilnius. Suddenly you see the dent of my body on your sofa in the living room, as if I had just got up and left. You even think that you got a whiff of my scent and you hungrily pull in the air with your nostrils, much like a huge excited dog. You find an observation of mine recorded elegantly with a pencil in the margins of your book, and having forgotten that the person who wrote it is gone, you sit near the telephone, determined to challenge me. It always appears to you that I am somewhere nearby.

Essentially that's how it is. I didn't go anywhere, I am still here. But most importantly I can write you letters. I believe that you will read them. I know that you'll definitely read them.

The Second: on justice and GGI, on our family and my teenage masochism

*Each person possesses their own unique
thoughts in their head, each spring has its
own water, each family possesses its own
customs and traditions, and each person
has their own words on their lips.*

Imagine the following landscape – like it was perpendicular
or horizontal like in those elongated Chinese paintings:
the unwieldy mountains with many flat spots, climbing
upwards, a rocky frozen waterfall and pine trees, the fine,
barely visible pine trees, all the slopes dotted with them.
It all gives off a scent of eternal tranquillity. It's almost
lifeless. You might think that it's a closed, untouchable
world if not for the narrow strip of sky – high above, right at
the top of the silk scroll. That sky revitalises the landscape,
creates a breach into another, different kind of world, it
makes you believe that there, beyond the mountains, there
is something more. But for me, the pine trees are most
important: this one here, in a somewhat larger square,
more or less in the middle of the slope, leaning over the
abyss, looking down sadly into the endless melancholic
gullet. That pine tree doesn't want to be a pine tree, it
thinks that it's not right, it feels that it was not born only
as a green shoot, which is destined to only turn into a tree,
it wants to be a waterfall or a sky, it thinks that it's not
right to just be a tree.

You say I made that up? You say there isn't a pine tree in
the landscape that thinks like that?

You're wrong, I see it very well, it's there. I was that kind of pine tree.

I always desired justice. I wanted everyone to be equal. I wasn't so naive that I would want unrealistic equality. I always understood that some people are higher, others lower, some more beautiful, others uglier, some angrier, others more gentle – I didn't desire to make them equal and make them the same. I didn't want to turn mountains into rivers and rivers into forests. I understood that mountains can't flow like water and rivers can't blow like the wind.

I understood that regardless of whatever kind of race (in the race of life as well), winners and losers are unavoidable. That those who win are either more gifted by God and their father, or prepare more tenaciously for the fight, and train more rigorously. For me, it didn't appear painful or wrong to lose. However, my very being screamed that everyone, absolutely everyone, is required to have equal rights to participate in contests, and what's more important – equal rights and opportunities to prepare, to train rigorously for them.

I know that you never believed in that desired justice of mine. I remember very well your favourite saying: "Explain to me what justice is, and I will explain to you why it can't exist." I myself liked the concept you thought up – GGI – God's Grand Injustice. You would always proclaim that GGI was the foundation for the world order.

But I believed in justice, I desired justice, I strove for justice. In other words, I didn't listen to my Teacher.

Not listening to honest people is characteristic of all of us Lithuanians. We don't listen to those who are worthy of teaching us. We most often don't even hear them and we don't acknowledge them. And not because we think we are so wise, not needing lessons and advice at all. It's somewhat worse than that: we still do listen to lessons and advice, however, only from those people who are marked with some sort of sign of respect or worth, without thought as to who marked them with that sign. We judge words according to the embossed sign of others instead of judging the words for ourselves and granting them a sign of wisdom forever. We are still a herd, easily handled by a clever shepherd.

I blame you for not doing what you had to do, but I forgive you to a certain degree because you are fated to live as a Lithuanian among Lithuanians.

Far too often I didn't listen to you. I paid dearly for that. Actually, a student shouldn't blindly echo his teacher; he learns from his teacher. You said that GGI is an irreversible and insurmountable thing, so you needed to live stoically despite GGI, but I strove to replace that GGI. Our ambitions weren't so different, and certainly they weren't contrary to one another. We both went along the same Path, but at one crossing you sat down to smoke, and I trudged on further.

And you're still smoking at that crossing, while I ended up here, where I am. And who knows (for the time being who knows) what is better? By no means do I think that my case is better just because it's mine. But I also don't plan on humbly giving up prematurely only because I am here now, and you remained there. That doesn't prove anything. That's still just one fact among a plethora of other conflicting facts.

It seems I started to teach you logic and coherent reasoning. Forgive me. By no means did I become ill with a superiority complex. I'm only repeating out loud the lessons I learned well from you.

GGI already expressed itself in all its glory in my childhood. Strange (or perhaps it's only natural), but you don't know anything about my origins, parents, childhood. You never wanted to know about that. You weren't interested in the least.

It seemed to me that you secretly believed that man's fate, his life, doesn't depend on the place and time of his birth or on his environment at all, that it doesn't even depend on his genes. While flying in the cosmic expanses of metaphysical problems, it seems you gradually came to believe that it was too far beneath you to admit to the influence of the mechanical assembling of one's genes or a specific environment on such a great creature as man. You would call man trash and a worm out loud. You'd intentionally belittle and disparage him. But in the depths of your heart you most likely hoped very much that he was independent not only of earthly things, but even from the gods. You worshipped man silently, but constantly ridiculed him out loud. Your unspoken inner lessons were always more persuasive than your noisy lectures.

I don't dare to argue with you: perhaps man truly doesn't depend on anything. However, I want to understand when I really appeared. Was that big-headed, big-eared little Levas really me? To be more precise – was there even a tiny fraction of the real me in that big-eared kid?

Even now I don't remember everything that I went through – even those things that I'd really like to remember. I remember only what I remember. Perhaps a person's memory is made like that: it only saves what the real "I" experienced, carelessly throwing all the ballast overboard, even events, which at the time seemed of utmost importance – if they didn't affect the real "I". So those things, which I remember about that big-headed, big-eared Levukas, truly are a part of my life. All of them are important, otherwise I wouldn't remember them.

We lived in a horrible basement flat in the Vilijampolė neighbourhood of Kaunas. There are hardly any of those apartments left now. A sports field kicked up dust outside the window. While staring out the window I would most often see only the legs of those playing football or doing the high jump. Angry, muscular legs. No, the window wasn't under the ceiling; we didn't live in a basement, but a semi-basement. I could reach the windowsill if I got up on a stool. The landscape outside the window was stretched out vertically like a Chinese silk scroll painting. There was a downspout waterfall and the unwieldy mountain of a bleak dark brown building. But there wasn't the faintest hint of a strip of sky even high up above, right on the top of the silk scroll. I would flatten my face against the glass, turn my head as much as possible, and see the fourth- and fifth-floor windows, but I was never able to see the sky. And turning around and looking back, all I would see were the faces of my family. Nor was I able to discern the sky's reflection in their eyes.

I'm ashamed to say it, but I barely remember my mother. I loved her, felt very sorry for her and now hardly remember her. Of course, I remember her face, her downtrodden eyes. I can still hear her teachings. However, all of that doesn't comprise an object, a whole person. In my memory the image of my mother is cloudy and dim. Sometimes it seems to me that she's hiding from me.

I really am ashamed, but I don't remember my brothers and sisters well, except for Stanislova. They were somewhat older and they didn't let me into their world. They distanced themselves from me, so they can't be angry at me. They never did get angry; in fact they paid little attention to me. I hung around alone, like that cat of Kipling's: my childlike loneliness wasn't oppressive. Like that cat I relied on myself and respected myself, because no one else respected me, no one appreciated me. That was painfully depressing and forced me to begin picking up on GGI without even knowing what it was. I looked at other children from the other yards with envy: they had it good. There was always someone who appeared and praised the sandcastle they had made or the paper boat they had folded from a sheet of notebook paper. But I was not respected and not praised. Perhaps it was precisely because of that I learned to respect and praise myself and not depend on the world's opinion of me. Perhaps it was precisely because of that I became independent and driven. However, at the same time I endlessly desired community and the most meagre of praise.

No one praised me at home. My father didn't have time

for that. I remember him the most vividly, especially his workshop. My father was a masterful jack of all trades, incessantly fashioning something from wood, metal, plastic or even stone. He would leave for the factory, make something there as well, and on his return start at once with a new order. My father was small, always with his hair cut very short, while his tired eyes were calm and colourless. Even when he spanked me for some sort of transgression, his eyes remained calm and colourless. He would carefully count ten whacks, and then would start working again. His workshop reminded me of the cockpit of a spaceship – there were so many woodworking tools, a woodworker's bench, and creations of the strangest shapes. During the day, especially when it rained, I'd play all alone in the workshop. At the time, my sister Stanislova had already begun to bring guys home, so she would shove me out of the bedroom. At first I would secretly stare through the keyhole. But the sight was not interesting. I would only see four naked legs, one on top of the others, one under the others, intertwined or spread open. I had already seen so many legs through the window anyway. When the neighbours informed on Stanislova to my father, it was probably the first time in his life he didn't go to work. He skulked with me in his workshop and then burst into the bedroom, having opened the door with a wire. It was the first time I understood how powerless my father was. All the drunken Stanislova did was laugh uproariously, while her partner, an athlete with a brazen look, demanded she return his money with a thundering baritone voice: he hadn't managed to do anything and had gotten himself excited in vain. Stanislova would take the money in advance. Such was her golden rule. I waited for my father to kill them, curse them, strike them down with a lightning bolt, but he only blinked with his serene colourless eyes and then quietly cried in his workshop. Even on a day like that he didn't stop working. He couldn't live any other way.

After that Stanislova went to Klaipėda to service the sailors. She later moved to Leningrad for the foreign guests at the Inter Hotels.

And my father continued to work. He couldn't live any other way. He had to feed the family.

"Remember child: work can't provide happiness," he uttered once. "However, it's necessary to work."

At the time I was already the best in my class, so I confronted my father. I told him that work is joy, an honour and spiritual necessity, that you need to love work.

"In my life I've never seen a ditch digger who loved his shovel," my father replied.

As the best in my class, I was deeply hurt by those words. From that night on I stopped respecting my father: his views didn't fit the moral code set by a builder of Communism at all. I had learned that code well. I had helped to make a display with its moral maxims at school. The display hung in the school lobby, next to the coat closet. You would see it just after entering. Along with the moral maxims, there was a worker who'd been drawn there, inviting all pupils to Communism with the broad wave of his hand. The worker looked a lot like my father because I'd drawn it. I'd drawn things for displays, wall newspapers and Komsomol newspapers my whole life. I was particularly good at various kinds of fonts. I was a true master at the most elaborate of fonts. I almost became a criminal because of that moral code display. I was ashamed to no end that the worker inviting everyone to a brighter future was my father, that ditch digger who hated his own shovel. I suggest that the picture be redrawn, but no one paid any attention to my offer. The display was mounted and stuck on the wall with adhesive. The Komsomol Committee didn't listen to the blabbering of a fourteen-year-old. Each morning that optimistic picture of my father would meet me at school and resolutely utter to me:

"No ditch digger loves his shovel. Work doesn't give a person joy!"

I couldn't stand it any more. I got the crazy idea to secretly disfigure that picture so it would have to be redrawn whether they wanted it or not. I couldn't do it in the middle of the day, so I decided to sneak into school at night. I was a very secretive kid, so I almost achieved my goal: there was no one to snitch on me. I made an impression of the key for the lock of the school's back door and gradually began to fashion a copper copy. There was enough material and tools in father's workshop to make thousands of the most elaborate safe keys. However, his workshop was suddenly sealed and afterwards taken away. After Stanislova's downfall it was the second largest misfortune of our home, though perhaps it saved me. If it hadn't been for the loss of my father's workshop, perhaps I would have become some sort of gangster, a safe-cracker. I was attracted more and more not by the smoothing of key teeth, but by the temptation of opening all kinds of doors. I even forgot about that ill-fated portrait of my father in the display. I dreamt more and more about opening secret doors beyond which riches and happiness awaited me. Goodness, I could have turned into a gangster of some sort.

Can you imagine me as a gangster? With a scarred face and icy stare? As is normal these days, I would have robbed worker cooperatives. Or I wouldn't have robbed anyone at all. Instead I'd have started racketeering. I wouldn't have written you any letters from beyond the grave. I probably wouldn't have got to know you at all. Instead you would have known me, looked at me with fear and a strange envy, as I came to a restaurant for lunch where everyone knew me and respected me – from the director on down to the very last dishwasher. I would have stepped slowly out of my Mercedes and walked morosely up the sidewalk, accompanied by bodyguards, looking straight ahead, not noticing trash like you at all. Can you imagine me like that?

Father's workshop was confiscated because of a complaint from the neighbours. I don't think they were innate snitchers. Perhaps they were simply annoyed by the humming of the wood saw. Perhaps they didn't realise that the authorities would take away all of father's material and tools and then slap an enormous fine on top of that for private labour activity.

Father died two or three months later. Mostly likely not because he didn't have the money to pay the fine. And not because we immediately started to live in semi-starvation without his supplementary income. I think he died of longing. Regardless of how and what he had said, deep in his heart he was a ditch digger who was fatally attached to his shovel. Upon returning from work, he would sit for hours on the couch and stare at one spot. He died of cancer, its spread had already eaten him up. From a clinical point of view, he should have died long ago, but he never had time for it: he had to work, feed his family. He couldn't do otherwise.

For days right before his death he was carving something out of the biggest of stones. When he was asked what he was making, he would reply, "God!" And perplexed he would add, "My grandpa was a carver of religious statues."

That was my father's only metaphysical behaviour. And the god ended up remaining unfinished. After that my mother used that rock to press her home-made sauerkraut.

My brother Zigmas supported the family for a couple years. He was a football player who played on Žalgiris and earned quite a lot of money. But then he broke his leg, got himself a job as a children's coach and was barely able to make ends meet. Later he became a horrible drunkard. I would see him spending his days next to the famous beer kiosks. His bones began to crumble from the drinking. He would spend his days around those kiosks, with casts and bandages all over him and a crutch in his shaking hand. When in the end he was run over by a truck, our family gave a sigh of relief.

"Dear God," mother said. "It will be much better for him. How much longer could he torment himself like that?"

I remember almost nothing from those years. They were like a toothache, and do you remember how your tooth hurt? You simply had to make it through the day, then another, and then again and again. More clearly I remember just one winter, probably the last winter of Khrushchev's rule – the one when white bread disappeared from the shops, but in spite of that sweet rolls were sold at schools. They could only be found at the buffets of Party committees, hospitals and schools. Probably it was then that I first understood what GGI is. They would sell ten rolls at a time to some people, and only two to me. I still didn't understand why that was, but I truly did feel God's Grand Injustice. I would take those two rolls home. I would carry them around for a long time, until nonetheless I would eventually eat one of them. Mother knew that I was able to buy two, but she wouldn't say anything. Most likely because I was supposed to become a doctor, a white-robed demigod. I was meant to be fed with rolls and not black bread.

And then GGI ensnared me from my head to my toes. While growing up I began to understand how I was dressed and how my classmates were dressed. It was better for the girls. They had to wear uniforms, so at least they all looked more or less the same at school. The uniforms for boys were constantly being made, designed and planned, but they were never able to get them right. Boys went to school wearing whatever they were able to come up with. All teenagers in Lithuania were happy because of this, except me. Because growing up I began to understand how I was dressed.

You wouldn't understand that, and I won't explain anything. You can smile as much as you like, but that was really GGI. Mother mopped the floor in three offices and all my other siblings earned money, but – Good God! – the way I was dressed! Stanislova would regularly send us money from Klaipėda, then from Leningrad, but mother

19

stubbornly would write on the remittance form "addressee absent" and take that piece of paper back to the post office.

But once Stanislova wrote a letter to me and sent the remittance in my name. She invited me to Leningrad, not simply for a visit – but for good. She was tortured by nostalgia: not for Lithuania, nor Kaunas, nor our yard nor our family. She unexpectedly felt a heart-rending nostalgia for her droopy-eared, big-headed little brother, who back then she used to push out of the room so he wouldn't get in the way of her earning money. In her photo, Stanislova was just like she was before: a pure blonde Lithuanian girl with cornflower blue eyes. The years had not left marks on her face. They didn't cloud her angelic gaze. She looked like a vestal virgin, but she had become even more beautiful. She was stunningly beautiful. She called me to her, she promised me a world of fairy tales, and I was supposed to become the little darling of her professional cooperative.

At the time I had no illusions any more concerning her way of life. My mother's formulation, "the loose girl", which earlier had raised a legion of questions in my head, had long ago made everything crystal clear. All the more when my classmates would formulate it somewhat more precisely: "Levas's sister is a famous Kaunas whore," they would say. "Now she has disappeared somewhere. Maybe they put her in jail, or perhaps she's getting treatment for the clap."

And suddenly I got her invitation as well as a remittance – a whole one hundred roubles. I had never seen so much money in one place. In her letter, Stanislova emphasised that it was merely small change for the trip. I was beset by excruciating uncertainty. Stanislova clearly did not keep to the moral code laid down by Communism, so I couldn't respect or love her. But while reading her letter, repeating her enchanting promises in a whisper, I felt that I was being shrouded by an unctuous, stifling mist. It was thick, almost tangible, it smelled of roses and French perfume. I didn't revel in the rewards in her apartment that could be clearly seen in the photographs as much as I dreamed about Stanislova's co-workers. The big-eyed vestal virgins surrounded me. I was their little darling. They caressed me with delicate fingers and velvet gazes. The undefined desires of those turgid teenage nights turned into a torturous nightmare. The vestal virgins were there, in Leningrad, they were waiting for me, and I was forced to toss and turn in my bed that reeked of sweat. They were suffering without me, and I was suffering because I was apart from them. I couldn't think about anything else any more. I secretly packed my modest belongings and left for the post office. The window for paying out the remittances only snorted and spit out murderous words, "Bring your mum or dad, child. They have to fill out a form."

I was only fifteen. I didn't have a passport yet. I couldn't decide my destiny yet. I had a cry in the little garden on a bench and slowly trudged home. No one had missed me, the basket with my belongings didn't raise anyone's suspicions – there was just about enough stuff for everyone to decide that I had been at basketball practice. I was tall and agile, I desired to become a star, but after half a year I stopped going to practice, as it turned out that I had a heart defect. That time I gave the remittance to mother, and she wrote "addressee absent" on the form and made her way to the post office.

After all, with a little help, I could have become a high-level manager of prostitutes. Can you imagine me as someone like that? Decked out with the most fashionable clothes from head to toe, with pockets stuffed with cheques, bonds, dollars and drugs? Meandering through the Hotel Lietuva lazy as a cat, scanning the room with a look that was at the same time both brazen and weary. I would be satiated to insanity, I would have half a million hidden under the floor of my summer house and all I'd dream of was escaping to Germany or England, taking a bag of diamonds or antique rarities as contraband. Can you imagine me as someone like that?

But at that time I was overcome by a frightening reality check. Finally I understood what I was preparing to do. I was preparing to travel to the home of a fallen woman and become a pimp of sorts. It was of no importance that the woman in question was my sister. Rather – it was important precisely because of this: this was all the more reason for me to bring her to the path of morality. But I had fallen particularly low: I was prepared to use the fruits of immorality in all of their poisonous sweetness. I understood that I didn't have the right any more to publish the Komsomol Spotlight wall placards: I had become trash, even if only in my thoughts, but I was just one step away from a deadly sin.* I was beset by stifling thoughts, I wanted to hang myself, castrate myself right then and there. I was essentially an exceptionally virtuous boy. Perhaps I was like some sort of seminary student, just without my own church, I still had to find it. I truly could have done something bad to myself, I was only saved by the class teacher. She was a rather youngish old maid with a hypertrophied mothering instinct. I understand that now, but at the time she was the holy confidante and confessor for all of us. I wasn't the only one – everyone would confess to her what they never would have revealed to either their parents or their friends. My class teacher examined Stanislova's photographs for a while, nodded her head and made an admonishing clicking sound with her tongue, and afterwards patted me on the head and strongly encouraged me to continue coming out with the Komsomol wall placards.

"You understood your guilt, Levukas," she explained. "Man cannot avoid making mistakes. It's important to correct your mistakes in time."

---

* Committees called "Komsomol Spotlights" were created during the Soviet period to uncover instances of people breaking Soviet law. Wall placards of the same name were placed in city centres and schools, listing those who had been fined or punished for their misconduct.

She ordered me to read as much real literature as possible, and if some impure thoughts arose – then I should exercise as much as possible. She was waiting in line for a flat to no avail and was renting a room from an old woman who was slowly going crazy. One flat was doled out to our school about every five years. Actually they had offered her the chance to buy a two-room cooperative flat, but she'd proudly refused it. The party, from Khrushchev's lips, had promised in a grand manner that one more step would take us to Communism, so only an idiot would pay for some flat with their hard-earned money, flats which subsequently tomorrow or the day after tomorrow there would be tons of – and for free. By the time the poor woman understood that there wasn't going to be any Communism in the foreseeable future, the queue for cooperative apartments had got longer than it had been at the beginning for communal apartments. Our class teacher slowly lost her mind entirely. I think she was infected by her landlady, though they say that mental illness isn't contagious. She began to write articles that denounced everything from beginning to end and take them to editorial offices in vain, not missing even the little factory newsletters. She was a harmless nutcase. I saw her for the last time in a bar. She entered the hall with a fantastic orange-brimmed hat with a pin denoting one having graduated from secondary school on the lapel of her jacket, ordered a mug of beer, put all of her cosmetic items on the table and began to do her make-up, every once in a while proudly looking over the reeking drunks in the bar.

Forgive me for going off the topic, but it always seemed to me that you had your head in the clouds. Your knowledge of real life was too inadequate.

Back then our class teacher had not yet gone crazy, and I obeyed her to the letter. I am trying to understand myself as I was at the time, that spindly-legged, sickly Levas, but I'm not capable of doing that. Now there aren't any teenagers like that. It seems to me that there weren't any like that left in those times either. I was the only one. At least, I didn't meet any others like that. It seems to me that I never tortured myself about it too much. I was used to living alone with myself and valuing myself. And when you told me your theory, that a person must first of all be himself, I settled down entirely.

After that unsuccessful vestal virgin odyssey I became absorbed with books. I felt immensely guilty before myself and the world. I desired to redeem my sins and improve. I wanted to prove to myself that I wasn't entirely lost. I soaked up the books suggested to me by my class teacher like dry moss soaks up rain. I devoured stories about real people and desired to become as much like them as possible. All real literary people sacrificed themselves and suffered, suffered and sacrificed themselves. After reading in the evening I wanted to whip myself with barbed wire. I had to suffer and sacrifice myself. That was the only way it was possible to become a true person. I was obsessively haunted by all different kinds of physical shortcomings affecting the main characters. I began to feel a metaphysical fascination for those who had no legs or were paralysed. I was totally taken by a tale called *A Story about a Real Man*. I dreamt of a lame person, someone without legs, without arms, who still achieved their goal – but I didn't really know what that goal was. I was especially enthralled by Pavka Korchagin. I would fume, desiring to spit in the face of all those nobodies and careerists that tried to hinder him. Looking around, I saw those kinds of people right nearby, within arm's reach. If they were like that, it meant that I was like Pavka. I was so damnably lacking in incurable diseases, physical shortcomings, endless physical suffering. I almost dreamed of being paralysed. Being healthy and normal seemed too insignificant. A person like that could not be truly great – that is what literature taught me time and time again. But I dreamed of playing basketball, being big and powerful! After all, it was right to go through life lame and ravaged – at least like the Gadfly from Voynich's novel.

In wanting to become a true man, first of all you had to cripple yourself – no one had indicated any other path. However, even in harming yourself you had to do it in a noble manner – by saving someone or building or fighting something.

Suddenly my heart began to flutter because of the constant pressure and excitement. For the first time in my life I ended up in the hands of doctors. They immediately found a congenital defect and were very surprised that I hadn't felt it till then. The doctors nodded their heads in deep thought, and I was secretly joyous. Finally I had acquired a physical flaw. True, it was a rather poor one, but after all my defect could still expand and become exacerbated. It could still chain me to my bed. I still had hope to become the Great Lame One.

I would very much like to see the me from those times from the outside. What was my expression like, what were my eyes like back then? What was going on in my head at the time? How did my behaviour with girls appear from the outside? After all, I could only love, as you understand yourself, painfully, hopelessly and of course without reciprocation. And better still – wither away till the grave because of the lost love of my youth. And better still – surrender my love to a friend, and bow out ever so quietly into the background. And better still...

The only problem was that I didn't have either a love or a friend.

Those masochistic ambitions continued to stay with me for a long time. Finally it was you who demolished them without even knowing it.

When you with that crooked smirk laid out your theory of a masochistic sensibility, that was the first time I wanted to kill you (but not the last). You spat and vomited into my soul. I looked at you like a priest at a vandal who had pissed on the altar. That was the bloody sunset of my illusions. Up until then I had thought that everyone, absolutely everyone, secretly admired the heroes of my youth. Only some had the courage to dream that they would also become like them, while others didn't dare. And you calmly, logically taught that Stalinist literature always propagated spiritual masochism. That a masochistic character, who was unable to realise any of their wishes and flights of fancy, had to enjoy the fact that they, despite being lame or deathly ill, were still able to match those who were healthy, and achieve what was totally normal for the average person through the worst suffering. That character, you taught, if he isn't lame, has to create a slew of artificial barriers in all spheres of life – from the personal up to the manufactured. "How does a normal producer of something act, having received an unreal, unrealisable plan?" you teased. He logically shows that the demands are too great. And how does a masochistic literary manufacturer act? He offers his plan to the contrary, which is even greater! Then he works nights, waist-high in icy water, triggers horrific catastrophes so he can get rid of them with superhuman effort. How does a masochistic person love? You ridiculed me relentlessly. He sighs, agonises, weeps, but in no way does he sleep with his love – on the contrary, it is also here that he creates artificial barriers for himself: he leaves for another city, recruits himself to the North for ten years, leaves his love to his closest friend.

I couldn't listen any longer. I wanted to kill you. I thought for a long time and very seriously whether it would be worth my while denouncing you. At the time you had already talked so much about everything that there was good reason to. That was the first great stain on my life: I really did want to denounce you. Of course, in 1970 you didn't have the threat either of Siberia or of getting thrown out of university any more, but still... I understood perfectly well what I was getting ready to do. It wasn't that I was trying to fool myself that I was protecting some ideals or demonstrating my loyalty and virtue. I consciously wanted to undermine you. I wanted to punish you in a painful way because you had earned punishment. You defiled the sacred, you had the gall to talk about Pavka Korchagin's sexual opportunities. I wanted to challenge you to a duel and kill you.

You need to know this. I couldn't have said that to you earlier. Remember, the resolute devastation of the ideals of strangers is always mortally dangerous.

By the way, it was the first time that I wanted to punish other people. I guess masochism very quickly and naturally turns into sadism. I wanted to hurt you. I asked myself angrily, Who are you? What right do you have? Your darkly angry face, your clever eyes, your entire being enraged me. Everyone explained to me year after year what a true man is, and with one breath you labelled that person a spiritual pervert. You can't even imagine how you insulted and wounded me. You ambushed me and pierced me in the tenderest spot in my soul.

However, you always had one wonderful trait: if you demolished something, you left neither ruins nor a bare spot. At once you began the building of a new palace – sometimes from new bricks, and sometimes even from the same ones. That time you were also consistent. You thrust a few good books my way. It's funny to remember, but I read *The Idiot* for the first time at nineteen. What's even funnier is that Prince Myshkin was also physically a cripple.

Sometimes all of it seems funny to me. I sit and put the events of my life in order, like chess pieces. At times I almost don't have the strength to take this game seriously. At times I don't want to write you any more letters. But I still write to you because I desire to help you. That desire is not entirely altruistic. I am already dead. I can't do anything any more. But you still can. You still can do a thing or two.

The Third: about the book of my life and heart defects, about phantasmagorical spores, a lie and the ruin of us all

Is one whose field is on the river bank,
whose wife becomes involved with another,
in whose home snakes breed, able to
contemplate calmly?

No matter how much I try to lay out my thoughts in an orderly manner, nothing much comes of it. The events aren't arranged in my memory the way they are in the current of life. They take on a totally different shade, a different weight, and smell differently. Unimportant details suddenly thrive and spread like baobab trees. Menacing tragedies suddenly turn into farcical stories, almost anecdotes.

I used to crawl out of that basement of mine in the Vilijampolė neighbourhood like some kind of worm. And I felt like a worm. An appalling fuzzy caterpillar, which deserved to be squashed. I was disgusted by myself; I didn't want to be myself. I didn't like my big head, my droopy ears, which I hid under my thin whitish hair. I didn't like my high-pitched and hollow voice, my thin lips and watery eyes. I didn't like that long-bodied caterpillar, that white fuzzy worm that crawled out of his cave each morning. His pale face, stuck on a thin neck, his fanatical eyes and fine white fluff on his chin. Good God, the way he looked! His pants had been washed to the point they were almost transparent, his shoes were still broken after having been repaired again and again, and his sweater mended with ragged leather patches. His cave was also disgusting: a bunk bed, cots and a creaking bed with iron balls on the bedposts, it was like the cell of a stifling prison, pushed halfway below the ground. Even the earth didn't want to carry him, chased him into the cave, oppressed and humiliated him. In his basement he was probably plotting against all of humanity.

He unavoidably had to be a jealous person, he had to be jealous, be jealous and only jealous – of everyone and everything. I couldn't stand him. I couldn't stand myself. I wasn't able to look in the mirror. That ghost from the mirror elicited loathing and hatred in me. A brain lay hidden behind its pale grainy eyes, cooking up a soup of the strangest of thoughts. That jealous man desired to be something like the protagonist of a novel, he probably wanted someone to write novels about him at some stage. On top of that, he was hungry for glory, he could even intentionally furnish himself with a physical disability so he could sandwich himself in among the heroes.

Could you stand such a person?

Of course, every normal person at times can't stand themselves. It's only stupid people who are constantly self-satisfied. But a normal person's hatred of himself is most often short-lived, and for the most part inward. I couldn't stand all of myself, and it was like that all the time. Waking up in that miserable musty bed, my first thought would be: I've come out of my sleep just the same as I was. It was only in my dreams that I was different: proud, graceful and elegant. I desired to be changed to my very core, but I didn't know in what way I should be changed. I desired a miracle; I believed that one morning I would awaken totally different. The boundless GGI stifled me, I had to conquer it, but the only way to conquer it would be by a miracle. I myself embodied GGI, so I had to conquer myself, but without a miracle it was impossible.

I didn't succeed in becoming a basketball star, and I wasn't able to even become the leader of my class. I lacked artistic abilities, so I remained a drawer of caricatures and satirical cartoons, even though I tried to copy the paintings of the great masters. While watching an animated film about the Ugly Duckling, pathetic tears would unconsciously flood my eyes. I had to find a sphere of activities where I was irreplaceable, although there doubtless wasn't anything like that in the entire world. So each morning I would wake up devastated and damned. Each morning I would wake up like Gregor Samsa – having turned into a disgusting bug. No one loved me, I was of no use to anyone. Everybody wished for my death. Perhaps dying was the best for me, because I didn't have any future to speak of.

You may ask why I'm writing about this. I myself don't even know. I am simply reading myself like some strange book. I can turn to any page and read what is written there out loud. I am a fully finished book, I know that nothing will change in those mouldy pages. I can be unbiased and impartial. I think that this book is instructive and useful. Perhaps that is why I am reading it to you – not in its entirety, just selected pages. Though they are hardly selected, it's just those that I randomly open up: I begin to read and I can't stop, as everything in this book is interesting. This book is my legacy, and you are my heir. Every person desires to leave something for the world. All I can do is leave my story, and leave it to you alone – you also contributed to it. Which is why you have to know how it ended up.

Perhaps I want too much from you? But I don't want you to do anything special; I don't want you to punish or take revenge on someone for me. All I want is that you listen to me. That isn't so hard, is it?

At once I see your squinting eyes and sarcastic smile. Alright, let's push that pride aside, there are other very simple reasons. I'm simply not finding anything else to busy myself with. Nothing concerns me now, I don't have any problems, everything's so clear-cut one could just howl. All I can do is to keep leafing through this book of my life – nothing else concerns me. Which is why all I can do is talk about it. All I can do is write you letters about it.

I care very little for the fates of saints and martyrs, or those of wise men and politicians. What concerns me more is my own fate.

It was you that taught me that each person's life is meaningful and complex like an entire cosmos. I'm explaining the structure of an entire cosmos to you – for fuck's sake, what more do you need?

Thoughts and events are rushing up like waves flooding the shore I'm sitting on all alone, and then they recede. The blue sky above drones like a sombre organ, there's too much of that blueness above me; it's compensation for the absence of azure in my childhood. I stretch out on the warmed sand of the shore and sigh heavily, because I've just crossed the finish line. I don't feel my body, because I don't need it any more, I don't feel my murmuring heart, which would be pacified by just a handful of the Bayer aspirins Father-in-Law procured. Handfuls of aspirin – in autumn and spring, in spring and autumn.

Now I am still thinking about my former health. Earlier I didn't have time for that.

I had a congenital heart defect, it was hanging over my head the entire time like the sword of Damocles. Even now I don't know what was defective in my heart – something about having too many partitions, or one was too small. I never tried to understand it that well. When a more talkative doctor started to explain it, I would immediately interrupt him. I didn't want to go deeper into the metaphysics of my body. I always believed in the mystical secret of the human body, perhaps I subconsciously didn't want to admit that a person is just a mechanism working away harmoniously or disharmoniously. That was almost the only categorical disregard of your teachings.

I can more or less imagine what you would do if you were me in this situation: you would ascertain the smallest detail of the workings of the heart as thoroughly as possible. You would surround yourself with medical books and cardiology manuals. You'd most likely even get a heart model – what am I saying, you'd definitely get one, I'd bet on it that you'd invent your own special one where the defect of your heart would be cast absolutely perfectly, that unnecessary or crooked partition. You would show this heart model to everyone with a strange joy, as if it were a virtue that belonged to you. And, of course, you would have courageously gone under the surgeon's knife.

It always seemed to you that a person's body was just a vessel, a mechanism, a machine, a coldly material object that had little to do with the person himself. You were fascinated with acupuncture, but you also understood that in a purely mechanical way: when some function of the mechanism got jammed up, you simply had to push the right button and this would fix the problem. You would get angry in a melodramatic fashion in which the body just got in your way: it always required food, drink, fresh air, and women, and what's more, it constantly broke down.

But for me, the body always seemed like it was brimming with a mystical secret. I didn't believe in any medical books, drawings of the nervous system or all those cross sections of internal organs. I didn't believe in any doctor. During their seven years of study they are fed the lie that the body is just a mechanism, the parts of which can be replaced with others or thrown out entirely. Could you trust people that think like that?

I always felt that the body – or rather its mystical secret – was controlling me. It operated in unpredictable and inexplicable ways. Having cut my finger, I would look for a long time at the blood coming out and feel that something irreplaceable and irretrievable was coming out with it. What intimidated me even more was someone else's body. When I started to become interested in girls, each thought about a woman's body made me shake like I'd been struck by electricity. The sexual act always seemed like a magical ritual for me, the merging together of two secrets into one short-term but all-enveloping secret, which could even spark a new life, a new mystical secret. My heart was not some sort of pump circulating blood. I always felt that it was the place where love and humanity lay. Just because of that I couldn't even think about mechanics in white lab coats digging around under the hood.

A person's heart can only be touched by wise men who have cleansed themselves from everything that is earthly, having washed not only their hands clean, but also their own hearts.

I can already see that you're opening your mouth to argue. Don't bother. You'll no longer convince me of anything now. My heart defect became a menace that hung above me like the sword of Damocles. There were many other perils I faced, but I understood that this was an unavoidable part of my nature; not even that – it was a part of my soul. My heart really did lack something – I have felt that since childhood. It lacked the ability to humbly resign itself to things, it lacked meekness and modesty. It possessed too much hollow glory, too much desire to feel its power and anxiety. My heart really was defective, though it was possible to live with such a heart for a long, long time, even though not particularly happily. All you had to do was not push yourself too much.

So what does medicine, or to be precise, cardiac surgery, have to do with it?

Yes, you're right, there were discussions about it – quite a few in fact. Of course, Father-in-Law was the one who started organising everything. And, of course, I refused.

I didn't explain my understanding of a person's heart, which is not supposed to be touched by the lancet of a surgeon, to anyone – they wouldn't have understood me, they wouldn't have even heard me out. At the time I actually didn't think too much about it. I was simply overtaken by fear. That fear wasn't just emotion without any clearer reasons. I was afraid in a very logical and well-founded way. I had already begun understanding the structure of our life. Father-in-Law helped me there, he liked to tell me such things, the kind of things I wouldn't have found out about anywhere else.

Now when the floodgates of information in your world have been opened considerably, many probably still can't believe that everything has deteriorated and come undone so tragically. So imagine how I must have felt knowing all of that long ago and unable to confide in anyone – they simply wouldn't have believed me. That's right, they wouldn't have believed me. After all, even the most hardened pessimists, who it seemed at the time made fiercely courageous assumptions, nevertheless, didn't reveal the true situation. That's how it is in every society, every community of people that is based on a lie – whether it be a group of pool hustlers or simply a family. But the average members of communities constructed like that don't even dream of the real depths of collapse and decay – not even in their worst nightmares. Those depths are known only by those who handle and select the lies that poison that community. That's how it is: if you want to lie, first of you all you have to know the truth. I contributed to society-wide lying, however: I lied only when I had the truth about the matter. Father-in-Law lied in a global manner and for some reason at times let me catch a glimpse of the macabre nature of our life.

So my fear of doctors was founded entirely on logic and reason. Not those specific people, the wonderful medical specialists that Father-in-Law foisted upon me. Not even the broken-down medicine – Father-in-Law promised to get me into the most modern special-access hospital.* I greatly feared that phantasmagoria, the spores of which got into everything, spread in the air, infecting all of us – those doctors, me, and even you. Yes, yes, even you – regardless of

---

* The Soviet elite had access to special hospitals and medical care that was unavailable to the general population.

whether you want to admit it or not. Though you were my teacher, you are still a human being, and no human is able to resist those poisonous spores. They not only penetrated people's brains, they even got into objects: the objects didn't want to serve people any more, they could break down or shatter most unexpectedly. And I was supposed to lie down on an operating table? So those people who were infected with those sinister spores would treat me? So tools imbued with those poisonous spores would touch my heart? So what if those surgeons were amazing professionals – they were infected, the disease lay hidden deep inside them, an outburst of it could erupt at any second, without them even suspecting it. No matter whether their lancets came from England or Sweden – and even if made of the most wonderful of Swedish steel – they could disintegrate during the decisive incision if they were exposed to air infested with those despicable spores.

You don't believe that such spores exist? Perhaps you don't know how to look at the mirror of the soul any more? And if you do – look at yourself. You are infested with those phantasmagorical spores, just like everyone else. They mutilated and ravaged your soul. Think about it: are you really supposed to be who you are now? Where are your books, where are your works, your star charts of thoughts? Where is your audience, where are your students, where are the mountains you've climbed? Is there a person, except for me, that upon hearing your name bows their head in respect?

If those despicable spores swallowed up such a talent as you – what should we say about us, we average mortals.

Look at that:

Mountains. They loom majestically, even from a distance they don't look toylike, even when it appears you could put them in the palm of your hand, they still remain mountains. The steep jagged precipices, the stunted dry grass and bushes, their leaves have all kinds of colours: there are yellow ones, red ones, brown ones and green ones. All of those colours are lacklustre, they are shrouded by the fog, and there's not a living soul around – just mountain sheep with twisted horns jumping from rock to rock, always climbing upwards. They hope to find something in those fog-covered summits, maybe it's there that people's secret aims, passions and sins freeze and decay. But there are no people here, just proud and elegant mountain sheep, continually climbing upwards though it seems there's no more place to climb – up at the top there's nothing but snow, sky and fresh air. Air, air, air, air.

We never breathed in fresh air, all we ever inhaled were those phantasmagorical spores. They mutilated our body, our soul, even our genes – so our children would be born already deformed. We didn't do anything when it was absolutely necessary, and hysterically did any old thing when it was necessary to rest. We gambled away our lives – to be more precise, I've already lost it, but you're still trying to save yourself, and you won't get anything done unless I help you. I can help you, I know Father-in-Law, though I don't know him fully.

I don't understand why he told me all sorts of horrible things, why he practically took pride in them. That I don't understand. Did he too feel the necessity to reveal the truth to someone? If so, I was of course the most suitable for that. I was like a pet parakeet which was headstrong and couldn't be tamed, as would be fitting for a wild parakeet.

But no, I still don't understand why he practically took pride in such macabre things. It seemed that he derived joy from the absurd, deformed life eaten away by phantasmagorical spores, like an artist derives pleasure from his brilliant creation. You could say that he invited me to admire it in his company. He was fascinated by it all, though I never understood WHAT was so fascinating. Some arrogant moron can be proud that he is better informed than others, the rank and file with a party ticket can revel in their comfortable way of life. But Father-in-Law was intelligent, you know that yourself now: he's not just clever or crooked – he's smart. What is there in that phantasmagoria that a smart person could find fascinating?

That's one of the most essential questions – perhaps you know or will learn the answer.

The Fourth: about prognostications and the meaning of a miracle, about rootless people and shot-putters

Misfortunes await birds soaring in space, experienced fishermen pull fish even out of the depths of the sea. What is foolishness, and what is the mind? What sense is there in hanging on to one's position? Even from afar, fate reaches us – all you have to do is extend your hand

How do you like the Hindu aphorisms I picked out? Maybe I will also take something from Lao Tzu or the *I Ching* – if I remember to. I'm not putting those epigraphs in order according to meaning, I simply grab the first one that sticks in my mind the most, and quickly write it down. I am hoping for a small miracle: that the aphorism will fit right into its own place. I'm used to waiting for miracles. There wasn't much else left to wait for in our lives.

The first real miracle of my life was my father's stone that looked like it had been carved by a master carver. I often rolled it into the middle of the room and kept looking at it until it began to glimmer in my eyes. I tried to understand why my father saw God in it. I tried to understand what that god imagined by my father was like, and whether my father could concoct any kind of god at all. Perhaps it seems like that to me only now, because actually I communicated with that stone for a particularly mundane reason. My mother pressed her sauerkraut with it. It was the only food I could always find at home. I would fill a bowl with that sauerkraut, stuff it into my mouth with my fingers and dream about a miracle. Someone had to come and do something good for me. That someone could just as well have been a god. I tried and tried to imagine him. But all those imagined gods down to the last one were fat and sluggish; they didn't care for people in the least. And they especially didn't care for teenagers from basements in Kaunas, teenagers whose only delicacy was their mothers' home-made sauerkraut.

The god of my room was also like that – cold as a stone, smooth as a stone, heavy as a stone. I came to believe in him because of my enforced loneliness – I didn't have the courage to join people my own age, as I felt uncomfortable and ashamed in their company. All of them were either well dressed or at least tolerably dressed, when they got hungry they all could run home to have meatballs or buy something delicious to eat, none of them were stuffed full of sauerkraut. But I was full of it – up to my neck, up to my ears, up to the top of my head, I hated it, I couldn't even look at it. Good God, I would eat it with my eyes closed, I grabbed it with my fingers. Or stared at my smooth, heavy stone god. It was my invention; I was used to imagining things since childhood.

In my childhood I didn't have real toys, which is why I played with my fantasies. And I also played with that masterfully carved stone, which was yet another of my fantasies. We were both united by sauerkraut, we both were steeped in its smelly juices. We were brothers, or perhaps something even closer. My room was dirty, a mess, horrible, while the smooth stone was as clean as a whistle. Even the reeking of sauerkraut didn't get absorbed into it. It was almost ideal. It really could have been a god. I don't think that a real longing for God could have appeared in me at the time. My parents were not religious, everyone in our family was indifferent to religion. Some of my aunts might have gone to feast days or Sunday prayers, but that was more of a habit and tribute to those around them. The educational system's atheist propaganda annoyed me somewhat, as it did everyone, but perhaps it achieved its aim: people who were deeply religious seemed almost abnormal to me. Indeed, much later when I began to research my family history, I found out that my grandparents had actually been woodcarvers who made statues of a religious nature. They made roadside shrines, which the eastern region of Aukštaitija was dotted with. That was just a myth, however, as the good-hearted rural dwellers cooperated with my research by telling me all sorts of increasingly novel facts which probably weren't true. They told me what I wanted to hear. I could fashion my grandparents as I saw fit. I discovered this when looking for my roots; people looked at me in wonderment and even with respect. Their stories made my grandparents seem ever more miraculous and mysterious. They weren't similar to people any more but rather to the heroes of myths and legends. When I understood this, I stopped looking for them. We don't need forefathers. We never had them. We are people who don't know our roots, maybe we don't have roots at all. We're artificial trees, planted into artificial soil, our roots were pulled and cultivated by hydroponics, fed by artificial juices. And we didn't wither away – we all grew up somehow or other. Only we aren't able to suck up the nutritious juices, we just wait for miracles from elsewhere.

I was also like that, I also waited for a miracle, but there wasn't anyone to create it. Perhaps that's why I latched on to that hapless stone; I also expected something of it, almost demanded something of it. At the time I was in the eighth or ninth form, it was exactly the time to decide what I was going to be, what I was going to do when I grew up. I wanted to do everything at once, move mountains and drain seas, bring forth a new sun and stop the winds. I was flying about in the skies, but the time demanded that I make a clear choice. I already understood back then that I had to become something, otherwise I would remain an empty dreamer and a loser. I wanted everything, but all I was was some sort of pale-faced nobody. I did well in school in most things, but nothing really attracted me. I waited for a sign from my stone. And in the evening, when my family members gathered together, I would go out for a ramble. Some of my classmates went to sports practice in the evenings, but my poor defective heart wouldn't let me join them. Others got together in the squares and played music at full blast from cassette players that had just appeared. All of them were well fed and nicely dressed. And I'm not even starting with the cassette players. I didn't have a place anywhere, I wandered the streets, looking for that ecological niche of mine, as if I could have found it right there, in that dreary Kaunas evening. I would return to my yard when it was already totally dark. They were switching off the lights at the sports field. And I always ended up meeting the same girl there. Her face was quite elegant, but she was the same height as I was, and at least twice as hefty. She also spent her evenings alone. She kept pushing her cast-iron shot in that drenched section of the field. She would stay on the field even after all the lights were turned off. In the dark I heard her heavy panting, then a stifled shout, and finally the thud of the cast-iron shot. That girl drove herself to extremes like a Kaunas Sisyphus of the night: she would fling that shot of hers, then bring it back and fling it once again. She was my friend of misfortune, she was my example. I always wanted to talk with her, but I didn't have the courage to. The only person I struck up a conversation with was her trainer. He worked tirelessly with her till it was almost dark, but then he left her to be on her own. I was convinced that she aimed to become a world champion, maybe her Sisyphean sweat has already turned into medals, fame and money.

"Last year Stasė took fourth place in Lithuania's national games," her trainer explained to me happily. "This year we'll be fighting for medals."

That news blew me away. The heavily breathing,

41

groaning Stasė was still only one of ten or so in Lithuania, meaning that she was one of a few hundred, or perhaps one of a few thousand in the world. She tortured herself, flinging that shot until it got hot – it even began to glow in the dark – in order to become one of a few hundred, or of a few thousand. And all I did was plod around the dark streets and think about who knows what. Which one in a few million was I supposed to become? And to become that I should have picked up my heavy shot and started to hurl it day and night a long time ago – to hurl and wheeze and gasp until I went crazy. If I wanted to achieve anything at all, that's what I had to do. But what could I hurl? My cabbage god, if nothing else. That blackish stone was the only thing in the house that reminded me of my father. His workshop had been confiscated, all of his tools were taken off somewhere. Perhaps in talking with the stone, I was unwittingly addressing my father, who hadn't explained anything to me while he was alive.

One way or another, something in that stone provided the answer. The summer of that year was wet and rainy, however that day dawned as a sunny one, though it was stifling. The sun was angry, I even felt the droning sound of the blue sky in my room, where I couldn't see it. I desired to ascend to the clouds, as I often ascended in my dreams, but I was sitting in my messy room and talking frustratedly with my woodcarver stone. I was bored and sad as never before. I desired more than ever that the world would say something to me, explain what I had to do.

"Say something!" I yelled at the stone lying in the middle of my room. "Give me a sign! Explain to me for crying out loud if it's worth my starting something, or better to just stay trash, a worm, or not live at all?"

I thought about ruin a lot. I killed myself in my thoughts in thousands of ways, but I died even more often not of my own volition. Misfortunes would come my way, I would drown, end up under a trolleybus or simply walk off into the distance and disappear into the fog. I didn't dream any more of getting into an accident and getting out of it injured, but still climbing out into the peaks. I began to crave only ruin. I was afraid of life, I was afraid of my future. I don't know why I started to scream at that stone on that particular day, but I do know that at the time I constantly thought about it.

The stone sat there inert on the floor, slow-witted and satisfied like some frog or jellyfish. I still managed to come up with the thought of how far I had sunk: here come up with the thought of how far I had sunk: here I was talking with a fucking brainless stone, I was even more insignificant than it was, I was the most useless piece of garbage, the wormiest of worms, a helpless kid from a basement flat without any spirit, without any powers.

The unseen blue sky droned on. The intense heat lazily pushed into my basement flat, flooded my brain, poured sweat on my face. Small bellows began to pump water into my temples. And suddenly I heard an unexpected rumbling and thundering. It seemed that the branches of some giant tree were cracking and breaking off. Finally there was a loud thud, as a piercing, spectacular shot was heard somewhere high up above, but the strangest thing was that this happened in the middle of my room. My stone gave out a piercing squeak and suddenly split in half. I was so scared that I stood motionless for a few moments as if I were paralysed. Then shaking all over, I approached the split stone and cautiously examined it. It split in half evenly, both separate pieces were smooth as if they had been polished.

I was calmed down only by the rain that had just started falling outside my window. Torrents of lukewarm water descended from the sky, drowning the heat-parched earth. It rained without stop for three days and three nights. I'll remember that rain my whole life – it was like a small deluge. It felt like I'd have to make a small Noah's ark out of planks.

However I threw out the split stone, as I was scared to stay in the same room with it, especially at night. I drowned it in the River Neris. As both its slippery halves plopped into the water, they murmured one and the same word, but I didn't understand it.

That was the only miracle of my life. I thought about the meaning of miracles numerous times after that, and it seems that I even thought up a thing or two.

What's miraculous about a miracle is that you can explain it the way it suits you. Everything is so well laid out in the world, so boringly explained, that whether you want to or not it's enticing to experience a miracle. There are no rules that apply to it, and you won't find an explanation for it in any book. No one will force their own opinion on you. You can explain a miracle as you see fit. That is what makes it a miracle.

But I didn't exploit that miraculousness. I was a staunch materialist, so I avoided mysticism when meditating upon things. I became a witness to the mysterious phenomenon of nature. As is well known, physics is the study of natural phenomena. So I became frantically interested in physics. I acted with immense pragmatism. Perhaps that was my big mistake. Perhaps it was precisely because of that my life took such an ill-fated turn.

I could have interpreted my miracle as I saw fit, and could have found in it metaphysical support sufficient for my entire life – God knows what I could have done with it. But all I did was squeeze enough out of that stone to choose a profession.

People who don't give a proper meaning to the only miracle in their life are sorely punished.

Essentially I am not writing you letters, but memoirs. Memoirs of a life cut short. And that's how they differ from all others – only elderly people write memoirs about their lives. But I'm still very young.

There's another essential difference between my letters and other kinds of memoirs: I am writing them for you. And you know a lot about me, I don't have to put everything down from A to Z any more, tell my life story in its entirety. I can recall only what is most important.

Don't be angry that I'm writing a bit incoherently, stopping for all sorts of details. You understand – I don't have anywhere to rush, and there are no details on earth. Everything in it is meaningful. What I'll write will remain, but the other things will be forgotten, as if they never were.

The Fifth: about class hatred and Jakovas Zundelovičius, about physics olympiads and Ortega y Gasset

The good become enraged for a moment,
the average for half a day, the below
average for a day and night, while the worst
never escape from their hatred.

Now I'll tell you unhesitatingly that a person's life rolls along the road of fate like a car that's always switching gears. In order to successfully navigate the hills and turns you need a different one each time. I found that there are many gears in a person's life, but now I want to write to you about one of them: hatred. I think that this particular emotion is no blacker or whiter than any other human emotion. It is one of the spokes which supports the wheel of the world. Without that spoke the wheel wouldn't turn, or it might even totally fall apart. You yourself liked to say: if love were enough, everything would be too simple. I agree – love isn't enough. What's more: enlightened emotions are not enough for a person's world to be stable. That automobile flying down the road of fate at times has to switch into a different gear, otherwise it will get stuck and sputter out. You wouldn't be a real person without fear or hatred, just a captivated and enraptured calf.

I am speaking so categorically because I briefly became such a captivated and enraptured calf on more than one occasion.

Sometimes it even seems to me that hatred is always very real, while love is often a little invented, embellished and dreamt up.

In any case, I want to talk about hatred now. Class hatred – that's what I have called it, and Marx together with Lenin shouldn't get offended by such a term: so help me God, I'm not attacking any structural theory for society.

I never became seriously interested either in economics or sociology. During my sweet youth all I was ever interested in was physics. It bewitched me in an instant, and I was amazed that up until then it had only been a boring school subject. Very unexpectedly, I experienced physics as a field of study that had been invented just for me. I was in the ninth form, and in the spring the student olympiads were to take place, so our teacher began to teach me readily. Suddenly it turned out that I was cracking the most complex of problems like nuts. I didn't even know how I solved them. I didn't have any clear plan, I didn't frantically start flipping through the textbooks looking for references. I just imagined the conditions for the problem so clearly that the answer would appear on its own, as if in some kind of dream. It was like I'd seen into that tiny world which was defined by the problem, and immediately understood all of its properties. Writing down the formulas or precise answers wasn't interesting any more, but I did even that thoroughly and attentively. I was always a thorough, somewhat pedantic person.

The physics teacher was stunned, and when I won our school's olympiad, my classmates also became interested in me. Before, I was called Spotlight for my drawings on the wall newspaper and Komsomol Youth publications, but now there was another nickname that stuck – the Head. At the beginning I was even happy and almost proud, but afterwards it became clear that a sardonic irony lay hidden in it. In giving me that nickname, my classmates were not as amazed at my talents inasmuch as they were making fun of how I looked.

"You know, whether you like it or not, there have to be a few thoughts in that kind of head," they would say.

Earlier on they used to explain that the emergency battery for the Komsomol Spotlight was stowed in the back of my head.

It was perhaps at that point I became a fighter for the first time. I had to wrestle not only with the math problems as well as my enemies at the various olympiads, but also with my family members. Once my mother found out that I had no intention of becoming a doctor, my mother immediately grabbed me by the hair. She became very nervous in the face of death. But the worst thing was that my brothers and my sister didn't support me. That was the moment I realised how much my privileged position had angered them. They worked day and night, and were unconsciously jealous of me; of course, they felt no hatred towards me, but they were also unable to imagine my wonderful future as their own. They understood life in a very material way.

"That's not a horse you'd want to put your wager on," Zigmas once said irritably. "I asked around: those physicists make peanuts and don't have anything to bring home. They all live in poverty and ruin their wives' nerves."

"Don't say that," Ona modestly objected. "If they were working at the Polytechnic, they'd be earning a pretty penny during the entrance exams."

My mother only moaned, "A doctor in the house is God in the house. He'd take care of me in my old age. He'd get medicine for everyone. And he'd bring a good sum of money home."

"He'd bring cognac home," Zigmas countered sceptically. "French cognac. Yuck – what crap! It's cologne, you can't even get it down."

"Depends on how you look at it," my mum lectured in an instructive tone. "Thank god, little Levas isn't some good-for-nothing loser; he hasn't taken to drink yet. If you say right at the start: I don't need cognac, just give me cash and it'll be fine."

"But I want to be a physicist! That's what I want!" I said almost crying.

That time I was deathly dumbfounded by my quiet brother Pranelis. Out of all of us, he was the most similar to Dad, and it seems he was just as modest as him, however his reply was rather harsh.

"We've all been slaving away here so you can be a doctor," he said clearing his throat. "Now pay your debt. You're in debt to us, brother. You have to pay it all back with interest."

His calm and serious speech shocked me, but what ultimately broke me was my mother's tears. She cried in such a hopeless and plaintive way that I promised to become a doctor right there on the spot. That was the only untruthful vow in my life. At the time I already resolutely believed that a person's body is not a mechanism which can be regulated and remodelled. I couldn't become a doctor – not even a psychiatrist. However, I promised that to my mother without a thought. Afterwards at home I would cover my physics textbooks with pages that I had torn out of medical atlases from libraries. Right up until she died my mum was happy that her little Levas was trying so hard to become a real doctor. I don't even know if I broke my vow; I had only promised my mum that I'd become a doctor – no one else – and when I got into university I had just laid her to rest. It was all the same to her, she died without being hurt by my conduct.

But my vow had been far too disingenuous. I hadn't even been thinking about medicine, all I'd done was dig into the bedrock of physics like a coal excavator. Throughout my life I was very persistent. I won the city physics olympiad, and began getting ready for the national competition, subsisting only on GGI, spitting out its bitter shells. They began preparing the winners of the physics olympiads from all the cities together in the evenings – everyone wanted to beat Vilnius. There was a guy named Zundelovičius who taught us – a smart-arse hook-nosed Jew. He really did know physics well, but the most important thing was that he understood student olympiads, the selection of problems and evaluation criteria perfectly. He didn't even teach physics; he taught you how to win student olympiads. And it was there that I once again got to feel the pitiful GGI. Zundelovičius paid almost no attention to me, I was a kid from the Vilijampolė neighbourhood no one knew; he devoted all of his competence to the whiz kids from the specialised schools.* The "specialist kids" had twice as many physics classes, they solved olympiad problems every day, they read university-level textbooks and went on about lofty matters. Among them, I really looked a moron. They would get to work on a problem, using the newest shiny instruments, using professional jargon, and never failed to show off. I'd take to those problems like a savage – with my bare hands quietly and frustratingly, without any magical spells and razzamatazz,. Most often I was the first to solve them, but I didn't even know how to speak up for myself. Zundelovičius didn't even notice me.

As they announced the lists of those going to the national olympiad competition, I was blindsided by a horrible injury. I waited for my surname, but it wasn't there at all. At first I thought that first they would name the whiz kids from the prep schools, and later continue with those from the regular schools. Then I really started to get anxious. I was still hoping that they had omitted me by accident, that it was some sort of slip-up, a mistake, a misunderstanding. However, the list was read through, and I had been left unmentioned.

"What about me!" slipped out of me in the total silence, and everything was in that exclamation: my basement, which you couldn't see the sky out of, the invisible shot-putter at dusk, the stone for pressing down cabbage that split in half.

---

* Schools with enhanced studies in certain areas, such as maths or sports, which were part of the Soviet educational system.

Zundelovičius glanced at me as if seeing me for the first time. Afterwards everyone who had gathered in the small hall looked at me as if seeing me for the first time. "You're not on the list!" Zundelovičius declared mercilessly. Yes, I wasn't there. They had put freckled Zenka on the list, who didn't know how to solve problems at all, however he was a cunning twat and was able to talk smartly. They put Nataša on the list, a quiet little girl, who didn't know anything at all – however, her father was a Somebody. They put everyone, or almost everyone, on the list – just not me.

I wouldn't say that my class hatred was born just then. Perhaps it appeared later, but that evening I felt that there was an invisible wall that stood between me and the others. An "invisible wall" – what a stupid and banal thing to say. That barrier that divided us was very subtle and complex. It was like we spoke different languages. It was like we thought in altogether different categories. It seemed to me that when all of them bit into a juicy apple, they experienced a totally different taste than I did. Or that a meadow after the rain or the dust of the old town smelt totally differently to them. They looked at me, but didn't see me, their eyes were not made to envisage people like me. I didn't have anyone to complain to, I couldn't be understood by them.

"Your victory in the city olympiad competition was a coincidence," Zundelovičius asserted even more mercilessly.

For a minute or so I turned into a horrible anti-Semite. That hook-nosed, sprightly-eyed Jew ran things here like he wanted. His unyielding eyes radiated surety in his self-righteousness and endless power. They said to me clearly: "Child, don't you dare resist, we'll deal with you! We'll deal with you like a goddamn Arab in the Sinai."

Have you ever noticed how characteristic it is for a person to seize on some trait of their offender? Have you noticed how quickly we start to hate Jews, Armenians or fat people, or tall people, or those that are different in some way?

No, I didn't sob, I didn't bite my lip till it bled, I didn't vow to take revenge on anyone. My feet took me right to the District Komsomol Committee, which was on the way home. Where else could I find comfort and support? I couldn't even mention physics at home, I had neither friends nor acquaintances, I didn't even know one of those older teachers who patiently took teenagers under their wing, guiding them on the winding path of life. I walked along the street, wiping the tears rolling down my cheeks, feeling like Pavka Korchagin, wronged by a horrible buffoon. So like Pavka Korchagin I went straight to the District Komsomol Committee: I behaved as though I were in a dream. I had never been there, but I boldly walked in, found the necessary instructor and even kept him back after his working hours. I addressed him without any long-winded talk, like Communist Youth from my favourite books addressed people:

"I come to you as a Communist Youth to a Communist Youth," I declared. "I need to consult with you."

The instructor was thunderstruck. That man, with his slightly puffy, unhealthy cheeks, obviously stuck in that particularly low-level post, dressed in a dark suit and pale tie – the eternal uniform of a functionary – it seemed he hadn't seen such a visitor in his entire life. He gazed at me like I was an alien from space. And that is what saved me. His bureaucratic armour fell in the blink of an eye, and he was left fragile and vulnerable. Though he was twice as old as I was, he didn't get angry at my informal address, and even put on some coffee. He sat with me for almost an hour and didn't interrupt me once. I drank coffee and talked, making up for my long years of silence. I don't remember what I said, my brain was made so light by the coffee that it was trying to fly right out of my skull. My thoughts raced at the speed of lightning, and as they struck each other ever new conclusions and generalisations were born. I spoke effortlessly, sometimes too much so. The boring newspaper articles and the political indoctrination I'd received in school fused together in my brain in a strange way, I spoke about GGI, though at the time I didn't even know of such a concept, and I spoke about the physics problems and Zundelovičius, about the olympiad competitions and Kaunas's honour, which shouldn't be defended by Zionist methods, especially if the winner of the city olympiad competition is wronged, the one who had the total right to go to the finals. I complained that no one respected me, I continued to ask – why don't they respect me, is it just because I'm the child of a labourer, only because no one fixed me up with a specialised school? Of course, I didn't say either "proletarian origins" or "Zionist"; it was that puffy-faced, red-nosed instructor who said those words, but in the end it doesn't even matter. What matters is that two days later I found out that I'd been included in the lists I had dreamt of. The instructor did not disappoint, he called the Department of Education, and my school, and it seems somewhere else too – Zundelovičius didn't go to Vilnius with us, we were accompanied by a totally different man who wasn't even a physicist.

Even now I don't know if I acted like a swine or not. That visit passed like I was in a dream, I poured out an hour-long monologue spontaneously, without even so much as thinking. I don't think that Zundelovičius's life would have become easier after that, but on the other hand, he only had himself to blame. I fought for myself, I fought for justice. I was right: at the national olympiad competition I took third place in my category, and I was second out of all the Kaunas students.

Let's suppose I hadn't dropped by anywhere, hadn't gone anywhere, hadn't won anything. Perhaps because of the wrong I'd suffered I would have dropped physics altogether. Would that have been better? And for whom would it have been better? For me, for Zundelovičius, or for the universal truth?

Incidentally, a few years later Zundelovičius hightailed it to Israel. If you left at the time, you had to pay out a good sum for all the diplomas, scientific degrees and who knows what else you'd acquired. Jakovas Zundelovičius spared no expense, spending more than 20,000 roubles, but he did escape to Israel. One of the few Lithuanian Jews to remain there. The strangest thing to me was that he chose a new profession. He began polishing diamonds in a jewellery workshop. Nothing stopped him from being employed as a physicist, he was even invited by Haifa University, but he became a diamond polisher. It appears that he had an as-yet-unseen, God-given gift for it. Perhaps it was actually I who helped him find that strange talent.

But I keep remembering that first visit in my life to the District Committee, the convoluted oration dictated in my brain pulsing from the coffee – and I grow anxious and feel ill. Earlier I didn't remember it at all. Now as I am writing you letters from the other side, I think about it more and more. I not only found support at that District Committee, it was there that for the first time I felt my own power. For the first time in my life I experienced that I can take revenge on those who hurt me, that I can overcome GGI. I had briefly broken through the invisible wall of GGI, I joined the society of student physicists, I even learned some of their jargon. It seems I became very similar to them. Unfortunately, I thought this until I was invited to Kornelija's place. In our group it was Kornelija's eyes that sparkled the most, and whose character was the best. She invited almost all the student physicists, because she had a place to invite them to. Her parents' house was enormous, you could get lost there. There were paintings hanging on the walls, while a grand piano stood proudly in the corner of the living room. She treated us to sandwiches with salmon and caviar, and offered real Burgundy wine to drink. This much I was still able to bear, but when the party warmed up, I experienced a shock.

Until that point only physics had been spoken about in our group, but that night they spoke about everything. It suddenly appeared that we were the inhabitants of entirely different worlds. First of all they flipped through Kornelija's new albums, Dali and Miró, said something about lines and colours, while I gawked at them like a complete moron. Salvador's soft clocks showed my dead time, the sardonic figures of Miró mocked me gleefully. Afterwards Gediminas played something sad and elegiac, everyone began to chatter excitedly about sounds, pauses and rhythms, someone recited Blake in English, someone spoke about prosody, sounds and caesuras, and I escaped from the living room and hid in Kornelija's father's office, but even there their life didn't leave me in peace, the spines of the books mocked me, lashed me in the face with invisible whips. It seemed to me that I was crying out of helplessness, tears rolled down my cheeks, but all there was was a painful emptiness in my head.

I wasn't jealous in a deep-seated way; it was more like sad, green envy. I didn't feel disrespected; they didn't intend to humiliate me. They possibly thought that I too had taken part in the conversation, that I had discussed Dali and Miró in weighty terms. I didn't feel shattered or offended; it was all just emptiness in my head, not like a desert, but a cosmic airless space in which life had not yet been born, where matter had not even come into existence yet. I knew for certain that nature cannot stand a vacuum, that sooner or later some sort of lump would appear in my head, some clot of matter. And it did appear, while sitting in the office that smelt of the dust of wisdom. That painful lump, that primary clot was my class hatred.

I keep planning on writing a letter more or less like this to Lenin:

Dear Vladimir Ilyich!
In following Marx, you spoke and wrote much about the class structure of society. About classes, their tasks and

their aims. You had in mind classes, describing them on an economic basis – according to their relations to their means of production.

Much was said to us both in school and at university about these classes – most likely not very deeply, most likely even somewhat primitively. But I understand a little bit about them.

But why did you lack the time to teach me something about other kinds of classes? Perhaps not classes, perhaps castes, groups, maybe strata – in other words, why didn't you explain to me anything about the division of people according to their souls, according to their relations to cultural values? Because there are such classes, they really exist. And such class inequality for a spiritual person is somewhat more painful than economic inequality. It's not so painful when you don't have anything nice to wear or to eat well as when you understand that it is your human soul that is naked and hungry, that you are a spiritual pauper, a spiritual cripple…

No, I won't send that letter either. Not because Lenin would get angry or be offended. They say he knew how to patiently immerse himself in the problems of the lowliest person. I won't write such a letter because I don't know exactly how to define what's tormenting me. But I will try to explain to you what that class hatred of mine was like.

I can't stand them with all of my heart – those professors' daughters, those academics' sons, I can't stand them because they had opportunities that I didn't have and couldn't have. In a sad, green envy kind of way, I was jealous of their grand pianos, home libraries, paintings, I was jealous of their knowledge, elegance, upbringing – everything that they got with their mother's milk. That was inaccessible for me. What I had to fight for, wrestle for with bloody hands, they got without the slightest effort – like a morning coffee in bed. What's worse – since they were kids they knew what they needed to look for, what to achieve, how to cultivate their souls. What for me was the most twisted of riddles or horrific of tortures was like an open book to them. No, I didn't think that they were showing off (and that could have happened!), pretending that all of their spiritual knowledge wasn't necessary or at least not necessary for me. I even understood all too well that, wanting to clamber up to their height, I had to think and improve, work day and night and even more. No, I didn't want to drag them down to my level (though such desires often win out!), I understood that I had to raise myself up. But what a sense of injury flooded over me upon understanding this! What a feeling of injustice it was!

I had to start as if it was a sports race, where everyone had to run five kilometres and I had to run fifteen. It was like I climbed up Mount Everest from its base, I climbed without any equipment and guides, while the others started from a wonderfully outfitted camp high up in the mountains with tens of Sherpa porters.

However, I was determined to prevail! Yes, yes, yes, prevail over all of the little professors and academic misses. I had to, I had a need to surpass them. Just like that – not catch up to them, but surpass them! I still had time and my class hatred pushed me forward. Yes, it was a hundred times easier for them; yes, everyone helped them. I went along unexplored routes all alone, at any moment I could tumble into the abyss, and yet I had to surpass them – they weren't pushed forward and upwards by such a powerful force as my class hatred did me!

I didn't dream any more about being lame or having one leg, paralysed and powerless. I had to be healthy and strong – as much as nature allowed me. I couldn't be distressed by trying to climb stairs that the healthy ones could run up in a few seconds. I had to train the muscles of my soul so I could conquer even the steepest of slopes, where everyone floundered.

I wrote a letter to Ortega y Gasset:

Dear Ortega!
I read your The Revolt of the Masses. Perhaps I didn't
understand all of it, but I most likely understood the essential
thread of your Thought. You believe that culture collapses
when the unclean masses try to adopt it. Perhaps, perhaps. I
myself also think it very wrong to belittle culture, to degrade
culture merely for the purpose of making it understandable to
as large a number of people as possible. However, you didn't
go down that road. You recorded that sad fact, and that was it.
   I would have considered you a genius if you had taught
us how one specific representative of those unclean masses
could attain a true spiritual culture without belittling it at all.
Yes, dear Ortega, the masses are always made from separate
units. And those units are not flies, not microbes, but people.
   It seems that the Talmud's assertion that each person is not
unlike a separate universe with a billion suns did not make
an impression upon you. Yes, a separate universe, and not an
element soiled by the masses element littered by the masses.
   Which is why I feel class hatred towards you, my honourable
Ortega. You are wise like all devils, however, you thought that
wisdom is your privilege and yours alone (that of your class,
caste, group, stratum).
   Each person who tries to create a theory based entirely on
the current status quo is making a very big mistake. There's
no status quo that can't be reorganised. It is a great mistake
for someone to stick a contemptuous label upon the vast
majority without even caring that purer and more humane
people than he himself will inevitably appear in that crowd.
Each person who is so greatly self-satisfied is making a gross
miscalculation.

I didn't divulge my term "class hatred" to anyone,
understanding how inexact and unclear it was. Those
words didn't mean what they normally mean. I was afraid

that upon hearing those words, people would be scared of me or start to loathe me with a different, contemptuous and wicked hatred.

I didn't divulge the meaning of my term even when you unexpectedly uttered it, when you told me, looking at me with a heavy, crushing glance:

"I feel class hatred towards them!"

Perhaps it's bad that I didn't explain anything to you then, but as you see, I can explain it now. At the time I was uncomfortable and even angry, because I had Father-in-Law in mind.

"It's not even a class," you shouted, "it's an indescribable societal conglomerate, you won't find one like that anywhere else. It's a nine-headed hydra: you cut off one head, and two grow in its place. That's our perdition!"

That time you, so cold-blooded and cynical, became infuriated. You were rarely overcome by emotions, that's why each outburst like that looked all the worse. You opened up to me when you still didn't know me very well. You took a big risk. You remember yourself – how easy it is to remember! – that at the time you could have, to put it nicely, ruined your life for such things.

Now they talk about it boldly and a lot. That hated class of yours is modestly called "bureaucracy". I don't know, maybe it all really is bureaucracy, and that's that. However, that word seems too tame to me, not expressive enough, not horrible at all. I applaud your trepidation: we need to think up a totally new word: one that is frightful, phantasmagorical, heavy – the kind of word which would give you the shivers, fill you with horror and instil a desire to do something.

From here, the other side, we can see a lot of things better than you can, as you struggle in a vortex of real events. I see that you are going along the true and right path. I see how afraid you are as you go along it. Believe me, for every person there's only one true path – the path of his own convictions, the path of his understanding of justice.

You understand everything correctly, my esteemed teacher. You are horribly afraid that the same ones, who so quickly have changed their masks, will begin to take us to new heights. That's how it happens most of the time unless a real revolution occurs. In more enlightened epochs, it is those who the people already know that speak out boldly – but the worst thing is that people believe them, obey their words, as for some reason they don't understand that those well-known figures attained honour and prospered earlier in the former phantasmagorical epoch. People simply don't have the strength to think about it, they don't want to worry their little heads – that's just the way they are.

If you shout the wisest thought in the world, no one will listen to you, and everyone will immediately ask, Who is this guy?

And I ask you, Who are you? What were you doing during all those phantasmagorical years? Why didn't you achieve your name being mentioned by a few thousand people, even a few hundred worthy people?

Why did you want to remain unknown to everyone?

Now you're running around with your seminal manuscript, *Perestroika in Albania*, but you've only succeeded in getting noticed and being praised by Father-in-Law.

Which, by the way, is no small thing. To become Father-in-Law's enemy is an immense honour. If you become Father-in-Law's enemy, you can claim that you haven't lived your life in vain. He is one of those rare people who focus their attention not on a name, not on the signature under some ideas, but on the ideas themselves.

I can understand why you called Lithuania Albania. You immediately felt the dissociation of Father-in-Law and his gang from the distressing events around them, the secret desire others had to undermine them. At once you unmasked their slogan, at times clearly stated, at times barely implicit: "Everything is so wonderful here that nothing needs to be changed at all." You sensed their demagogy, often garnished with national motifs: you hear, here in Lithuania, everything took place in a well-thought-out and correct way, and as for the nonsense happening elsewhere, let them deal with it, as all is well here! When their thrones shake, they unashamedly resort to national demagogy so that nothing can change anywhere, just as in Albania.

You're right on that point, Tomas. We can see everything very well from the other side: the entire great buzzing country split into an endless number of small, closed-off and self-ruling Albanias, where the little local kings just want one thing – that nothing changes anywhere.

The Sixth: about the feeling of security and the great community, about the chubby-cheeked bigwigs on television, indifference and internal emigration

> *The rivers flow to help others, cows give milk to help others, trees bear fruit to help others, good people perform their works to help others.*

I want to write to you about the human trait that separated you and I the most. What I have in mind is the feeling of security. I say "feeling of security" because I haven't come up with a better description for it. It's a vague concept, but I'll try to explain it. You'll understand me. You really will understand me.

You yourself talked a lot about it, though to tell the truth you approached it from the other end. You would talk about the ability to always stay true to yourself. But that irresistible urge to defend your personal self-consciousness regardless of the circumstances, to stay yourself in principle, is contrary to my "feeling of security". I'll no longer put quotation marks around these words from this point on. We know each other far too well to argue over terms. It's important to understand what we're saying to one another.

Everyone needs a feeling of security. What is characteristic of man is the desire to feel protected in a team, a group, a crowd, the desire not to remain alone against the entire world. Do you understand me? You most likely don't, because you are an individualist through and through. You only feel safe when you are all alone. I never knew how to feel this way. I always tried to help others, receiving their help in return. I suffered in childhood and as a teenager precisely because I couldn't find help and protection from others. Which is why the world scared me so much.

After all, it's not as though teenagers are madly joining societies for no good reason, into any kind that comes along – they just don't want to be alone with themselves. La Bruyère once said that all of man's misfortunes come from his inability to be alone with himself. I was always permeated by this kind of inability, which was an ill-fated, devastating handicap. From childhood on, I remember a horrid fear of the world growing inside me. No one taught me to be alone with myself, to be myself, and you appeared in my life too late. I was not taught that either in school or at home. I used to look at my sister and brother with envy: Zigmas socialised with football players or other athletes, they lived in a community, they overcame their fear together. Ona socialised with other weavers, they went to dances together, had their secrets and common goals. My classmates were divided into groups and subgroups, if one of them uttered a word, they knew well that they would be supported by at least a few people. I was the only one as lonely as could be.

Who was I and where could I fit in?

Someone else might have taken pride in his independence, but inside me there was a fear, a deep black fear that just kept growing. I didn't feel safe for a minute. No one defended me, and I didn't feel as if I could defend myself. The so-called freedom to stay uncommitted and to not listen to any instructions didn't make me happy at all. I strongly desired protection. I could depart for the most difficult battle, but not alone – only if I went with others. I could move mountains, but only when I was surrounded by like-minded people, only if I was with others. Otherwise I wouldn't have felt safe.

People that are smarter and greater than I most often

look for answers alone, but then suffer horribly because of their loneliness. It's true, they aren't choked by fear, but experience utter anguish, unable to find like-minded people, or at least listeners who could and would want to understand their thoughts and aims. The average person doesn't care about such things. I think what they care about the most is a feeling of security. The great ones weep that their ideas suffocate in solitude. The average ones quake because they aren't able to live alone.

Do you understand me?

I'm not talking about love, not about someone close to you who understands you. I'm talking about the feeling of security that is provided by a community. I'm a bit nervous, because I can't describe what the most important thing is in this matter. I'm waiting for a clear thought to suddenly pop into my head and solve everything, but it's just not there. I'll try to explain everything to you pragmatically, rationally, though such an explanation doesn't explain anything, even to me.

I'm the kind of person that is inclined to sacrifice my personal freedom, a part of my individuality, to a community of some sort, blindly obeying its rules and discipline, just so in turn I will get what I need the most – a guarantee of security. If misfortune would fall upon me, if I am pushed up against the wall, a person like me won't feel as if he's a goner, he knows that the community will help him and not leave him to his own devices. You have to pay for that, often very dearly, but no price is too high, when you are paying to feel eternally secure.

This kind of person agrees to sacrifice a part of himself, so the remaining part will always be protected.

There's only one alternative to such a path – your path: each moment remaining yourself, not sacrificing even a hint of your being, however knowing the entire time that in every case, in every situation no one will help you, you'll be responsible for yourself, and it will be you that fights and you that loses. And you'll never be protected.

I'm speaking logically, perhaps even sensibly, but I'm not talking about what I need to talk about. I still don't know how to say it. You understand, it's as if you had asthma, you constantly lack air, the eternal fear of choking torments you, and you know very well that only a community can save you, only in it could you feel safe. When you're attacked by yet another bout of suffocation, the community will lend you air, immediately provide you with a pillow of oxygen, without which you'd most likely meet your death. It's as if you were swimming through an endless sea, waiting with horror for a murderous cramp, alone you'd immediately drown, and, being a member of the community, you would know full well that a boat is sailing nearby, from which a lifebelt would always be thrown down to you. That feeling of security is the most important thing of all, you'd pay anything for it.

I was precisely that kind of person, it would be stupid and dishonest to pretend that it was otherwise. Most people are like that, they just pretend they cherish and nurture their individuality immensely, but actually they become stronger only through feeling the support of the community.

I always looked for a community I could be a part of, which I would at least have to sacrifice something to, the goals and aims of which would be the most decent and virtuous.

Most important is the price of that feeling of security. In wanting to obtain the protection of a community of murderers, you need to kill people. In wanting to ensure the support of homosexuals, you need to become one.

I don't know why this is, however, in this world the most monstrous people are often part of the most powerful communities. If you want to ensure staunch protection, you have to become a monster. And that is where the tragedy lies: all sorts of mafias and criminal clans provide the most solid protection.

As a teenager I tried to be a part of the community of athletes, but my deformed and defective heart didn't allow me in. I got myself involved in the community of physics students at school. This community, it seems, was ideal, you hardly had to sacrifice anything, all you had to do was give yourself up to physics, and that's it. But I didn't become a part of it. I felt an overwhelming class hatred towards the members of that community, I couldn't step in time with them, I could only fight against them. I fought honourably, sticking to the methods of a gentleman, but this was hardly a solution.

You can't feel safe in a community you feel hostility towards.

What's more, I always doubted if a group of intellectuals could be a true community. It seems that it can't. Intellectuals are far too individualistic. They are not inclined to sacrifice themselves, they value themselves too much. No true community is possible without sacrifice, without helping others.

Somewhat later, when I had already finished university, I was spellbound by a divine physicist and theoretician, a Jew with the Russian surname of Solovyov.

"You're as pure as crystal," he declared to me. "You could be a judge."

Hell, I certainly wasn't pure as crystal! But I didn't argue.

"I am a lone wolf," Solovyov the Jew confessed, "and like a wolf, I feed on the meat of dead animals."

He was sad, as if he had lost everything, his face darkened and his cheeks were sunken. Solovyov's sister Riva had just died.

"What kind of monster am I?" Solovyov said anxiously. "During the funeral and after it I was tormented by a single thing: that this could prevent me from doing my physics. Can you imagine? That's exactly how I judge everything: will it help me to do my physics or will it be a barrier to it? Can you imagine? I go to watch football matches, but not because I like football. Only because watching it helps me do my physics. I shout, I relax, I think better. I judge everything in that way. I'm no longer a human being, and only the devil knows what I am. What am I trying to achieve by this? Fame? The meaning of life? A Nobel Prize? What's all that for? No, I'm asking you: what's all that for – for me myself?"

So that's what real physicists are like. In vain I got ahead of myself to assert that you didn't need to sacrifice anything to the community of physicists. Can you become a part of that sort of circle? Why, you yourself won't fit into the physicists' community.

By the way, all of us, whether we want to or not, belong to one big community – the Lithuanian nation. Later I'll write to you about it.

"Dear Sir or Madam," "Dear Mr or Mrs So-and-so," or other formal address – such words would be truly sacrilegious here. I don't even know how to address him. Perhaps I should address him like some American would – Uncle Joe?

Uncle Joe!
I am writing to express my hatred towards you. And don't think that, having successfully passed away, you have forever avoided your duty of reading such letters. I think that's your punishment: you'll be forced to solely read such letters until the end of eternity. You'll do nothing else – only read condemnatory letters.

I won't analyse your legal, political or moral guilt. Others have done that and will do it a million more times. I'll analyse just one tiny aspect pertaining to your metaphysical guilt. I'll express my hatred towards the principles on which you founded your community.

I won't even mention the crimes of your gang. Yagoda, Yezhov, Beria and the like, you know, were unique monsters, but I'll also leave them to others. What shocks me most are the principles of that community of yours. You took away the main foundation for any community for the people around you – the feeling of security. No one could feel safe being near you. You devoured Bukharin in public and Kirov in secret. Even those whom you didn't manage to chew up, you still kept them in this state of horror and stress. You kept the wife of the country's president imprisoned, and numerous relatives of the members of your circle. You didn't even spare the family of your right-hand man, Molotov. No one could feel safe next to you. In this sense you really were unique, the twentieth century doesn't know another like you. Even Hitler protected his own.

That's your horrific metaphysical guilt. You violated the eternal principles of all communities. If a person can't even expect protection from the community he sacrifices himself to, then it's impossible to live in that kind of world.

I became a part of the Komsomol apparatus imperceptibly, as if by accident. The doughy-faced instructor of the District Komsomol Committee, my saviour and Zundelovičius's tormentor, showed up at our school with a huge commission and struck up a pleasant conversation with me. At the time we were being constantly hounded by all sorts of commissions: you see, our Komsomol secretary had got into a fight at a dance while drunk, but the worst thing was that at the Komsomol chapter he threw around famous names and threatened the militia, though in reality he didn't know any high-ranking officials at all. Then those people, who were peeved that their names were being dragged in the mud by some whippersnapper, badgered our poor school. But no commission could do without my instructor. It appeared he had a taste for tormenting people.

I can't remember his name for the life of me, just his eyes. They were beautiful, sky blue, but entirely gazeless. It was like he was looking intently at his interlocutor, but it was a gazeless gaze. I'm trying to remember if he looked like that a year ago, when I went to him to inform on Zundelovičius. Who the hell knows – I didn't look him in the eye at the time. Now he was walking the corridors of my school and sticking his nose everywhere: his round, doughy face would squeeze through the door, but his eyes, it seemed, couldn't see anything – they had no gaze.

It was that gazeless person who proposed to appoint me as the secretary of the Komsomol. I was easy-going and kind, I had a pile of prizes from the olympiads, and I had been involved in the Komsomol Committee since I was little – I was always making wall newspapers and publishing the Komsomol Spotlight. But what the gazeless person emphasised the most were my proletarian origins.

Later I used to see him on the TV screen quite often. He was always teaching everyone something or other. He had climbed quite high up the steps of the nomenklatura, thrust his way on to the TV screen and was still giving instructions to everyone. He still appeared to have that same gazeless gaze, however everything was overshadowed by his cheeks. Those cheeks got bigger each time: they expanded and grew, until finally they were resting on his shoulders, spread out to the sides, covering the entire screen. It seemed that they would soon cover the entire world. That instructor – now not the District Komsomol instructor any more, but something more – stood out for his truly unique cheeks. I didn't take note of his name – it's even strange in a way: after all, I'd heard it or seen it written so many times. Maybe that person simply didn't have a name, just like he didn't have a gaze?

Even now his fuzzy figure often shows up on the TV screen. If you want, you can see him. He didn't disappear anywhere. He didn't even change his vocabulary, all he did was stick in a few newfangled terms. He continues to sow those phantasmagorical spores throughout all of Lithuania, ones which gnawed at us and repressed us for years on end. Tomas, you're right in writing that nothing can change in Albania. To hell with them, if only it were really possible to exile all of them to Albania!

I've slightly digressed. After all, I was trying to tell you about the Komsomol, my first community, and not about some breed of gazeless people with doughy cheeks.

Upon being appointed school secretary, I still didn't feel like I'd become part of some grandiose community. The only thing that amazed me was my rise – both its substance and form. In those youthful times, I was still able to feel the grimaces of the great lie. None of the students, none of the teachers were planning on nominating me. There was talk about various candidates, but no one mentioned me at all. However the doughy-faced instructor asserted himself, and it was me who was unanimously chosen. I was even a little offended: after all, he didn't even know anything about our school or our activists. I wanted to decline it, but I was taken aback by everyone's indifference. They could have raised their hands for anyone, but they didn't care at all. I decided that I shouldn't care either – all the more since I had less than a year left in the school. Nevertheless, in those times I was still able to feel the grimaces of the great lie.

I was formally appointed secretary, so I carried out my duties formally. I cared somewhat more about physics problems and the library of Kornelija's father. Much later, already after my studies, Kornelija told me how she had gradually begun to detest me. I would spend entire days at their house. She got used to my big head and enigmatic glances. She wanted me to pet her, but all I did was explain the books I'd read to her. At the time I still didn't know anything about women.

I didn't know about anything at all.

Life didn't go particularly well for Kornelija. When her father was arrested, it seemed that the poor girl was about to go crazy. Even I was surprised: her father was a true scholar, a smart man – why did he need those bribes for the entrance exams? Only later did I understand that he despised his salary; he considered such a salary for his talents and hard work simply a mockery. He died in a hard labour camp. The legend goes that some savage prisoners wagered and lost him at cards and stabbed him to death, though he may have fallen from some scaffolding. And poor Kornelija went downhill insanely fast. After her father's property was confiscated, she couldn't understand how she could survive alone on her own income. She tried to earn money with her beauty, later with her brains, and in the end tried to combine both of those advantages and became a professional secretary to high-ranking officials. The very last time I saw her as she was losing her youthful beauty, smoking cigarette after cigarette, knowing all too well that her best days were over (if they could be called her best).

I really do feel sorry for Kornelija, in those days she was one of the few who weren't indifferent. The intuition of an aimless life and lack of a future hovered above all of us like an obscene bird of the night. It seemed that the younger people were, and the broader and more varied a future that was supposed to stretch out before them, the less meaning they perceived in their lives. I always saw it that way – perhaps I was naive, but I was never stupid. I at least desired something undefined, at least I strove for something or other, but my contemporaries, it seemed, lived in a kingdom where time stood still, where striving for anything was hopeless, because each goal required changes, but once time had stopped, nothing could change any more. That indifference, that peculiar non-existence was an incurable disease engendered by those sinister phantasmagorical spores. You and I hardly ever talked about this, we talked about loftier matters. Speaking about it seemed too trivial – like declaring with a serious face that trees are made of wood or that air is a mix of oxygen and nitrogen. That phantasmagorical epidemic was a fundamental, irreplaceable fact of our existence, and that's that. Perhaps you lived without sensing that horrible epidemic at all. You had the unique ability to talk only with smart people or, precisely, to get a little spark from the mind of every person. I was always amazed how you tried to squeeze out a few fairly wise sentences from the stupidest of people. However, it was all a game, a pretence, perhaps even a self-indulgence. But in reality you – forgive me, teacher – didn't know our everyday life. You grew and lived in a strange reservation of intellectuals, and that's not much better than living on an Indian reservation. It's an anachronistic, unreal world. Your customs, your rules for evaluating people, even your language were only suited to that reservation of yours, while you didn't even try to talk with people from elsewhere. There was a lot you didn't know and didn't care to know. Which is why I am explaining things to you so thoroughly, things which for most people are evident.

I was relentlessly bothered by the fact that my contemporaries didn't have any goals. I couldn't understand this at all. I didn't understand why no one (almost no one) wanted to become that evening shot-putter, grunting and panting in the dark, a mad physicist, even writing formulas with his spoon while having soup, or an ironic wise man like you – the truth be told, not everyone could achieve this. They didn't want anything; they said the hell with it to everything beforehand. They declared in advance that everything – absolutely everything – has no meaning. That everything in the world is a pretence: duties, medals, wealth, even love.

"Snitches!" long-nosed Henka would shout in the dance hall, imitating some Russian rock group. "I looked at you and saw – you are all snitches! You look like people only on the outside, but inside you are all nothing but snitches!"

It was apparent that he had in mind not himself or his

friends, but the grown-ups, first and foremost his father, most likely. His father was the city committee's instructor on cultural issues and successfully fought against rock-and-roll, which was just coming on the scene. But his biggest achievement, the quintessence of all of his work, was the constant frustration of the Drama Theatre. Henka's father choked that poor theatre in a quite masterful manner, I'd say even with a passion. However, his son, with just as much delight, fought with his father and his colleagues, until finally he was severely punished: one night, one he had probably prepared for for a long time, in the middle of dancing, he suddenly declared:

"And now we will sing you 'Socrates's Blues'. Socrates was the first to publicly say: people, look at who is ruling you!"

I didn't register a single word from that song, but that evening for the first time I took a good look at Henka. His nose really was impossibly long, and perhaps it was just because of his gigantic height that they didn't call him Gnome Nose. His eyes were small and on closer inspection looked foolish, his face flat and plain. However that evening it struck me that he wasn't quite like most people. He had a strange ambition, an indescribable aim – he had yet to be infected by those phantasmagorical spores. After that evening his group was finally dealt with in short order. They were almost accused of anti-Soviet activities, and Henka's father had a mild heart attack. Not because of his son, but solely because of the threat to his career. That man didn't follow any biological laws – he could have sacrificed his own son, if it would have helped him to climb one step higher.

No one defended Henka, no one helped him, the public were up in arms for maybe two weeks – until another group began to play for the dances. That by the way was the time when the dances I remember started to vanish – discos began to appear, which didn't need either lyrics or live musicians.

I tried to stick up for Henka – not with words, but with my actions. I invited him to form a new group or sing solo during our Komsomol evenings. He looked at me like I was a complete idiot, and just brushed me off. Afterwards for a long, long time he loitered around Freedom Avenue, growing longer and longer hair. But finally he got work in the most conservative of variety show ensembles. Later I would see him with a tuxedo-like jacket and bow tie under his neck. He looked rather elegant, though his nose remained hopelessly long.

Though I wanted to save Henka, I myself didn't make any kind of protest. I always wanted to unite people, and not pit them against each other. Actually, at the time I liked Henka more than most of the others. He had an ambition, and, looking at other people, I always thought that they were the same snitches as those Henka growled about. To be more precise – not even snitches, just aspiring ones.

They were weak-willed good-for-nothings – that's what they were. They declared contempt for everything, while their contempt was expressed by total inaction. At the time there wasn't any "compote" yet, the name for Lithuanian heroin, it was enough to have a small handful of psychotropic pills and a rather simple philosophy. The words "internal emigration" became popular at the time. I don't know where the dishevelled and arrogant "internal emigrants" heard that term, but I saw its real meaning perfectly well. It was a great alibi for doing nothing. If someone wanted to do nothing, then that's what they did, and when asked why they weren't doing anything, they would reply enigmatically: "I'm in my internal emigration." I didn't want to be associated with them. They didn't go anywhere. They were frozen in place.

You, of course, are secretly mocking me, even though you are trying to keep a serious facial expression. Oh, I didn't want to associate with those "internal emigrants", but getting involved with the Komsomol apparatus was just the thing for me? I understand your derision, Tomas, because you were one of the few real emigrants, without any quotation marks. But understand me too. I wanted to live and do something. Maybe I didn't exactly choose my path; it's more likely it had already chosen me. Now when the plugs have been taken out of many people's mouths, everyone – mostly those whose mouths were never plugged – suddenly became very wise and *en masse* began to see again. The Komsomol is a formal organisation, the Komsomol apparatus is a breeding ground for bureaucrats, and so on and so forth. They are all clever, they understand everything so well that it's even scary. I already understood a lot back then, I felt the overwhelming power of the horrible spores, but at least I'm honest and admit that I didn't have any big objections to it. We all – yes, yes, all of us! – were so stuck on the idea that the status quo was totally unshakeable, that we didn't pay attention to the endless nonsense. I also didn't pay attention to it, just like everyone else. I simply tried to at least do something, at least achieve something. I didn't foster any naive hopes, I didn't think I would reform everything in a way that befit a reform. I wasn't attracted to a career in the apparatus at all, I was interested in the Komsomol as a community of young people. It was what it was, and I had enough brains and a sober understanding to not even dream of dramatically changing its structure. But I was also not ready to become a passive, faceless part of it. It seemed to me – and it seems to me now – that everything can be changed only by the people themselves. It seemed to me that if it's me that comes to a community – with my own aims, desires, ideas – it means that I am required to enrich it, to improve it with my participation itself, all the more with my conscious efforts.

Don't laugh at me. It's you I'm writing to, because I believe that you won't laugh at me. Perhaps I am not particularly wise, perhaps I am not very educated, perhaps my thoughts are not all that splendid and unassailable, but at least I'm not lying either to you or to myself. For me there's no sense in lying; I don't want to lie, even by accident. Which is why I avoid any sort of rambling, I'm trying to lay everything out as logically and simply as possible.

You can unravel the ramblings, if it seems to you that everything was somewhat more confusing than it seemed to me. Yes, I truly did believe, being an honest, sufficiently pure and persistent person, that if I took up the work of the Komsomol, I would most certainly be capable of changing and enriching that community. It's understandable: I didn't hold delusions of grandeur, and I wasn't readying myself to change that entire massive organisation. But I honestly believed that I could definitely change my surroundings: the youthful community of my school, and later on that of my faculty or technical university. I was sure of it and I saw like-minded individuals alongside me.

Perhaps you remember how we got into an argument, and without my noticing you wrung my secret out of me: I thought that in the Komsomol organisation, no more than twenty per cent were real Komsomol youth, while the rest were ballast.

"And me, what about me," you asked, squinting craftily, "am I a true Komsomol youth?"

Already back then I respected you a lot, already back then you were my example in many respects. But I was always honest, that was one of my great misfortunes.

"No, you're not a true Komsomol," I spat out, swallowing the saliva from my nervousness. "And you most likely never were."

You howled with delight, and I couldn't understand why. I didn't know that you actually weren't a Komsomol. I was used to the fact that everyone had Komsomol membership – except for hooligans, criminals or religious fanatics. After all, they weren't even accepted for studies at university.

Such are the paradoxes of life: I respected you, I almost worshipped you, you were an example for me, but I was not ready to accept you into my community. Believe me, you could see from a million miles away that you didn't need a community of any kind, even if you would get into one by chance, you'd immediately deface and dismantle it. Perhaps even without noticing, without any intentions, but you'd unavoidably dismantle it. Such was your nature: you'd take everything apart, look not for unity, but for differences between people, until only a little group of individuals was left from the community. You understand the world that way. That's fine for you. As you said once yourself, you are a party unto yourself. Such people are rare, for the absolute majority of people a community is essential, like water or air.

Much foolishness or crimes are done by people just because they end up in the wrong community and through their weakness blindly obey its rules.

I think I have the right to maintain that – after all you know what my last community was like.

The Seventh: about you and about Virginija, about strange coincidences, which are infinitely commonplace, and the ever-vigilant eye of Father-in-Law

Whoever stands on their tiptoes doesn't stand too long. Whoever goes with big steps doesn't walk too long.

While writing I keep trying to imagine your face and envision your eyes. Most often I remember you as I saw you the first time, though now you are totally different, your face is wrinkled and tired, and your eyes don't radiate that limitless belief in yourself. When I saw you for the first time, you were standing on a podium, accepting the laureate's cup for the physics olympiads, and looked at the hall with the careless glance of a ruler. But what I noticed the most was your unbelievably long curly golden hair that lay on your shoulders and draped across your back. That time I saw you from afar, I didn't even register your surname.

But three years later I saw you in the corridor of our faculty. I was new, still a green freshman, everything around seemed strange and new, but what I noticed the most was you. During a break between classes you were standing in the faculty lobby and smoking. Suddenly someone came and made a few jokes while showing you some books or notes. But you stood there with the careless expression of a ruler, nodded your head to some, explained something to others, pointing your finger at those books and notes, or smiled listening to the jokes they were offering up to you. Though you had cut your long hair, I recognised you at once.

I asked an older student who you were, and he raised his eyebrows in surprise:

"Man, that's Kelertas!"

There wasn't even anything left to ask after such a reply. At once I envied you, but at the same time I was overcome by an unconquerable resolve: I promised myself that if in a few years some freshman asked an older student who I was, he would be told with the same wonder: "Man, that's Levas Ciparis!"

That first year of studies I had never felt so alone as then. God knows, I felt like an alien, like the hero of a fairy tale, sent out into the big wide world to carry out a metaphysical task: go to a place you don't know, and bring back something which you know nothing of. I was all alone and infinitely sad. And during every break you stood under the sign "Smoking Forbidden", smoking incessantly and glancing at me with your malicious-looking eyes like some demigod, observing with indifference the commotion of lesser people and their hopeless efforts. You most likely didn't even pick me out from the rest, but for some reason it seemed to me that I was the one you were following carefully, secretly judging my behaviour. I can now admit: I tried to make you like me, and when it came to doing something well, I first thought about how you would evaluate it. It was naive and laughable, but probably only natural. My mother had died in the spring, and my brothers, having heard that I entered the university to study physics, just shrugged their shoulders. I didn't have any real friends. I needed to lean on someone and follow someone. I invented an exceptional friend, a living example. Thus I invented you. You were to blame: you seemed such a bright spot in that colourful mixture of faces at the faculty. Your face was contemplative, somewhat angry and exhausted – suiting that of an exceptional friend wonderfully. Already back then I was addressing you in my thoughts, sending you silent messages.

However, a lot of time had to pass before I could address

you directly, and no longer telepathically. That first year of studies still seems strange and illogical to me, though perhaps it was natural, and fateful. A great destiny awaited me in Siberia, which I travelled to after my first year, having signed up for a student construction brigade. Later they would say that I had been preparing for it all in advance, that I was targeting a career like targeting a bullseye. There was talk that already at the time Father-in-Law's hairy hand was raising me up. That's all nonsense. I didn't even know Virginija at the time. I went as a regular member of a construction team. My goal was clear and simple: I needed money. Those construction teams got paid well. In one summer I could earn at least around two thousand roubles, which back then was the most important thing in the world to me. I went to hunt for money, good money, and not glory, a career or a girl named Virginija. I was lacking everything: books, clothes, even food. I tried hopelessly to feed myself somehow from my stipend, but for other things I had to earn money. They didn't take first-year students as lab assistants, so at night I would go to the railway depot and load wagons. It was hard for me, as I was not strong. However, I was as stubborn as the devil. While dragging a sack of sugar or lifting a shovelful of coal, I convinced myself each time that that was my biggest battle, that it was precisely this sack, this shovel that was the most important obstacle that I had to overcome. If I didn't overcome it, I wouldn't achieve anything in life. I learned how to do hard physical labour by the sheer force of will. The muscular guys next to me couldn't bear it, but I kept going. Only I constantly listened to my deformed, defective heart. It would become angry and pound, it didn't want to work at that rhythm, but I would persuade it. God knows I would talk to it, at times I would order it, and sometimes I would beg it to not fool around, asking it to beat normally, not to stop yet. And it would obey me, sighing sorrowfully and skipping a beat, but finally it would start beating evenly and regularly. I could stand one such night a week, and that was enough to earn a second stipend. The summer was supposed to save me, it was supposed to turn me into a rich man, almost a millionaire. After the summer, I was supposed to be swimming in money and nourishing myself with truffles. Summer in Siberia was my great fulfilment and my dream, as well as my greatest victory. Siberia had disfigured the lives of hundreds of thousands of Lithuanians, but it was supposed to compensate me for all that, and give me gratification.

But Siberia didn't want to give anything for free. We built cowsheds and warehouses of some kind; we needed to work twelve hours a day, sleep in tents and eat who knows what. That was normal for me, but some of the Lithuanians started to wimp out and complain. The leader of our team was an alright guy, but he desired humane working conditions. He didn't understand Siberia – it was like a ghostly beast wanting blood or at least bloody sweat. Even the simplest of cranes was just a dream, as you needed to go at least twenty kilometres for materials, and go like you were going into battle: whatever you won was yours. But because our commissar wanted humane conditions, he wrangled and argued, waved the contract around and sought justice. It was like he was a trade union leader squandering all of his efforts on the fight for workers' rights. He didn't understand the ghostly beast's rules of behaviour: it agreed to pay well, but only for horrendous hardship. It wasn't and couldn't have been otherwise.

You'll perhaps say that I simply came to terms with the rules of the game. Yes, I always knew how to follow the rules of the game, but at that time that wasn't the most important thing. The sky that summer was fiercely clear, the light of the sun penetrated the grass and leaves, it was almost like you could touch it, it trickled through your fingers and you could drink it. Right after starting to work in the early morning, I'd become light-headed, I felt that

I too was drinking in the light of the sun like a plant, that I didn't even need to eat, I could work, work and work as long as the miraculous Siberian sun shone. I worked and worked, others joined me, while our commissar continued to rebel, argue and tilt at windmills, until he threatened to strike. No one would have stood for a strike, stopping work simply would have meant terminating the contract. As luck would have it, a correspondent from the *Komsomol Truth* newspaper came knocking, and he suggested to our team that we should choose a new commissar.

"I wouldn't advise you to return home after terminating a contract," he spouted, taking swigs of 100-proof grain alcohol as he did. "You'll be the laughing stock of all Lithuania. The Komsomol Youth were scared of hardships! The Komsomol Youth demanded soft cots and the best sweets!"

Our commissar was tall and handsome. After a month in Siberia he'd managed to grow a nice-looking curly beard. Being a leader suited him. He proudly surveyed everyone, and with the voice of a great actor, he asked who there aimed to take over his post and what they would do once they had replaced him.

And that's when I couldn't hold it in any longer. There was only one thing I understood from this gathering storm, but I understood it very clearly: if we beat it out of there, we wouldn't earn a kopeck, and deserters wouldn't be accepted on to other teams – not this year, not next year, not ever. I knew that I had to stay there and persuade the others. That was the only way. I had to campaign for their support, force them, hypnotise them.

I'd often run through various speeches in my head before falling asleep. I persuaded and taught everyone lofty intelligent things. But for the first time, I really did speak up. It wasn't hard for me, as I was so dead tired that I didn't feel the reality of events, and could easily have thought I was dreaming. I don't remember how I persuaded all of them, all I know is that I resolutely stated: we can build not only everything that has been envisaged, but also lay the bricks for yet one more cowshed on top – the collective farm really lacked that. Thinking about it in real terms, it was most likely nonsense but at the time I was not able to think in practical terms. On one plate of the scale was the ruin of all of my hopes, while the forgotten dilemmas of my teenage years fell unexpectedly on the other: Pavka Korchagin, the legless heroes and artificial hardships, which I wanted them to create. I spoke like some character out of Stalinist Realist literature. I invited them to the building of that damn cowshed like we were going to conquer space.

Most likely we would have gone to rack and ruin or starved to death, however, the wonderful tribune and new team commissar Leonas Ciparis was swiftly supported with good publicity. Our correspondent was not only taking swigs of pure alcohol; he knew a good story when he saw it. The spontaneous elections for the new commissar were immediately announced in the press of the entire district, and the committee secretary of the district's Komsomol flew in by helicopter. Suddenly construction material and as many tins of military meat as you wanted appeared. They improved our working conditions somewhat, and we worked our tails off. Only our former leader and another four bearded guys flew home, calling me a strike-breaker.

I didn't even try to understand what they were muttering; I worked away and knew that now I would definitely get my money. That's what happened. We built all the cowsheds and warehouses and yet another cowshed on top. I, as a commissar, was given 1800 roubles for the summer. I could live without worry for two years. However, that wasn't the most important thing. I finally felt the sacred feeling of community. For that month and a half our Komsomol team was a real community, I managed it as I saw fit. It seemed to me, and I was right, that no big fights ever broke out – even while handing out wages. I came to believe that my ideas and dreams had a purpose, that they had a real foundation.

But the most important thing that happened in Siberia was that I met Virginija. I didn't pay attention to her right away, but gradually began to notice her more often. She was mysterious and solitary. The longer I looked at her, the more I failed to understand what had brought her there. She didn't look for friends. She wasn't short of money: you could see that from everything about her: her clothes, her things, her whole behaviour. She was not used to hard work, but her cooking was unbelievably good. She wasn't beautiful, she really wasn't. I remember that well from the summer – afterwards I could no longer judge her or compare her to anyone else.

I would look at her and then forget her for a time, I would start thinking about her before falling asleep and then a few days would go by before I even noticed her. And she walked alone most of the time. She was equally nice to everyone, equally attentive to everyone and equally unavailable to everyone. As Ramūnas, the full-time cynic at our team's headquarters, declared, you could smell a good breed in her at once.

"Either she's a duchess of some sort," Ramūnas explained, raising his index finger, "or she's a member of a powerful, secret sect! Just take a look how she believes in herself, how she manages to stay above others the whole time, not offending anyone. She's like a princess. Throw a pea in her cot and you'll see!"

As a commissar, I had to do a little less physical labour. I was always running to transport canned food from the military unit with a Uazik truck from the kolkhoz. I always saw Virginija in the kitchen. It started to become apparent to me that she was like me. Just as quiet, she also had her secret aims, and she also couldn't make them public. I felt close to her, but still didn't dare to strike up a conversation with her, as there were always people around when I ran into her. I was shy around girls. I was both attracted to Virginija and intimidated by her: she would look you up and down with her big brown eyes and say nothing. You could try all you wanted, you'd never guess what she was thinking. Maybe she wanted to talk to you, or perhaps she was secretly mocking you. A sorrowful secret enveloped her the entire time. One Sunday I met her by accident a bit further away from the tents and the building site in a forest next to a brook. We didn't work on Sundays, such was my own strict order. No keen types or money-grubbers had the right to touch a single brick. I knew very well from my brother the football player that if you did hard physical labour, total rest one day a week was necessary. I told my team that even God rested on the seventh day. They were amazed: a Komsomol leader had invoked the authority of the Lord our God. I remember that for good measure I added that man's nature demanded that we rest on the seventh day, that man's organism is based on a seven-day biorhythm, which would be disrupted if we didn't rest. That was a total invention of mine, but everyone believed it. On Sundays the team snored away till noon, and on my orders no one was woken up for breakfast. And yet I liked to spend those mornings wandering around the surrounding countryside. It was on one of those mornings that I found Virginija crying.

Till the end of my life I didn't know how to comfort crying women. In that instance I simply came to her and began to talk about the sun, which was beating down that morning. I told her about the rays, which one could drink, and told her how they help me work and then the books I could buy with my summer money – and by chance I hit my target. I comforted her, because I didn't even try to comfort her. She caressed my cheek and said,

"You're nice."

It would have been better if she hadn't touched me. From her hand, some kind of wave went through me, perhaps it was electricity or perhaps an even stronger energy. Or perhaps it went from my cheek to her hand, I don't know but that touch shook me, and shook her, and it was not some unpleasant tremor, it was an entirely different tremor, the kind that tempts you to experience it again, and again, you wanted her to caress your cheek once more, to feel that sweet tremor once again.

It was much later that I read *Romeo and Juliet*. I'm not embarrassed to admit that I read it so late – there are so many who have never read it (they're so unlucky!). So I read *Romeo and Juliet* and at once I felt that the same tremor had shaken Juliet – that trembling, that electricity or even stronger energy pierced right through the whole play – I don't remember either the dialogue or any beautiful words from it any more, but I remember the trembling, the electricity, because it was exactly the same as the electricity between Virginija and me.

It's difficult now, sitting around here on the other side, to once again experience those old feelings. What's more, I don't want to write to you in an emotional manner. If I'm to write a memoir, perhaps I need to keep to the rules of the genre: surrendering to your emotions or revelling in them doesn't suit memoir, but there's a lot from that strange summer that I can't forget. What you could say about Virginija had to be more than would suffice for any other wife; she truly wasn't that kind of love or that kind of wife. When I was seized by that miraculous but also frightening tremor, I was overwhelmed. I couldn't bear a moment without Virginija, she became what my hand or heart was to me, or like a yet-unseen, indescribable organ, which I didn't realise I even had until that moment, perhaps not everyone had one, just people in love. I accepted her as a gift, as a reward, for a long, long time I had been alone and empty (without that indescribable organ), but suddenly I felt I was brimming with something. If that's what love meant, I was brimming over with love. That love (or how would you call it?) flushed hopelessness and fear out of me, and eclipsed that God's Grand Injustice of mine.

Until then I had been afraid of revealing myself to anyone, as I had neither friends nor teachers, but I wasn't embarrassed in front of Virginija: I told her everything about me, not to get her to like me, but simply for one reason: that she would get to know the real me. I don't know why I trusted her so much. You'd have thought me entirely unacceptable to her: we were different in all things. And she didn't encourage me to make this grand confession: she didn't show me any goodwill, she only looked at me gently with her big brown eyes. But I trusted her totally – perhaps because love really can conquer the eternal fear of the alien other, perhaps because love extinguishes loneliness.

I felt that she was just like me. She was my total opposite and that's why she was like me, or – if you like – that's why she was my other half of the Platonic apple. That Sunday she was crying out of despair. She had come to Siberia only to avoid being recognised, so that no one would know who her father was. She had achieved this, keeping herself wonderfully incognito, but she had fallen into the worst possible despair: no one paid any particular attention to her, no one wooed her. It seemed that her worst suspicions were coming true: in Vilnius the boys would be hanging off her just because of her father, just because of her last name. She'd gone there, poor girl, to be part of a work team with the idea of being courted, but the guys worked like horses for twelve hours a day and then on Sundays they all snored till noon and dreamed only of getting enough to eat. She had wanted to test herself without realising that once they got here even existing couples put all their love aside for more easy-going times. She didn't believe me: she thought I knew who she was.

I think that she also felt class hatred – a strange reverse hatred of herself. Being the daughter of her particular father greatly hampered her life. Thus we were total opposites, but at the same time we were very much alike. I was also hindered the whole time by the fact that I was the child of my parents. In our fairy tale it was I who was Cinderella, she was the prince, but the fairy tale was a bit strange: I didn't need either a miraculous carriage or a crystal slipper – the prince in this story had to pretend she was a beggar. I sought Virginija without even suspecting that I would also gain Father-in-Law. You understand – someone like me definitely couldn't be interested in who someone's parents were.

After returning to Vilnius, I couldn't endure a day without Virginija. But as it turned out, she left for the Crimea for a week to recuperate. I plodded along the dusty corridors of our faculty, feeling the odd glances of my classmates. For some reason I didn't see either respect or amazement in them. Those glances were judgmental and perhaps even a bit suspicious. A large majority of the physics students already knew who I was, and without hesitating pointed me out to those who didn't know me yet. I unwittingly had won popularity, just not quite the kind I'd desired. I carefully read the article in the *Komsomol Truth* by the correspondent who had visited us in Siberia. I didn't see myself there. There was something written about a man of steel who had turned the young people towards the eternal struggle for light. The article was full of phrases like "integrity of principles", "victory of ideals" and "defeat of indifferent fellow travellers". The three columns on the second page were crowned by a photo: me and Virginija opening up military canned food and smiling like calves.

Then I met Father-in-Law eye to eye for the first time, without even suspecting that he was Virginija's father. The commissars on the construction teams were invited to a high-level reception, which he also attended. The reception was rather democratic, I felt quite free, but Father-in-Law was slowly walking around among us, occasionally stopping near a group of people to talk with them. He also stopped near me, giving me a broad smile, and turned to his assistant who was darting around the hall like an eel, always staying at the host's beck and call.

"This is Leonas Ciparis, whom you enquired about yesterday," I heard the assistant's helpful, velvety voice and didn't even ask myself why such a person should enquire about me.

"It's a pleasure to meet you, young man," Father-in-Law extended his hand to me. It was clammy but it wasn't soft or limp, which I had unwittingly expected.

Father-in-Law's entire appearance was uncharacteristic of a high-ranking official. He was of handsome build, tall, even taller than me, and his blond curly hair, with elegant waves combed back, was like yours. God knows, I instinctively thought that if he were to grow hippy hair, he would look like you. His eyes were piercing and held no mercy.

"I think we'll meet again, young man," he said and smiled.

He stood with me for quite a while, all four of the journalists buzzing through the hall managed to snaps their cameras. Father-in-Law once again smiled and slowly made his way through the hall, accompanied by his eel. That time he didn't leave much of an impression on me. I was pleasantly delighted, and that was all.

But then the miracles began. The commissars of the construction teams were awarded medals, with two even getting Orders of the Sign of Respect. Perhaps a week later, I opened up the newspaper and read that one of the recipients was Leonas Ciparis. What's more, three days later I was elected secretary of the faculty's Komsomol. But the biggest miracle, the one which made the greatest impact on my life, awaited me a week later. I was moved from my communal dorm room to an improved two-person dorm room. When the dormitory commandant brought me to the new room, I expected to see anything and everything, but not you.

You sat next to the window smoking, though it was forbidden to smoke in the rooms. I was astounded that you didn't even try to hide your cigarette, you gave the commandant a friendly smile and asked nicely,

"And who is this little freshman here?"

"It's your secretary!" the superintendent blurted out angrily.

It seemed to me he was somewhat upset that he was so clearly disregarded, and left, slamming the door.

"I'm Levas," I said with dry lips. "We're going to be roommates."

You didn't go to the trouble of introducing yourself, you looked me over casually and nodded haughtily. And then I did the stupidest thing that I could have done: I asked something that had preoccupied me all year:

"Why did you cut your hair?"

I couldn't have known that I had stuck a hot iron rod into your heart. I was the infant who hadn't heard the famous story about your hair getting cut. Your face even twitched. You let out a sigh that made the windowpanes shake, and exclaimed with a snort,

"Young people today! What planet are you from, kid? Never heard of the military training department before?"

That same day I asked around about the famous Kelertas trial. With utter horror I heard a story about how upon being forced to cut your hair by the military department, you brought it to court for violating your constitutional right of personal freedom. I don't know if you understood that it was an act of someone from another world. I would have been less surprised if someone had told me that in your spare time you flew to outer space. I would have been equally amazed if I'd found out that you were from Mars and had only stopped on Earth temporarily. And I found out about the consequences of your Mars-like behaviour: the court didn't even consider your complaint, but for some reason the rector took away your increased stipend for half a year. Your hair was cut nicely just like everyone else's. And I, having just stepped into the room, with one foot put all my weight on your callused heart.

"What planet are you from?" you repeated, and I broke into a cold sweat.

That first meeting heralded much of what was to follow. I, a faculty secretary decorated for services to the nation, immediately felt like some poor insect before you, like a featherless bird, like empty space. Clenching my teeth, I vowed to myself that someday I'd be your equal. I didn't have the slightest idea whom I had to equal, what I had to strive for. At the time I had absolutely no idea who you were.

It was only then that I realised for the first time that my duties, even my medal, didn't impress anyone – it caused scorn, if not indifference. For a long time, I couldn't understand that. Surely the active engagement of a person in society was never a shameful thing – it had been respected by the ancient Greeks; it was respected by all European nations. Only in the sleepy Asiatic empires frozen in time was it something not respected. That's what history told me.

I turn the pages of the book of my life and can't get over how much coincidence figured within it. I could have ended up on a different work team, where I wouldn't have met Virginija. If I hadn't read all those books about crippled heroes when I was a teenager, I never would have made that idiotically triumphant speech to my team. If I hadn't been moved to your room, my life would have taken a totally different direction. I wouldn't be hanging around on the other side and I wouldn't be writing you letters. I can't imagine what I would be now. Most likely a contemplative henchman for Father-in-Law, ready to carry out any order he should give me. I emphasise – any order.

You're to blame for my life going in the direction it did. It's not because of the somewhere you directed me to that I find you guilty; it's that you didn't direct the rest of them anywhere. You were always waiting for something; you sat on a rock off to the side and smoked. You didn't do anything; all you did was let others understand that you knew what needed to be done. That's even worse than being dumb and simply not knowing how to do anything. That's maybe even worse than being a loafer and consciously causing mischief.

Why when teaching others didn't you ever teach yourself anything? Having raised havoc inside me, you didn't take an interest in where it would take me, you didn't take any interest in my fate at all.

Now you've finally acquired the courage, finally you got up from your rock, but why do you think that someone will listen to you, why do you think that Father-in-Law will be scared of you, why do you think that it's precisely you, who hasn't done anything for years on end, who just smoked on that little rock, that can turn everything in the right direction for everyone?

Perhaps I'm not exactly coherent, perhaps even biding my time here on the other side I'm giving in too much to my emotions, but it seems to me that you simply didn't have the courage, you were fearful of doing something. Which is why you were never dogged by any sort of coincidences – after all, when you don't do anything, nothing can happen.

I did something the whole time, I didn't stand in the same place for a moment – which is why I was tortured by those coincidences. Natural coincidences. If I hadn't read particular books as a teenager, I wouldn't be me. If I hadn't been moved to your room, I would have found you myself. If you hadn't existed, I would have thought you up.

Tomas, I know that there are no coincidences in the world, I know that everything in it is rule-bound. But why – my God – were those rules so ill-fated for me?

I was also a coincidence for Virginija, but it was me she met, it was me she fell in love with, it was me she felt bound to. At the beginning it was hard for her. The poor girl would deceive me when I accompanied her home. Of course she couldn't take me to her real home on Čiurlionis Street. So I had to accompany her to a high-rise of flats not far away, where she would disappear up the stairwell, stick her head out the window to see if I was already leaving, and then follow me without me seeing her. On my way to my dormitory I would pass her house. Afterwards Virginija told me that there were two things she was most afraid of. First of all, that she might be accosted by hooligans, and I would have turned round and found that she was following me. But what she was even more afraid of was that while passing her home, I might turn off near it or peek over the fence. That would mean that I knew whose daughter I was escorting every evening. Thank God, I didn't have the slightest clue who the stucco fence belonged to. I didn't see any houses or streets at all, all I was doing was dreaming about the next meeting. That's how I walked around, as if in a dream the entire autumn, not even suspecting that I was being closely watched by Father-in-Law's unfaltering eye.

Unfortunately, even from the other side I can't ask Father-in-Law why he didn't reject me, why he didn't destroy me. Why he didn't pick a better match for his only daughter. After all he touched me carefully with his invisible fingers, took me apart bone by bone, knew every detail of my life. He examined me like the Eye of Providence. Many times, I felt like I was being pierced by the gaze of his eye.

Perhaps Father-in-Law really had some sort of supernatural powers?

Tomas, be careful now, his eye is following you without respite!

He will deal with you yet, Tomas; he will definitely deal with you. He can find the rubbish inside you or in your past, and then he will certainly dump it in your path, threaten you with it, hurt you. He could do worse: he could find some weak spot in you, which is unprotected by any sort of armour, strike at it and force you of your own free will to obey, recant and sell out.

Or he could do the worst thing of all: prove that all of your (all of our) efforts are weak and futile, that everyone has been too eaten up by those phantasmagorical spores, that no one will be able to defeat him any more – he will be the one to defeat us all.

It seems to me that the following would be the worst – if he'd let you and all of us act the way we want, but would provide us with the evidence that we can't do anything any more, that those damn spores have already eclipsed our brains, our nerves, our hearts, our....

The Eighth: about perverted morals and deformation of merits, about collective breathing and runaway physicists

The only thing in this world is misfortune, and happiness does not exist – we call being saved from misfortune happiness.

I can still see those mountains in front of me, those craggy slopes, overgrown with crooked pines, I see everything like in a painting, I see little people climbing up those slopes: bent over, dead tired, but persistent. I was also climbing mountains, at least that's what it looked like to me, but now I am beginning to have increasing doubts about that. I am trying to take a close look at those mountains of mine and I ask myself more frequently: weren't they all fake? They were very similar to real ones, shrouded by the real mists of the human spirit, but they were fake, not real at all. I constantly think about it: was my climbing just a massive mystery, where everything was falsified and mystified? After all, a perfect imitation can fool not only the viewer, but also the very participant in the act. After all, you cannot only falsify mountains, but also fool the climber himself. That's what the worst thing is. I could really have climbed it all, panting and falling down with fatigue, not even suspecting that the mountains were fake, and consequently also my efforts. What a painful thing to discover! Can you imagine how painful that would be?

Sometimes I tried to argue with myself: who would need that strange deception, why convince a person that he is conquering real slopes and ravines, if others know in advance that it's all just a fabrication? And then I tell myself: perhaps it was necessary, perhaps the mechanism for scattering the phantasmagorical spores needs those like me to appear, smoothing out the fake slopes, but truly thinking that they're climbing Mount Everest. Such a painful discovery! Can you imagine the pain?

Sometimes I want to pin Father-in-Law up against the wall and force him to tell me if he really was the one who ordered the baton to be passed to our work team, and for that medal to be conferred on me; had he really read the article in the *Komsomol Truth* and seen the photo of Virginija and me. It seems our team really did work well, it seems that we truly had earned our reward, and that my name too had resonated unexpectedly loudly... It seems that I didn't get anything for free or unearned, but doubt always gnawed at me. Somehow it had all happened so very quickly, so very unexpectedly, but when I found out who Virginija's father was...

I'd definitely need to pin Father-in-Law up to the wall and force him to tell me. I'd need to accost him and frighten him so that for once in his life he'd have to say what he was really thinking, so that he'd finally give himself away like he gave himself away to you not long ago. I could force him to tell me, I just need to try very hard.

Do you know who I am? I am everything and nothing. I am that fly buzzing by your ceiling, that smoke outside your window, that flower resting in the vase on your table, I am each object and even each sign. I am everywhere – as much as I am in the thoughts of each person; I could find my place in Father-in-Law's thoughts and accost him unawares, intimidate him and force him to give himself away.

Do you understand what the worst and most laughable thing here is? I am wandering like a spirit without a place, I dream about appearing supernaturally to Father-in-Law – and why? Only so I can finally find out the most banal thing: whether my mountains were fake, whether I wasn't painfully fooled.

You see, our team really did work well, we really did earn our laurels, and my surname was made quite well known because of that article…

For crying out loud, one of the saddest things in our lives is that in the Brezhnev era all of us – all of us! – began to lose faith that one could earn anything in an honest manner. If even I doubted that – what do you think my colleagues thought? For them, everything was obvious – a strike-breaker, the future son-in-law of Father-in-Law himself – the paths for assholes like that are lined with roses. That's what they really thought, they couldn't think any other way, because life taught them that you can't earn anything by being honest.

If I would write a letter to Brezhnev, I would start it like this:

To the great despised Leonid Ilyich!
The most appalling and derisive merit of yours was that you turned the morality of society inside out. A person who was distinguished with prizes and respected, had to be ashamed of his prizes, because everyone unavoidably thought he was rubbish, a bootlicker and imposter. A person who had done honest and proper work, could await only derision, humiliation or even punishment. You turned the morals of society into such a mess, that that was an even bigger mockery than calling that economic catastrophe of yours "mature socialism".

Did you notice – I am not theorising. I am writing letters only about what I experienced in my own skin. I'd say that I am a thinker-naturalist – it doesn't come from the word "nature" but from the word "naturalism".

Everyone suffered because of those perverted morals, that deformity of merits. A person wants to be recognised, he desires to be appreciated, but what can you do if all the criteria are mixed together into a phantasmagorical cocktail, and nothing means anything any more? Is a national award a high appraisal of your work or is it politically befitting recognition that one can whine to get, stand in an unruly queue for, or get in return for some idiotic task? Tomas, I don't think that it is only a societal thing, an external thing; it's also man's internal chaos. I repeat – every normal person desires to be appreciated, but if there aren't any criteria for evaluation – an internal chaos arises. I really do think that, Tomas. You don't know any more what do to and why it's worth doing, you don't know anything any more, you start to have painful doubts as to whether your very own misty mountains are fake or not. You start to search for your own criteria.

I also searched for them. I searched persistently for collective breathing.

I wanted to unite people, give meaning to the community I had found myself in. It could have been a good community. As I already wrote to you, I never had global aspirations. I'm talking only about our faculty.

I tried. I really tried. I never put my nose up, never acted either like a manager or someone bearing a medal. I always remembered our Siberian community, I wanted to create something like it in Vilnius. I thought for a long time as to what brought us together and united us there. We were like a single family there. I'm not putting on airs or speaking in slogans. It was really like we were one family. We weren't united by a genetic likeness, but something even deeper, more important. Genetic likeness is only a biological thing, but we were united by a collective breathing. It was as though we had started breathing together in one breath, it was like one heart began beating in all of us. Don't laugh – I'll tell you sincerely that it was a splendid thing. It was like love. There's a deep meaning hidden there. That collective breathing established real criteria, ones which our collective breathing prized, that were really valuable. It seemed to me that there was nothing more important than finding that collective breathing here at home as well. But at home that community of ours slowly began to dissipate. At the beginning, upon meeting one another, we would almost hug each other, a week later we had already cooled to each other somewhat, and after a month we barely greeted one another on the street. I saw how the faces of all of them sank, that collective breathing weakened, each of them began breathing in their own way, to their own rhythm, perhaps even with their own air, which they would never loan to another.

That whole community of ours soon died out like a holiday romance. I haven't experienced one myself, but they say that that's just how they are: wild passion on the beach, sleepless nights and sighing, and a month later, upon meeting the object of your limitless desire, you don't know what to talk about with them.

They all explained to me that that was the only way it could be, but I couldn't and didn't want to believe it. I felt that this collective breathing was a living creature, that we ourselves had taken its life away, killed it. I couldn't understand at all how it could have died. Petrelis, one of the most tenacious guys from my team, explained it like this:

"Man," he said to me in a friendly way, "if you went to work somewhere in the steppes, in the taiga, as far away as possible from people – I would be the first to go with you. It's all different there. But here," he waved his hand dismissively, "here the phantasmagoria kills everything."

At the time I had no idea what to say to him. It was only afterwards I understood what the most important thing had been there. He thought that collective breathing was only possible somewhere far away, in a small team, that you needed to escape as far away as possible from Vilnius, from all of our lives, and create a romantic work sect.

I thought otherwise. I thought that it's possible, that it's necessary to find that collective breathing right here – with us, everywhere, in every community. I didn't want to run anywhere, and I wasn't attracted to hard physical labour at all.

The very idea that collective breathing could only be achieved by abandoning oneself to hardship, to working without rest, by just working yourself to the bone seemed completely absurd to me. I was already influenced by your teachings. I wasn't fascinated by that lame-boy romanticism any more, it didn't seem to me that honest goals and a collective breathing were possible working on an empty stomach up to your waist in ice-cold water any more.

After all, that collective breathing has to appear on its own while living a normal life! I believe that even now.

You planted that thought in me, and then you abandoned me. I searched for that collective breathing until the very end – and you know yourself where it brought me to. I tried to inspire others with it as best I could. I never wanted to impose my breathing rhythm on others, on the contrary – I was ready to adapt to each community that had a goal. However, I didn't see any kind of communities like that around me. A community of rock fans flourished, the societies of beer guzzlers continued to multiply, all sorts of pseudoscientific communities formed, they whipped up empty controversies and mindlessly rearranged what already existed. Even you didn't manage to prescribe a good community for me, while you refused any and all of them out of principle.

Of course, there was still the physicists' community, but a massive disappointment awaited me there. It was my second year of studies, and it became totally clear to me that I would not become a good physicist. No, my victories in the student olympiad competitions were not accidental or invented. They were real, but they simply showed one thing: that I was good at solving already formulated problems. That talent didn't disappear anywhere, and I was able to easily collect good marks. However, I couldn't be a true physicist. I didn't know how to formulate new problems, discover new tasks. That was immediately made clear to me as soon as I came face-to-face with real physics. I could have written a term paper on a topic chosen by my advisor, a Bachelor's thesis, most likely even a dissertation. I could have become an exemplary employee in science. But not a scholar. It turned out that for that I didn't have the God-given talent.

You're to blame for the fact that I understood that very early on. You, it seems, never intended to become a physicist, but you were visited by the biggest stars from the faculty. Regardless of whether I wanted to or not, I matured and was permeated with the scents of physics, surrounded by those rising stars. Those guys played chess without looking at the board, listened to your albums, tried to play jazz themselves, but most importantly, they fantasised the whole time, concocted something the whole time. The most fascinating questions would come to them like they do to five-year-old children.

"A fly!" Izia would shout happily, pointing at the windowpane. "You think it would fly in an airless space?"

"Of course not. The very principle of how its wings work presupposes the resistance of air," Raimondas would reply. He always spoke in a sophisticated way.

"If there isn't gravitational pull, it will fly," Misha said, summing it up, "based on the principle of reaction."

"You're full of it," Izia said angrily. "It has to resist molecules of some sort. Elementary mechanics. If there are no molecules – there isn't any reaction. It won't fly in an airless space."

That was how their arguments would start about action and reaction, Newton's Third Law and the devil knows what else, while at the same time they thought up new tasks: could you dig a hole in a state of weightlessness, could a fly apply the principle of reaction, and finally, something that was totally off-topic – do flies reason? Everything was of interest to them, and they could conjure up a riddle at any time from anything.

I kept quiet most of the time, perking up only when a clear task had been formulated. Then I would crack those tasks like nuts.

"I'd definitely take you on as an assistant!" Misha once declared in amazement. "You're more useful than any computer!"

As always you smiled enigmatically, but those words got stuck in my head for the rest of my life. I thought about my fate as a physicist. Perhaps I wasn't totally stupid: at least I understood that I wasn't meant to become a real physicist. I didn't feel that limitless childlike curiosity for everything as they did. I wasn't able to look at everything as though it were full of the most fascinating riddles. All I could do was be an attentive solver of other people's tasks. You immediately agreed with me when I expressed my first doubts about a career in physics.

"Of course you won't be able to," you snapped back categorically. "You and physics don't mix at all. Physicists are at play throughout their life, but you're too serious. You don't know how to play. All you could do is be a helper: someone who gives detailed accounts of other people's games."

I winced at your words. Sometimes you showed no mercy. Most of the time you had no mercy. You cut down my belief in myself when it was barely sprouting, but you were wise as well. You taught me. You taught me at least two things. The first – it's not worth it for a lame person to dream about a career as a ballet dancer or tennis player, and the second (and the most important) – that you shouldn't cry over your deficiencies, but try to turn them into advantages.

By the way, the people that visited our room later emigrated in droves. Almost all of them were Jewish, they got Israeli visas, but left for the US. Even Raimondas had a marriage of convenience with a Jewish woman and took off after them. It was better for them like that: there they got more of everything – more money, more freedom to wander through the world of physics, somewhat more opportunities to play their favourite games. The community of physicists is a worldwide community, there they found their own collective breathing, but here something would constantly take away that air from them.

Back then I was neither a dogmatist nor a fanatic. I didn't condemn them, there was just one thing I didn't understand: why did they let them go so easily, I'd say even, willingly? Why didn't anyone try to stop them? Offer them more money, more freedom right here, not take away the collective breathing they dreamed of. All of them were fantastically smart and talented guys – you know yourself, Izia got a Nobel Prize at thirty-five. Why did they let them go so willingly?

I could have understood if they let go of or even pushed out some political enemies or criminals who only wanted riches – but those guys...

I would probably continue my letter to Brezhnev like this:

Your absolutely worst mistake was that, upon establishing yourself in power, you began to recklessly parcel out the country's spiritual riches. That is somewhat worse than the export of nature's riches. Spiritual riches can't be recreated or substituted with something else.

You let a great number of scientists, inventors and thinkers in general go without any concern. Scores of writers, musicians and artists. Some of them ran away themselves, but that didn't upset or horrify you – in fact it only strengthened your infinite tranquillity. As far as I understand, all you needed was "silence and obedience to God" from everyone, as they say. No other criteria existed any more. But only idiots can observe "silence and obedience to God" their whole life. A person who has at least a faint spark of spirit will speak up sooner or later. And you need to listen as closely as possible, and not try to shut his mouth, even if he speaks of very unpleasant things. A wise person truly does deserve at least to be heard out.

In writing this way, I think of you. You didn't go anywhere – perhaps only due to the fact that you didn't have any concrete opportunities. You sat here like some black box, collecting thoughts within yourself, asking yourself questions and answering them yourself; you let it boil inside you, you lived inside yourself – without any exit to the outside. It seemed to me that that is precisely the mechanism of schizophrenia – boiling inside, totally isolated from the outside, without checking one's thoughts and ideas against reality.

Tomas, why didn't you write books, why didn't you pass manuscripts around or go abroad, why didn't you do anything concrete for all of us, you just sat on that rock smoking? That's all people like Father-in-Law needed – for you to stay quiet. Don't tell me that if you had said something – if a hundred or a thousand people like you had spoken up, I can't believe that even then nothing would have changed here – that everything would have plodded along just like it did?

The Ninth: about a phantasmic quandary and ant syndrome, about my marriage and our separation

Time will pass and your friend will become your enemy.

And your enemy will become your friend. The ego trumps all.

If you'd acted, perhaps you would have achieved something. I acted for both of us (after all, I did listen to your teachings), I acted for many, but I still did little. I was just a tool in someone's hands, perhaps the hands of the great handless person. Imagine that you think you're climbing a mountain, but suddenly you see that you're sinking in a swamp. That what you considered to be the pure air of the mountains is in reality smelly sludge. Are you saying that could only happen in a dream? Our lives must be an oppressive dream, where anything could happen.

The first time I felt I'd done something essentially out of kilter was when I was brought into the dormitory board. We didn't do anything positive, all we did was check the rooms and catch people living there illegally, the so-called "rabbits". There were a lot of those illegal inhabitants, and I really didn't think that there could be so many of them. I couldn't understand why we were catching them. People didn't have anywhere to sleep, so they would clandestinely spread out a cot and doze in their friends' rooms – God knows, like rabbits, with one eye half-open. And we would catch them, make life tough for them and bring their future up for discussion. Why? What for? I immediately brought this up at the dormitory board meeting, but there came the infallible response: that's what needs to be done, those are the instructions.

That must have been when I noticed for the first time those people infected by ant syndrome. Ordered by the government, they could do any idiotic thing, without giving any thought to what they were doing, without comprehending, sincerely not comprehending in the least the nonsensical nature of their actions. It's a unique syndrome. Generally in life these sorts of people act totally normally, it seems they are able to think things over, doubt, and evaluate their behaviour. But just as soon as they find themselves in a community of some sort, something blocks a part of their brain. It becomes impossible to talk with them, they don't understand what you're saying to them. I was horrified by how many of them were around me. Of course, they weren't the only people around.

Our raids were organised by a guy named Šakėnas, a well-fed guy with somewhat deranged eyes, who wore a beret pulled down over his eyes at all times of the year. He was not infected with ant syndrome, instead he was a little poet of terror. He should have been born earlier, when he could have been an NKVD officer and the bard of nocturnal raids. He would announce raids at the most unexpected moments, catching the poor illegal inhabitants or those drinking beer in their rooms with an unprecedented inventiveness. Those round-ups were one of the most important aims in life for him.

You can't imagine the eyes of those who got caught. I felt like rubbish, I felt like a part of some secret, unnamed repressive apparatus.

"How many scalps did you bring home today?" you'd enquire sweetly, after I'd returned gloomily from a night-time raid.

I could have killed you each time for your smart-arse attitude. You really were a unique individual. I haven't met another person in my life I could have loved so much and wanted to kill so often.

"You have to feel joy in the duties you've carried out," you explained affectionately. "Each scalp of yours is one more brick in the collective edifice."

Of course, you were the one who described the ant syndrome, just a bit later, during one of our grand night-time conversations. You explained that, along with such types, there are also people who are functions and then there are those who are simply idiots.

"The problem of morons is a problem of the era," you affirmed.

"Why?" I asked like a stubborn idiot.

"Because they don't decrease in number. They grow in number. And that's already total ruin."

You sat half-naked, lit up by the dim light of the street lamps in the evening falling through the window, listening to your shortwave radio through your headphones, which you got when I moved in. You would stare at me contemptuously, as if saying, It's none of your business what I'm listening to, you can kiss my ass. That's exactly what your eyes would say – until I suddenly confided in you that I was hopelessly in love with Virginija. I surprised myself with that sincerity of mine.

Nevertheless you are a good person, regardless of what you sometimes pretended to be. When I opened up my heart to you, you suddenly began to regard me differently. It seems to me that we Lithuanians are too introverted, too rarely willing to talk about things. We lived together in one room for almost a year, but who knows what kind of person you thought I was. All I had to do was open up, and right away you stopped making fun of me, you talked to me almost as your equal at times. I remember even asking you why such changes had taken place.

"You have a vision," you explained dryly. "Before I thought that you were simply a pushover."

I really don't know if I had a vision. It seemed to me that I just had a feeling and an aim. As Lezama Lima would say,

I was seduced by the eros of unreachable distances. I wasn't able to be in one place, I had to go forward, conquering any and all barriers. I wanted to create a community, I didn't even know what kind, but certainly a good, cosy community. My class hatred had melted away long ago. I didn't look at those who had been given somewhat more in advance humbly any more, but more like from above. I calmly contemplated if I could lean and rely on them, and I always ended up deciding that I couldn't. They simply became drowsy and lazy in my eyes, they didn't move forward. But I needed companions. I felt like a young prophet who still didn't know what he was supposed to profess, but felt certain he was destined to be a prophet. I was just held back by those hapless traits of my tiny dominion: those night-time raids, the meetings concerning all those lawbreakers. I didn't want to punish them. I didn't need people whom I had to force to come with me. I dreamt of a truly honest, voluntary community, whose laws and rules everyone would obey willingly. It was then I spun my theory about the twenty per cent of Komsomol members being real Komsomol Youth. I didn't want to bring along individualists or frauds, careerists or the indifferent. But what I suffered from the most were those infected by ant syndrome. I couldn't understand at all why out of all the people around me, they were the most numerous – among my committee colleagues or on the District Committee.

Now that everything has changed so much where you are, it's important to not make a crucial mistake: that of saying people infected with ant syndrome are curable. As far as I understand it, that's what you wrote in your *Perestroika in Albania*. I also heard that Father-in-Law tried to convince you how profoundly wrong you were.

Don't let yourself be fooled. Ant syndrome is an incurable disease, those people were secretly inoculated with a ruinous broth of those sinister spores, their brains are teeming with those spores. It's not possible to cure them any more, the disease can subside only to flare up later and become three times worse – at the worst, most fateful moment. Such people need to be removed as quickly as possible from all places where they can rule at least something. You are totally right in writing that no revolution wins if it keeps the same people in the same places – as happens in every Albania, thus in Lithuania as well.

Believe me, I know those people up-close, and not in theory, like you. They are more detestable than the most detestable theory. They are ill. They are even unable to take responsibility for their actions.

I understand that humanism doesn't allow them to be destroyed spiritually. And I am not suggesting that. They can do various jobs very well. Let's say, they could work in a gardening cooperative or a carpenters' cooperative.

I failed to come down with ant syndrome, I had a strange immunity. The more I was weighed down by my environment, the more determined it made me. I did this and that – you know yourself, sometimes you'd glance at me, smile and nod your head.

"Well, well," you'd say sadly. "Well, well."

You were right as always. I was frustrated, I felt stifled, but nevertheless I achieved a few things. Ultimately the popularity of Physics Day was clearly down to my own actions. What's more, I...

I started to write something that wasn't the most important thing, which was that even the smallest of achievements demanded a superhuman effort. The most important was that I, brimming with the most sacred of aims and desires, constantly had to act in a sleazy or moronic way. I didn't understand why I had to run after those poor rabbits, why the dormitory rules turned it into army barracks or a monastery. I didn't understand why I had to preside over the stupidest events at the faculty or repeat meaningless phrases, looking like the village idiot in everyone's eyes. Why did I have to make those who didn't pay their Komsomol Youth dues feel ashamed, and then almost beg them to still pay, as if without all of those who aren't paying, the Komsomol Youth would fall apart and collapse? But the hardest thing to understand was why the Komsomol Youth leaders only cared about those bloody papers in which you could write whatever you wanted. God knows – my job was evaluated according to my abilities to make things up and create artfully written reports. Writing a good report was only a little easier than writing a good short story. And it's no different in the sense that readers don't care in the least if you experienced the story described, or if you made it up from beginning to end – it was the same for my superiors in the district committee, who didn't care in the least whether my report had anything in common with the reality of the faculty or if it was totally made up. Whether I wanted to or not, I started to plunge into conscious lies. I played a strange game, because that's how everybody behaved. Even you didn't explain to me why that game was necessary, what the essence of it was. Why bother lying if the liars know very well that they're lying, and those reading those falsehoods also know that it's only lies. You called it the perplexing phantasm, you said that the higher the position a person has reached, the more he believes in that phantasm. You surmised that from a certain level upwards, state officials didn't know anything about reality any more, replacing it with that phantasmic world of papers. At one time I was at the point of believing that, but then I came face-to-face with Father-in-Law, who had a rather high post, but knew about everything rather better than you and I.

Even you didn't manage to guess the secret of the perplexing phantasm, but I'll try to. It seems to me that those people ill with ant syndrome, or the people who merely serve as a function, do not lose their human needs and traits. They simply live in a twisted world, like

110

in Carroll's *Alice in Wonderland*, but unwittingly try to maintain those human traits in that Wonderland. They very much like that twisted world, they are fascinated by it. They are enchanted with themselves. But all of those paranoid reports, the whole perplexing phantasm of that world in general, perform the functions of an aesthetic. For them, those phantasms are an art, a miraculous music of the spheres. They find it very beautiful to think that they know how to invent everything so elegantly. That they perceive the phantasmic world they've constructed as a work of art is something I was greatly interested in, and I read a lot about similar predilections. For example, in the Mandarin palaces of China, all life was endlessly dramatised – from rituals through to the details of their clothing. Everyone had a role in this theatre dreamed up from the ground floor and would experience endless satisfaction and fascination with that theatre, and also with themselves.

Think about it. Perhaps this thought will help you improve Perestroika in Albania.

Now I'm spouting about common societal traits, but at the time I was concerned with entirely different things. The unavoidable moment for falling in love had finally come for me and Virginija. There was no sense left in us. When we met up, we didn't want to talk about anything; we immediately went to the closest secluded spot to make out, but no caresses helped at all and within a few minutes we were so full of desire that we could have made love right there and then, on the grass or a park bench. We never talked about it out loud, but it was obvious. The poor girl couldn't take me home to her empty house, she couldn't even borrow someone's key. The luxury of the home of any of her girlfriends would have instantly given away who she was, and Virginija was still desperately trying to hide this.

You were the only one I could confide in. I felt ashamed and weak, and I almost didn't understand what I was saying.

"Levas!" you said to me tenderly. "You know we have a room, and I go back home often."

Your simple and natural offer seemed sacrilegious to me. I was talking about love to you after all. Love with a capital L, and you... My God, how innocent and upstanding I was! How fearsome I find that now.

"Levas!" you said even more tenderly. "Love doesn't exist entirely to mess up a person's nervous system, making him go and drown himself. Love exists to continue the human race. You are both simply normal people, not heavenly angels. Believe me, I'm also talking about Love with a capital L. I'm starting to get jealous."

When I stammered the news about the empty room, it seemed to me that Virginija breathed more easily. I don't know why I'm telling you this. Perhaps because of what happened in the entryway of our great merging. I was already dreaming about our secret conjoining of bodies, I was already caressing Virginija's naked breasts, I was already... I gave a shudder, because suddenly a triumphant Šakėnas invaded my dreams with his ever-present beret and the entire night-time raid brigade. Even I wasn't left out. For fuck's sake, I came to capture and check myself! I couldn't do anything – just as I was touching Virginija, Šakėnas would stand before me in all his glory, blinking with his slightly maniacal eyes.

The thought occurred to me that I ought to give myself a good whipping.

Finally everything happened without any miracle, simply and without any fanfare. After it was over, Virginija began to bawl, and I comforted her like an idiot, kept giving her my sacred oath, until finally she washed herself and with a shaky voice told me who her father was.

It all seemed very silly to me. I just snorted, but a few days later the laughter stopped, and I had to meet Father-in-Law officially.

By the way, it's not worth talking about the further fate of Šakėnas. Yes, yes, that very same Šakėnas, the respected editor. Perhaps you noticed that even now, as the gates have been opened, Šakėnas for a long time didn't get involved in the common commotion. Just when it became indecent and even dangerous to stay quiet, his newspaper organ began to spit out fiery condemnatory articles. Šakėnas immediately understood that the hour had arrived, when he could take it out on people. His somewhat maniacal eyes once again shined victoriously. After all, it wasn't important to him whom he was terrorising, all that was important for him was to feed on human flesh. Now he is tearing apart the enemies of perestroika.

Father-in-Law received me in his home office. After two days I had not yet recovered from the shock, a state that still enveloped me when I went to see him. Father-in-Law was both wise and perceptive. He had barely glanced at me when he pulled out a bottle of Camus and glasses from his home bar. After the second shot, I was fit to converse with anyone.

"I won't ask you anything," Father-in-Law reassured me at once. "I know everything. And how long has Virga been pulling you along on her string? Ever since that construction work in Siberia?"

He really did know everything, even what had happened the day before yesterday. His relationship with his only child was very open and honest. That was perhaps the only sphere of his life where he acted honestly.

"I just want Virga to be happy," he said firmly. "I've followed your career, and I like you. I even like your naive idealistic excesses. As far as I understand, you are entirely independent, and you won't drag your brothers and sisters into our family."

He spoke about our marriage as if it had already been decided upon. What blew me away the most was that he had investigated my life down to the last detail. I saw him leafing through my application or some special dossier that he had ordered to be made. He knew more about me than I knew about myself. For example, Father-in-Law told me Stanislova's address.

"I'm warning you straight off – no hysteria!" he declared. "You're not the kind of person who would immediately start milking me. It's more likely that you would get it into your head to live in a tent and not take one rouble from me. That would be naive. Since childhood others have had quite a bit more than you, so you'll just be taking back what belongs to you. You can think of it as winning the lottery. You'll get a flat right after the wedding. I won't promise you a car – there's no sense in showing off to your students. Of course, you don't even know what they're saying about you. If you need to go somewhere a bit further out – I can let you use Kaziukas."

Kaziukas was his driver. I had the chance to spend some time with him too.

It was probably then that I had reached the highest point of my private idealism, afterwards I only slid lower and lower. Now I'm justifying myself, though I don't really want to do that. I am speaking, of course, about our separation, perhaps the most unpleasant event in my life. I call you my teacher, and probably at the beginning you were surprised about that. When I understood that for the very first time, I myself was greatly surprised. I lived with you in one room for almost two years and didn't consider you any sort of teacher. All I wanted to do was to argue with you, I wanted to kill you hundreds of times. I understood that you are my teacher only when I broke off from you. At the beginning I didn't want to admit it at all, your teachings only caused irritation. But soon the irritation passed, and I was overcome with horror.

You possessed me like a spirit, like some sort of ghost (now I can partially pay you back in kind). Through suffering, sweat and tears I would squeeze out some idea, it seemed it was paid for by my pain, and my pain only, and I was proud of it. I valued it like a treasure, but I would suddenly understand that you had already said exactly the same thing. Through the greatest ordeals I would get hold of some book, read it with pleasure, torture Virginija with that pleasure of mine and suddenly it dawned on me that you had frequently suggested I read that book ages ago. Unfortunately, a person only truly appreciates those values that he's lost. Your monologues in our dormitory room appeared to go straight in one ear and out the other, but something must have got stuck somewhere in my subconscious. Your thoughts slumbered in my brain, and while snoozing they awaited the time that they would become understood and needed. They would tumble upon me just as I started to think about my life and the entire world. Slowly I surrendered, came to obey you, admitted that you were my teacher. It was only then that everything fell into place, I breathed more easily and could live in peace. I was already consciously trying to remember your monologues, consciously searching for answers to your philosophising about what seemed in their most abstract forms like things that didn't concern me at all. But what I thought about the most was our separation. Believe me, that was more of a blow to me than it was for you.

I have to add one important thing here, which still doesn't give me peace: you have to answer for what you did. You most likely weren't looking to be anyone's teacher, however, your subjective wishes are not important. What's important is what you did objectively. If you were constantly sowing your thoughts, you have to answer for what sprouted from them.

When you said that you switched to philosophy, I wasn't surprised in the least. Rather it was strange to me that up to that point you still hadn't dropped physics. You talked a lot about personal freedom, about the need to be true to yourself, but you continued writing your diploma thesis as if nothing was going on, though you were interested in all sorts of things in the world, just not physics. If you were cautiously asked about it, you'd shrug your shoulders and mumble on about how you didn't consider your study years lost time at all. It always seemed to me that you were fudging a bit. In any case, your switch to philosophy cheered me up more than it surprised me. You eagerly made use of the new campaign inviting as many natural science students as possible to philosophy. Your candidacy didn't raise any doubts, our philosophy lecturers remembered you very well, however…

After finding out about your most important concern at the time, I became speechless. I thought that it was a bad joke, then I thought that perhaps there was something I didn't get. But the situation was clear; they couldn't accept an entirely non-party student into the philosophy department, and you weren't even a Komsomol Youth. You had to be accepted into the Komsomol – and as quickly as possible.

I was so used to the fact that everyone was a Komsomol Youth, except for criminals and religious fanatics, that I couldn't get a word out, unable to find anything to say.

Very recently we had argued a lot about my work and my future. I knew well, even too well your view of our organisation. At once I remembered all of your scoffing, even derision. I didn't take it too much to heart, because I thought you were one of us. Making fun of yourself is allowed, but when it appeared that you were an outsider… All of your talk, all those statements suddenly took on a new, unpleasant and disdainful significance. And you didn't even blink when you asked to be accepted into what you called the "glorious ranks". You didn't feel the change in my behaviour, in my glance. Being as clever as you were, you didn't sense the strange rupture inside me. You were calm and self-confident, because everyone supported you. Even the dean mentioned in passing that the Kelertas issue, you'd find, would be sorted out without any problems. The philosophy department pressed me politely by phone: supposedly they needed to print the lists of employees for the new academic year, so if it wouldn't be a problem... I was enraged by the absurdity of the situation; no one cared about my convictions, no one cared what I thought about you, everyone considered your acceptance a pure formality, which unfortunately you couldn't do without. I wasn't all that naive or stupid, but nevertheless I was blown away by everyone's indifference. All of them thought that your acceptance was all just fiction. They thought that all I had to do was include you in certain papers and issue you a membership card. They hurried me without even stopping to ask what I thought of all this. And not because they would have considered me wasted space – simply they were certain that I thought the same as they did.

But I thought otherwise!

You acted properly, you didn't mock me, you didn't broach the subject at all. But each one of your glances, each smile affirmed to me: kid, your illusions and aims are naive, no one needs them; I'm not to blame that I ended up having to overtly expose it, it just simply turned out that way. It was proved by every movement of yours, each melody hummed under your breath. It seemed to me that you'd totally forgotten when the office meeting was set for. When I reminded you, you raised your eyes full of surprise to look at me:

"Ah, yes, yes, I remember," you said without any conviction.

You said that and went who knows where; it seems you went to a beer bar. And I led the office meeting, quivering from the hurt. I guess I had realised something, or that I was going to discover something very, very soon, and that discovery was going to slap me in the face like a wet rag. I uttered the usual words, I listened to the usual answers and clearly felt as never before that I was acquiescing in a grandiose sham and taking part in an absurd play, that all of our talk and beautiful words were of no use to anyone, and most importantly were of no use to us either, that we were play-acting for someone for whom that play-acting was also useless, that...

"The last question on the agenda – Comrade Kelertas's admission into membership of the Komsomol," our minute-taker Veronika declaimed in a sing-song voice.

She said "admission" firmly and clearly – an event that has already taken place is talked about like that. You strode into the auditorium with a crooked little smile and stopped to lean against the wall. My anger even blinded me. I thought that you were mocking us. It was only later I realised that you were simply drunk.

You didn't poke fun at anyone, you had simply agreed beforehand to go with someone to the bar and weren't going to put off drinking a few beers for some trivial nonsense. You really did stay true to yourself, but in that case, you had to expect that someone else might want to stay...if not himself, then at least the formal winner.

Without a doubt, I did not stay true to myself on that ill-fated late afternoon. Out of a sense of justice, I should have made more or less the following short speech:

"Comrades! We all know Tomas Kelertas, we know many of his virtues, but I will not talk about those here. I have to tell you one important thing: I know Tomas Kelertas better than all of you. We have lived in the same dormitory room for two years already. So I consider it my duty to inform you: Tomas Kelertas considers the Komsomol Youth a formal organisation that is of no use to anyone and had never planned on belonging to it. The circumstances simply have come together that oblige him to be standing here in front of us. We do not matter to him, and he couldn't care less about Komsomol Youth. But he needs to go through this formality, which for him is a mere formality. Our dean and philosophy lecturers consider this a formality. I don't know, perhaps you think the same? However I cannot consider this a formality. I think that Tomas Kelertas does not possess the right to be a Komsomol Youth member. And I am telling you this unhesitatingly, however pathetic it may sound. We'll be making a spectacle of ourselves and making fools of ourselves, we'll be admitting that we are simply clowns and marionettes, and that those who mock us are one hundred per cent correct. I don't want to be a clown. But I'm not the only person who decides things. I've told you what I think, and the rest is up to you. I won't even demand that my opinion be recorded in the minutes, as it's just important for me to express my thoughts on this issue."

Saying something like that would have been honest. But, as you remember, I just asked for your CV, stuttering the entire time. You cast an angelic look at me, smiled with your Gregory Peck smile and said,

"Yes, of course, it's written, just Salvinija hasn't typed it up yet. But I'll bring it tomorrow, then we can attach it."

I was seething with anger and pain, but it seems I asked for recommendations quite calmly.

"Ah, yes, the recommendations. They, well, here... Well, even when people get married they find the witnesses at the last minute... Men who'll give me a recommendation?"

You turned to the members of the office, once again flashed your Gregory Peck smile, and it paralysed all of them. And after recovering, they nodded their heads for a moment, they could write any kind of recommendation for you, because who would want to disappoint Kelertas, Kelertas of all people?

"So, the guys will sign, they'll have them by the end of the meeting," you explained amiably.

With a breaking voice I asked for the application.

"Ah, yes, of course, the application," you said, digging furiously through your pockets. Ultimately you found a ballpoint pen, grabbed a sheet of paper. "The application is coming right up."

It wasn't even this mocking theatre performance that killed me, but that ever-present smile from the face of a movie star. I couldn't admit you into my community, and it seemed that you understood that, because you didn't hurry to write that application at all. If I had surrendered, I would have lost all respect for myself. And yet I wasn't ready to say my speech, so I acted opportunistically and postponed your admission to the next meeting.

"We'll discuss it when the documents are sorted out," I must have said.

I understood very well what I was doing. I knew that now you wouldn't be admitted to the philosophy department. I knew that I was ruining your life, but I couldn't act any other way. Even the empty-headed members of my office understood that there was something important at work here. They all fell silent, and I ended the meeting.

I wandered the streets for a few hours, choosing the words I'd use when I next spoke to you. After all, I needed to return to our room. That was the worst thing. I needed to return and live with you for a few more months. I was worried. I was tormenting myself, but I would have looked you straight in the eye. I was ready to rise up against the entire world. Suddenly I acquired courage – right in the nick of time, I was certain that our battle had just begun. I was ready, if needed, to tell the dean to his face what I thought about his attitude towards our organisation. I was determined to write a letter to the Moscow Central Committee, an article for the newspaper, I was determined…

None of that was necessary. You didn't return that night at all. You didn't return to our room at all. The next evening when I came home, I didn't even find your things there. It seemed like they had evaporated. It seemed that I didn't even think anything; I was just surprised that they had disappeared so quickly. It appeared that you were helped by your colourful community of physicists. Probably it was the last time they saved you – afterwards all of them scattered around the world. You were the only one to remain in Vilnius.

And out of my hopelessness, I made the journey to visit my sister Stanislova for the first and the last time in my life. In a huge flat on Nevsky Prospect she seemed like a Madonna of royal blood, though in fact all she was was a whorehouse madam of international standing. Businessmen who had regular business in Leningrad knew her cooperative better than the Hermitage. Stanislova knew four foreign languages, but she had forgotten a lot of her Lithuanian.

I showed my disapproval of her and got slapped with a wet dishrag across my face.

"My little brother, you can't stand us, as we don't fit in with the majority," she said to me proudly. "We sell our bodies at best, but not our souls, as is usual. And who are you? You're the real prostitute. We've heard a few things about your work, we've heard a few things about your marriage. You're the prostitute, but me – I'm an independent artist."

For a long time afterwards I wanted to take revenge on her. I made horrible plans for retribution. But what could I do to her? Even Father-in-Law's ambitions paled in comparison to Stanislova's. I tried to forget her, but remembered her just one time – right before the end.

And my marriage was happy, almost blissful. Father-in-Law barely interfered in my life, or to be more precise, he interfered only as much as was proper. I didn't have to worry where Virginija got money for her dresses, I knew that I would always be fed, dressed and have shoes, that I'd find a way to buy books, and I didn't need anything more. Our flat was not very big – a couple of average-sized rooms, but it was right in the centre.

I still ask myself why I accepted those almost unearned gifts so naturally, without thinking about it. You see, you don't have to search for elaborate explanations here. A person always thinks that he is getting less than he deserves, and whatever he gets, he most definitely deserves. I didn't notice that, I didn't think twice about it. You were no longer near me, so no one could make fun of me or teach me any more. I simply lived, worked a lot and loved my wife.

I loved Virginija with a calm and decent love. She really was close to me. She was my second half, probably the best half. We fought only so we could make up as quickly as possible. Living together on an everyday basis just got better and better. Sometimes it became scary – how long could that bliss last?

The only thing I didn't know anything about was her preoccupations. She was interested in linguistics. What's more, she studied Eastern languages, so with Father-in-Law's efforts she even went to study for a time at the Institute of Eastern Languages. I didn't know anything about that field of activity, the names Whorf and Sapir didn't mean anything to me, nor did the hazy musings about Montague grammar. All I knew was that she was definitely as smart as me. She soon soothed my sorrow at our separation.

"Levas," she said sternly, "you were far too dependent on him anyway. Good God, sometimes I was jealous. I felt horrible when I saw the eyes you looked at him with, how you hung on his every word. You definitely needed to split up from Kelertas. You can't depend on one person like that. You made him up, Levas. He's not like that. You made him up."

Even I used to think that I exaggerated a bit in thinking you to be so great. I thought so much about you, I fought with you so much in my mind that you totally lost tangible realness. I was so racked with torment that I had ruined your life. You received a free diploma and started doing who knows what. You wasted your time to no purpose because of my stubbornness.

"Could you have acted otherwise?" Virginija asked me calmly.

"No, I couldn't have."

"So what are you tormenting yourself for? That he won't

understand you? When it comes to that, I think he'll understand. You won't surprise him with anything. He's as smart as a whip. Kelertas won't go to ruin. He's no martyr. He's not one of those who disappear."

She was right. You didn't disappear alright. It seemed to me that the difficulties in trying to get into the caste of philosophers perhaps even helped you, that's the way it seemed to me.

That's it, that idea, that mood! I really wanted to remember it, to feel it again. Even now, while calmly writing you letters from the other side, sometimes I unwittingly start to fully justify the painful and despicable things I did to others. That's a ruinous feeling, most likely one of the traits of ant syndrome: the irresistible urge to call your repugnant actions charitable acts. It probably wasn't me, more than likely it was something else inside of me that began to think more or less the following: of course I tripped you up, I hit you below the belt without warning, but it was totally acceptable, totally allowed, and my repugnant behaviour, you might say, even helped you, as it steeled your resolve and will. So I didn't even do anything bad at all; that unquestionably repugnant behaviour isn't actually repugnant behaviour at all, but rather its absolute opposite – an immensely moral and admirable act... Thinking like this, you don't even feel where or in what place their defective substitutes push out the real concepts, the real feelings. You really don't understand where the problem is, one of many rotting, reeking problems, which are scattered about in our life. I'm not sure who I should write to about this. Perhaps Suslov?

Citizen Suslov!
This time I'm not prepared to examine your role in the history of the Lithuanian nation or your post-war endeavours – and not because I'd be afraid to or want to avoid it, it's simply because for the time being I know too few facts about

it. Presently I am more interested in other aspects of your endeavours.

For many years you were considered to be the primary ideologue of the country, which is why I think you should take responsibility for one strange phenomenon, which is firmly entrenched, unassailable and overwhelming. I would call it the sublimation of sadistic repugnancy.

For many years a firm methodology of hounding and laying waste to people was entrenched in our country. The roots were undoubtedly hidden in the Stalinist system, but even after Stalin's death they were not severed, and that ill-fated plant continued to branch out, and produced poisonous blossoms. A person could be taken down in the pages of the press, in the speeches of officials, in all sorts of internal testimonials and reviews, in closed meetings, and finally in all sorts of complaints, even anonymous ones. That treatment of people was usually dressed up as conscientious and principled criticism, but it had nothing to do with criticism. Criticism is an open argument, when one person states something, and the other can reply. But your sanctioned and legitimised "criticism" meant ruin. If it was an artist that was criticised, that would mean an unofficial ban on his work, if it was a scientist the loss of all his positions and if it was a social figure, his total exclusion from any and all activity.

That system for denouncing people was universal, but it's not about its structure that I want to write. I am more interested in how the ethics and customs of relationships between people developed. The system of denunciation elevated a certain group of people whom I'd call professional denouncers. They could be the full-time advisors of the high-ranking officials, art critics and science administrators. They appeared to possess real duties, but it was all just a cover. Their real work, their profession, was taking people down.

The time of these people (at least for the time being) seems to have passed, but they're still around. And the most important thing is that their wrong-headed ethics live on.

They were always perfectly aware that they were lying, that they were doing horribly repugnant things, but they weren't ashamed at all. They were sated and satisfied when their caste prospered, and that's not hard to understand. But there's something else I don't understand – why did they remain calm and satisfied when their caste was publicly castigated? You see, what's strange to me, what I really can't understand is that even now they aren't ashamed in the least, even now they're not the tiniest bit afraid. They sleep soundly, which is the worst and most amazing thing about it. You'd have thought that they would be shaking and constantly jumping up in the night, drenched in a cold sweat – after all, all of their work was one long chain of sordid behaviour, and their innocent victims now could peacefully settle their scores with them; not take revenge, but settle their scores fairly. However, professional denouncers sleep soundly. They're not afraid of anything at all. There must be something essentially warped in the very system of practical ethics, if those people aren't afraid of retribution at all. What's more – even today they feel they are in the right, they justify all of their ghastly work soberly. I'd say they don't even remember it, and they're certain that they've always acted correctly. That's what I simply cannot understand.

What did you do to people, what did you do to their minds and morals that things like this could possibly happen? Share your experience with me. It's indispensable for the study of psychology and perhaps even psychiatry. It's a special selection process. Tell me your secret – how do you breed such people? Is it simply a psychological effect or are such people bred by methods of genetic selection? Will their children be born like that or can you still change them?

The Tenth: about my son and my soul, about Father-in-Law's stories and dead bodies that weren't dead bodies, but the most important of all – about my first end

"Your son is you, you caused him to come into this world," wise men say. Look at your son, and you'll see yourself – look at yourself, and you'll see your son.

This letter will probably end up being very long, because there's a lot I want to say. For a true memoirist, it may make sense to spread all of those events over a few chapters, but I care more about recreating my life for you than retelling everything in chronological order. In my life it all happened to me without rhyme or reason, and quite mercilessly, so I'm just going to dump it in your head. It'll all become clear for you – if, of course, you want to understand it.

I was just beginning to wonder: what do you think about me, what did you think about me during all those years when we didn't even meet, didn't talk at all? Perhaps I appeared naive and ridiculous, or perhaps you forgot all about me long ago? Perhaps you look at me from the heights of a radically changed life, and you only see me as a tiny ant, a creature from those accursed times, a creature not even worth wasting time on?

Don't think about me like that. My sad story could only perhaps have happened in such a strange, phantasmagorical time, which now is modestly called the time of stagnation. But I wasn't given to stagnating and encouraging others to stagnate; I was a participant in history, whereas the truest stagnaters are still alive. So perhaps my story still has meaning today, and will have meaning tomorrow, and... Think about it.

Everything became jumbled up in my life when my son was born. I've already written that everything belonging to the body seemed spiritual to me, almost mystical, so imagine how I was affected by a new life, the appearance of a new body. I was blown away and fascinated; a new life in my house was a miracle that had happened to me alone, the only one in the history of civilisation. I am not exaggerating one bit – that's exactly how I felt. First of all I began to consider with horror whether I had passed on any of my defects to my son. My heart defects – in both the literal and figurative senses. Until then I had felt responsible only for myself – Virginija was a very strong woman, and I didn't need to support her. After my son was born, I felt responsible for him or, in other words, for the whole world.

Living is hard for someone who is responsible for the whole world.

I looked after my child and in my thoughts I continued to argue with you. I tried to convince you of something, though I knew that you couldn't hear me and, it seems, won't hear me any more. Raising a child is hard work. All the time I was dragging myself around short of sleep and often talking out loud to myself. I was suddenly overcome by the horror that I wouldn't have anything to pass on to my son. I still hadn't decided what I was going to do with my life, and now had to think of what I was going to pass on to my son. When you disappeared, my everyday worries unexpectedly became my entire life, its content and essence. To my horror, realised that I couldn't talk and think about anything except those worries. Previously I would have occasionally sunk into a different, more complicated world that was somewhat more elevated than the mundane everyday, a world of conversations with you. When you vanished, all that was left inside me were everyday worries, organisational troubles and the nonsense of writing reports. I began lying more and more often and more and more hopelessly. Every day I continued to find new absurdities in my life, new deceptions and new inanities. Is that what I had to pass on to my son? I felt that soon I wasn't going to be left with anything that could be passed on to him. Gradually I began to feel that I was losing, irretrievably losing my immortal soul.

"Soul" is a strange and unfathomable word. I thought sometimes that it doesn't have meaning at all, but other times that it was the only meaningful notion in the world. I think that a person doesn't always match up with his soul. I'd go so far as to say that they don't match up most of the time. I think that the entire life of a person is an effort to retrieve his lost soul.

I myself tried to do that my entire life.

There are quite a few people who don't need a soul at all. It was absolutely necessary for me – for myself, and also so I'd have something to pass on to my son.

I don't know if love alone is enough for the soul. Love is a lot, really a lot, I read the miraculous words of St Paul on love a thousand times. I experienced love myself, I lived it. Perhaps it alone isn't enough, perhaps you can't breathe in love all the time.

I know your opinion on the matter, as you always repeated that line from Camus: if love were enough, everything would be too simple.

I loved Virginija. Then I loved Birutė. I loved my son like crazy, that big-headed droopy-eared Levukas. They say that parents sometimes for no reason start to morbidly doubt whether the child is theirs or not. Looking at my son's big head and droopy ears, I could rest calm in the knowledge that I wasn't going to be seized by that kind of paranoia. But then I feared for Levukas's heart all the more. I was dreadfully afraid of taking him to a cardiologist. Thank God he inherited his heart from Father-in-Law's side. Father-in-Law's heart was as durable and long-lasting as a diesel motor. Perhaps, I said, the soul always prefers to snuggle up to a poor, sickly heart?

I very much wanted to keep my little Levas from having to look for his lost soul. I wanted that so much that I began to examine myself with suspicion. I always believed that the first spark for a person was lit by his parents and grandparents. If my grandfather hadn't been a woodcarver of religious statues, I wouldn't have become the kind of person I was.

I was suffering because I was trying to guess what kind of spark I was going to light in my son's heart. I loved him very much.

I was still looking for that spark or perhaps something more along the lines of a flint that could start it. Each person is a seeker, but I was an exceptional seeker. Perhaps because my daily life at the time was sorted out. I had time for my seeking.

People shouldn't have serious concerns about earning their daily bread, otherwise they'll only look for bread, and not for their lost souls.

The end of my studies was approaching quickly, and I suddenly realised that I didn't have a clue what to do. I tried to sit down and think about it, but the monotonous flow of events carried me along unhindered. Our life was already planned in such a way that we wouldn't have time to sit down and think. I no longer understood what I was doing and why I was doing it. I dropped out of the physics community altogether, as no one wanted me as a physicist. I couldn't even talk with my course mates – we spoke different languages. All of those years they had done a particular job, gathered themselves into a particular community, in which there was no place left for me. Whether I wanted to or not, I thought about what I'd done during those years, who I could have a friendly chat with, who I could confide in.

All I could do was talk with those same paper report

martyrs from other faculties. Some of them were pretty nice guys – for chatting or having a beer. There wasn't one I could mention the idea of a grand community to – or the feeling of security and the ant syndrome. I couldn't even hint at such things. I also interacted with the district committee instructors and secretaries, but had no interest in chatting to them – in a friendly way or otherwise. Not one of them had any lofty goals or similar foolish notions. As far as I could see, those people were dead. I tried to prove to myself that I wasn't, that I was at least trying to achieve something, so…

Inside I was persistently striving for who knows what, but it became utterly unbearable when I sat down and came up with what I had actually accomplished. I had organised a Physicists' Day three times, and it had become popular all over Vilnius. I had got a group of windsurfers together, supported a few rock musicians, and also set up a few amusements for myself. However, that really wasn't it. All those things were just fun and games. With such ambitions, I could, in the best-case scenario, become the director of the Sports Palace, but I'd dreamt of becoming a prophet! Yet no one listened to me. The windsurfers and rock musicians didn't feel any gratitude towards me, nor did they even talk to me – after all, I wasn't a windsurfer or a rock musician. Other people in general couldn't have cared less about me.

To tell the truth, there is one more significant thing I did – in a proud and principled manner I disfigured your life, and in doing that I did something worse to myself – I drove you out my life.

What else did I fill those four years with, after the construction work in Siberia?

Mostly lies, fabrications and nonsense. For some reason I made myself believe that a noble goal could be reached by fictitious means, that the nobility of a goal sooner or later would compensate for everything. I was naive. I was an idiot.

Imagine the following scene from a non-existent film: a wretched, bald man with an oblong head and dressed in black or grey clothing is hidden behind piles of papers – paperclips, forms, circulars – and is going through those papers over and over again, moving them from one place to another. A piece of paper constantly falls on the ground, the poor man coughs, crawls clumsily under his desk, lifts the paper up, cleans the dust off it, leans on the table and smiles faintly. You'd think that he's happy. That bald and crouched-over man is surrounded by paper flowers, paper dogs and paper birds. He pets those paper dogs, he loves them, because his soul too is made out of paper.

That is what I saw as I looked in the mirror of my soul.

Probably I needed to go to you, get down on my knees and beg for your advice. Pride didn't allow me to do that. I was still trying to retain my pride.

I was still trying to fool myself, and didn't admit even to myself that I had been doing one particularly horrible thing all of those years. I passively supported the universal lie that was flourishing unabated. Subjectively I was striving for something else, I was going on about lofty goals, but objectively I was supporting a kingdom of lies. I adapted to it and it swallowed me up.

I was already prepared to become a worthy son-in-law for Father-in-Law.

In the meantime I had not ascended the steps of the secret hierarchy even to the level of Father-in-Law's driver Kaziukas. Officials' drivers don't sit in luxurious offices or presidiums, but they are immensely important people. Now that all sorts of denunciations and *exposés* have become so popular, journalists shouldn't be digging through papers or hanging around elite circles. If they're looking for juicy material, they should talk to those who were driving the officials around. They're full of information that you wouldn't find in any secret archives. They know absolutely everything. Drivers and all sorts of assistants and people carrying briefcases – they are a closed society, a Masonic lodge, they know one another through special signs, from facial expressions, from the secret glimmering of their eyes.

Father-in-Law's driver Kaziukas was one of those omnipotent Masons.

He was a small, heavily built man, and his hair was always cut very short. He reminded me of my father in some way, perhaps because of the fact he was working all the time, though his work was rather suspect.

He had become part of the car, he was a centaur – half man, half vehicle. Even when he got out of his Volga and stood on his own two feet, I sensed that he might switch gears somewhere under his armpits and speed off down the street at a hundred kilometres per hour. It seemed like he had a wound-up spring inside him. No, he didn't run around like he was wound up too tight; he wasn't loud, he was quiet and contemplative, but there was certainly a wound-up spring hidden inside him. He was the embodiment of activity. He was Father-in-Law's legs.

Once I drove with Kaziukas through all of Lithuania. He was driving me from Palanga, and at the same time performing his primary duty: collecting tributes for Father-in-Law. I sat in a limousine with tinted windows, real leather seats, a radiotelephone and a Japanese television. I had been too long in the sun and was slightly light-headed, so everything seemed a tad unreal. I briefly felt like I was the real owner of the limousine, and looked contemptuously at the shitty little cars as we passed them one after another. For the first and only time, I felt like I was the centre of the world. That afternoon I ruled the world and viewed it disdainfully through my squinting eyes. I was ashamed, I'm even ashamed now that I remember it, but that's how it was.

We drove along the mysterious zigzagging routes and collected tributes. In one place we got smoked vendace, at another French champagne, at a third fantastic custom-made hunting cartridges, and finally mysterious packages whose contents were probably the very essence of power, its alluring force. Kaziukas would pull up at some factory, luxurious house in the country or the party's district committee building and park. He would smoke a cigarette without turning the motor off. And at once an indulgent figure with a package would suddenly emerge from a door. Kaziukas wouldn't even turn towards them, but just point to the boot with his thumb. He would occasionally get out visibly annoyed and return cursing: those arses don't even know how to put a package together properly. And he would get particularly angry if a meek figure didn't show up at once on his arrival. He would pump the horn in rage, the limousine would howl as though it were alive, and someone would come running, almost stumbling, and guiltily lowering their eyes. All of those people were gazeless, that was their defining feature. Kaziukas would get horribly angry at those who weren't on time, and the perspiring district committee secretaries, who would bow in front of him, could have licked his shoes or done who knows what. Capriciously, I was draped over the back seat and kept wanting to order one of them to get down in the dust on their knees. Any of those gazeless people would have done it, it wasn't even interesting to demand it – it was so clear anyway that they would have got down on their knees, not in front of me, but in front of Kaziukas. I understood that the district boss in this secret hierarchy was Father-in-Law's driver – there was no comparing them. Everyone was quaking as they awaited Kaziukas, and a secret service appeared to be tracking the progress of our limousine and its arrival time down to the nearest minute. We collected tributes, a sacred ritual, and the smallest mistake or slip-up could offend Father-in-Law's shadow which was lazily hovering over our Volga limo. We checked a few lakes closed to the public – one for fishing, another for hunting ducks – and we checked other hunting grounds. Finally we threw a couple smoked chickens in the back seat. They appeared so miserable to me that Kaziukas immediately sensed what I was thinking and explained, "This is a rare delicacy! They are marinated and smoked by a Heroine of Socialist Labour. The woman really earned her title: no one else in the world smokes chickens like she does."

We stopped to swim at a small closed lake and tried the chicken. It really did have an extraordinary taste, the taste of power and rapture. When we drove further on in a drowsy state, the other cars moved to the side, giving the road over to us. The traffic inspectors were giving us a salute as we whistled through the country at a fantastic speed, and that afternoon I really did feel almost all-powerful.

That afternoon I looked at the entire world from above. And at those poor physicists, forever slaving away at their strange problems. And at you, my teacher: that afternoon you were just a poor dishevelled little man, who would spit while he talked, and go crazy about lofty matters that no one cared about. I could have crushed you all with the movement of a finger, I could have squashed you all like fleas.

At first Virginija couldn't talk to me at all, but afterwards, when I for no particular reason pulled her into my arms, she just sighed and moaned out of satisfaction.

"You've never been like that before," she said to me after everything. "You were like a god."

If that evening I'd started a second son, he would probably have become the ruler of the universe.

The sobering-up came that same evening. You made me sober. Without wanting it at all, quite against my will, I remembered one of your teachings.

"When you see those kinds of riches," you explained to me back then, "when you meet a prosperous man, always think about the price those riches were acquired at, and consider whether you would agree to pay that price."

Father-in-Law definitely wasn't stupid. He was and is just as clever as you. His piercing gaze hides a formidable mind. He would amaze me just like you did. Among the men in power, he always looked like you in the faculty's teaming hallway – like a conspicuous stain on a colourful carpet. He was physically strong and not the least bit senile. He played tennis ferociously, and older women swooned at his voice. He liked absurd jokes and made up great political anecdotes. Just in my hearing, he invented maybe ten different variations on the subject of Brezhnev's eyebrows, some of which I later heard other people telling each other in the street.

It would be easy to disparage some senile halfwit or soulless opportunist, who only cared about their privileges and other shiny objects. Father-in-Law was not like that at all.

You can admire him and even respect him in a way. Without a doubt, you need to fear him. It probably isn't possible to only love him.

His attitude to me was cool, but he was amiable. He didn't focus too much on me, but he also didn't allow me to be forgotten or feel cheated. He let me operate on my own, but would clean up the place of operation. As far as I can tell, he was simply monitoring me. He wanted to figure out who I was and what I was worth. He was too clever to elevate his son-in-law only because he was his son-in-law. Now I understand that he was deciding what he was going to offer me – either a sinecure or the epaulettes of his aide-de-camp.

Sometimes I think, How would you have acted if you'd been in my place? And at once I reply, You could never have found yourself in my place for many reasons. Then I pose the question in a different way, What is the most exquisite, most refined thing I could have done? The most refined trick would have been to conscientiously fight for the epaulettes of his aide-de-camp, find out his secrets, examine his security system, and then cruelly annihilate him.

But then I immediately ask myself, What would I have to do afterwards?

Now it seems like that "afterwards" has come. So what are you planning to do, having listened to Father-in-Law's remarks on your *Perestroika in Albania*, and having heard everything he dared say to you?

That question of the price you'll have to pay is to be found in the fairy tales and myths around the world. You'll pay with your soul.

Those father-in-laws haven't been hunting for their lost souls for a long time, and I think they've forgotten about their existence.

One of man's greatest misfortunes is that his body and even his brain can manage perfectly well without any sort of soul.

But at what price?

At the beginning I didn't want to believe the various stories about Father-in-Law, but then there were so many came out that it was impossible to ignore them all. There were too many living witnesses, too many people wronged. They all complained, lamented and condemned Father-in-Law. When I was told about the grisly horrors he carried out during the post-war years while practically a teenager, I even wanted to put together a dossier on him. Maybe he thought that gathering a dossier on others was his privilege and his alone, I wanted to show him that the reverse could also be possible.

However, I changed my mind pretty quickly. I'm not and don't want to be Father-in-Law's biographer. And also the dry description of other people's pain never leaves a mark. With the expression of an overly satisfied snob we read about endless suffering, torn-out entrails and severed heads, but it barely leaves an impression on us, unless a grand master of the quill writes it. But everyone will talk of how they cut their finger in an especially vivid, convincing and painful way. How the blood gushed out, how it hurt and how that horrible wound didn't heal for such a long time!

That's how man is made: in reality he only empathises with his own pain. So I too will only tell you what I experienced, the other stuff you can figure out on your own. You'll have no trouble filling in the missing details in Father-in-Law's portrait, as you never lacked perceptiveness and imagination.

I will start with some details, such as the following: Father-in-Law sits in his office, looks tenderly at his interlocutor and promises him generous support, care and protection. But just as soon as his interlocutor closes the door, he calmly dials a telephone number and orders that man to be done away with. A detail? Probably. Every politician's daily bread? Most likely. However such details tormented me my whole life.

Yet another detail. I was once visited by a neighbour from Kaunas, a former hooligan on our street. He bravely carried his cross, and took care of his sick mother and supported his sister who'd been injured in an accident. I was shocked when I found out that he still lived in the same kind of basement flat I'd lived in way back when. I had somehow forgotten that such things existed. He asked me to intercede, but not for himself. He begged me to save his brother, an economist, who had thought up some sort of experimental system, which in one factory had produced miraculous results. The brother had undergone all the Stations of the Cross, languished in court, even taken things as far as Moscow, and ultimately almost defended his idea. He wanted things to be better for all of us. He was one of the upright communists – an increasingly rare species in those times. But suddenly he was relieved of all his duties and almost convicted of who knows what. My former neighbour continued to show me the conclusions of the scientific committees time and again, and cried real tears. He insisted that Father-in-Law could fix everything, as his economist brother wholeheartedly believed in Father-in-Law's mind and power. His brother felt that enormous GGI. He stood on the verge of suicide, and only Father-in-Law could save him. My guest told me everything so convincingly that I almost began to cry.

I steeled myself to go to Father-in-Law officially for the first time. That economist seemed like one of our own, he had a sacred mission, and wanted things to be better for all of us. I prepared for the visit as if for an exam, and looked through the documents my neighbour had brought me, repeating the process ten times. I was a little proud of Father-in-Law and – there's no sense in hiding it – of myself. A person who was backed into a corner was searching for justice from not just any person, but from Father-in-Law himself. People believed in him. And I was the mediator by which justice would be re-established. I clearly imagined how Father-in-Law would hear me out with interest and glance at the documents. Perhaps he would seek out some further expert opinion. I could clearly foresee how he would re-establish justice, and I would have contributed to that. I naively imagined how that economist's production model would begin working better and better, how gradually the entire system would correct itself, and how…

I was green, very green. Father-in-Law listened to me without interruption, and then swept the documents I'd brought him off to the side. He knew about that person, but wasn't planning to correct this horrible injustice at all. The concept "justice" didn't exist in his mind. So is that economist right or not? I asked, but Father-in-Law couldn't even understand what I wanted to know. You see, Macaitis (the economist) had committed a faux pas, some sort of subordination. He hadn't listened to some order, which had been expressed in the form of a recommendation. What's more, he had complained to Moscow. But was he right? I asked, and why was he attacked – not just him but also the most important thing, his system, which could have been beneficial to us all? Father-in-Law truly didn't understand what I wanted. It was as if he were saying, What injustice, what undeserved personal ruin, and furthermore – what guy are we talking about? That economist had been purged and didn't exist for Father-in-Law. As far as I understood, at one time he had stood in Father-in-Law's way, and then he'd died, disappeared into thin air. In Father-in-Law's eyes, I was a necrophile. I had dug up this man's rotting carcass from the ground and demanded that it be washed, polished and worshipped. I was a nutcase. The strangest expressions of my craziness were my inexplicable fiery assertions about "the benefit for us all", "morality" and "how can we punish a man who brings us only goodness and virtue?" Father-in-Law answered me very clearly that this seeker of justice and disturber of the peace was not useful FOR US. We were speaking different languages, and our brains worked according to a different logic.

I was overwhelmed by apprehension. I started to lack air, and my sickly heart began to beat irregularly and tonelessly. I had understood long ago that the disappearance of Macaitis was in accordance with the rules, sanctioned by Father-in-Law himself. But I no longer understood what those rules were, the ones by which such people were purged. That economist Macaitis was in somebody's way, but who could he have been obstructing, if he was merely trying to make things better for us all? That much I understood, even without being an economist. Who was he obstructing? For a long time that question wouldn't give me peace, and sooner or later I had to ask who were "us all". And then I had to ask who were the "not us". Even later I had to ask which of those groups did I belong to and which was I helping. And then I had to answer that question myself.

It turned out that I was teetering on the border between "us all" and "not us". It turned out to be even stranger than that: I wanted to find justice "for us all" while becoming a part of the "not us". It turned out that I was pursuing the sacred aims of "for us all" while using the methods and rules of the "not us".

Thus I remained dangling between heaven and earth: I was assigned a position as a physics lecturer in a big technical school. And, of course, I quickly became the Komsomol secretary of that school.

At the time I was essentially doing nothing. Would you call giving lectures on the more banal elements of the physics syllabus, participating in the even more banal Komsomol meetings and writing phantasmagorical reports as doing something? If I did anything, I did research into Father-in-Law. You could say I attempted to try his clothes on – after all, if I stopped dangling between heaven and earth, then that was going to be my best future option.

Up till then, Father-in-Law hadn't seemed entirely real to me – no more real than to the average newspaper reader. Though I saw him close up, heard how blissfully he panted while scratching his chest hair, and observed how he ran up the stairs to the fourth floor like a young man. I could play chess with him and even win – he didn't become angry at all and wasn't a sore loser, in this sense he was almost poetic. It was more fun for him to lose, while having come up with some elegant combination, than win a boring and tedious match. I could never comprehend that man. He was clever and by no means shallow. He was a handsome older man without a soul. He was a monster with a great number of pleasant traits.

I would always remember how you complained back then, "We have so much fallen out of the habit of colourful people that when we meet a multifaceted person we get totally confused. Our life is so monotonous and the people so banal that we've totally forgotten the variety of the world. We are so used to one-dimensional people that when we meet someone different, we no longer know how to act or what to think."

It seemed that you were talking to me about Father-in-Law.

I never did comprehend that man, I didn't understand his credo, his aims. Others often said to me that the desire for power wins out over all other feelings, but I don't believe that. A person has to have more complex aims than a desire to be the head of the pack. That's characteristic of animals, but such a refined and complex man as Father-in-Law simply had to have more complex global plans.

He is a metaphysical being. He has some sort of secret intentions, but I never succeeded in decoding them.

Only gradually did he begin to manifest as a genuinely metaphysical being. I was in awe of him as the first human was of a magician. Perhaps all magic derives from a lack of knowledge. That's what happened to me with Father-in-Law. I examined his work almost unconsciously, but of course I couldn't find out about anything in its entirety. Even the most talented interrogator for particularly serious cases with the whole of his powerful apparatus wouldn't have been able to find out everything in its entirety. But I did have an advantage over such a hypothetical interrogator. I could rely not only on facts, but also on my feelings, intuition and imagination. After all, I wasn't collecting case material, and I wasn't planning on divulging it publicly, but even then I may have been preparing to write you letters.

I wanted to warn and protect you.

Father-in-Law seemed like a massive octopus, or to be more precise – like a centopus, carefully hiding his endless tentacles, each of which slithered over vast distances and branched into even smaller tentacles. While trying to grasp the end of one of them, I discovered to my surprise and horror that the end was usually attempting to reach me.

Simple as that: it would even reach for me, a small-time Komsomol functionary. On numerous occasions I tried to figure out how some idiotic ban came about, or how some unwritten order appeared and then gradually became a law. I got tangled up in imaginary threads for a long time, rising higher and higher along the cliffs of the hierarchy, until I was amazed and horrified to find that the threads unavoidably led towards Father-in-Law's office. Gradually it began to appear that he ran absolutely everything in the world. It seemed that there wasn't a ban, a humiliation or a demagogic slogan he wasn't sticking his nose into. I understood and understood very well that it shouldn't have been like that; after all Father-in-Law was not the person of highest rank, but all of those threads led irresistibly towards him. It seemed that he was undoubtedly the highest in some secret, distorted world, and his tentacles were spread out in an oppressive metaphysical space, which was ruled by rot and those poisonous phantasmagorical spores, which had infected absolutely everything, including people's minds, and even objects. In that oppressive space the putrid spiritual corpses of the dead were scattered here and there: the corpses of people's souls, the corpses of thoughts and ideas, the corpses of propositions and reforms.

That was perhaps the most important thing: those reeking corpses. If they hadn't existed, you could have considered it to be all in the realm of fantasy, a creature of my excited nervous system. But those corpses were too real. They were evidence that this phantasmagorical space brimming with decomposing, poisonous spores really did exist, that those secret tentacles existed, and their outcomes were very bleak.

Those spiritual corpses opened my eyes.

If all of Father-in-Law's tentacles, their many-sided offshoots, were still slithering, passing on information, pushing people or holding them back, I would have understood the work of this massive and powerful organism as a biological imperative, showing the nature of the ruling organism and its laws. However, there was no biological purpose to what this organism did: it killed creatures it didn't feed on. Those tentacles, those offshoots quietly choked people's souls, thoughts and ideas, propositions and reforms, and then left their gasping bodies to dismal decay.

Father-in-Law's entire path was sown with those unseen, horribly reeking, decaying corpses. I'd find out about the efforts of the more progressive teachers to reform the schools at least slightly – and soon after it would turn out that Father-in-Law had quashed all of those efforts. I found out about historians' attempts to raise the curtain surrounding the most fundamental moments in Lithuania's history at least to some limited degree – and immediately I would discover that all of their desires were masterfully killed off by none other than Father-in-Law. He constantly worked with the hands of others, but you could recognise his handwriting on it at once, the marks of Father-in-Law's iron grip remained on the bodies of his spiritual victims forever.

Gradually I began to understand more fully what I should have understood much much earlier: Father-in-Law himself spread those phantasmagorical poisonous spores, which destroyed absolutely everything: thoughts and ideas, people and even soulless objects, weakening even stainless steel, even the indestructible ceramic of the cosmos.

My Father-in-Law was a prosperous breeder and spreader of those spores. He was like some mushroom, feeding off the juices of us all.

I don't agree with calling such people simply bureaucrats. Such an ordinary word doesn't measure up to the task of describing them. You have to think up a special, threatening, phantasmagorical word for that – the kind that they themselves really are. Such people gather into strange sects that are incomprehensible to a sober mind, they recognise each other at once – perhaps from some secret signs, perhaps from their smell. They are dangerous, you need to fear them.

If I could, I'd send a telegram to all the people of Lithuania.

It should be delivered to every flat and to every dormitory. This is what I would write:

Be wary of them and, for God's sake, don't think that they're easy to overcome. They won't give up easily. You have to fear them. You need to judge them accordingly. They aren't afraid of any sort of spell. A fight with them is not a gentlemanly sport. It's war. A serious, long and dogged war.

You can't do without corpses in a war. Yes, corpses. Let's say, people who've drowned.

I have to write to you about this. That event helped me to come to a decision. That event shook me up.

I remember, it was an autumn evening, I couldn't fall asleep for a long time, and eventually I sat down to write you a letter. It definitely wasn't the first one – perhaps the tenth one, perhaps the twentieth. I was still asking everyone what you were doing and how you were. You nevertheless got into the doctoral programme for philosophy, fraternising with your colleagues, horrifying them with your ideas and musings. They approved your dissertation topic which took some effort, and having dreamed up several turgid formulations, they essentially fabricated everything. However, after they'd heard what you were planning on writing about, they all took fright: it was obvious that such a dissertation "wouldn't pass muster". But you were perfectly fine with it. You knew how to feel great, though you also knew how to be sad. You knew how to do a lot of things. You knew a lot of things.

I kept writing letters to you, wanting to ask you something or other. On that ill-starred night I wanted to ask you whether an honest man can take a dishonest path, if it's practically the only available path for the simple reason that there is nowhere else to go. To join in the procession, all the while secretly hoping to be able to turn everyone in the appropriate direction sooner or later.

There was a lot more I wanted to ask, but I was interrupted

by the incessant ringing of the doorbell. Visitors never called at our house at night, so I was quite surprised when I saw Marius, our neighbour from the second floor, standing in the doorway. He was young but had already gained a good reputation as a surgeon; he was perhaps the only younger man in our building, which was made for the elite class. All the rest were old enough to be my parents.

Almost pushing me aside, Marius stumbled into the room with a partly drunk bottle of cognac. He himself grabbed some glasses from the cupboard, poured some for us both and only settled down after I tossed back what felt like a double.

"I didn't sign!" he exclaimed in the voice of a gravedigger.

Then he trembled all over – from his cheeks down to his fingertips – and poured himself some more cognac. I had never seen a person tremble like that before.

"They're just bringing them in continuously," he uttered gloomily. "They've been laid out on the basement floor. They don't let our staff near them; all kinds of militia as well as indeterminate lowlifes are bringing them in and piling them up. You understand, they wouldn't even let us... they just insisted that I sign. But I didn't sign! Some had no documents but were somehow identified. Relatives are swarming all around the clinics. There's commotion everywhere, and that son of a bitch locked me in an office with him and tried to force me to sign. He alternated between threats and offers of sacks of gold. But I didn't sign!"

I questioned him in a logical and relatively calm manner. Maybe you heard something about it – rumours about the pontoon bridge over the Neris, the one near the concert hall and the sports centre, had been buzzing around Vilnius for a few days. That little pontoon bridge couldn't support large flows of pedestrians. Normally it would be closed after concerts or sporting events, but that night someone didn't do what they were supposed to. Someone failed to put up a barrier with a warning, or maybe he put it up but there were no security guards on duty or perhaps it was something else – in short, hundreds of people suddenly thronged to that rickety pontoon bridge in a rush to cross to the other side of the river and the small bridge inevitably collapsed. Afterwards, I questioned numerous witnesses; there were quite a few of them. Some people floundered about in the shallow waters and waded to the shore, many struggled in full view of everyone, and others were dragged by the current into whirlpools. It was dark. You couldn't make sense of anything: women and children were screaming, someone was shouting for help, and the scene was completed by the sight of a phlegmatic middle-aged man who, like the captain of some ghost vessel, was floating down the middle of the river on a pontoon that had broken off from the bridge, and proudly looking left and right. This much I found out later.

But that night Marius sat across from me and explained something else about those people who had drowned. They were taken to the clinics and laid down right on the floor. Only then did the real catastrophe, the real phantasmagoria, start. There were not supposed to be any drowned people. No catastrophe of any kind had taken place, not to mention one with victims. Marius was on duty that night, and so the clever guys twisted his arm and demanded he sign a stack of death certificates.

All of those people who drowned, down to the last one, were supposed to have died from pneumonia. They died at home because a doctor had not been called in time.

"They kept trying to break me again and again," Marius repeated. "They cornered me. They talked so much and so convincingly that at times I thought I was seeing things and that dozens of people really had died from that strange pneumonia. But when I looked once again at the drowned bodies dripping on the floor, I knew all of it was real. And they continued to try and force me. But I didn't sign."

We guzzled down that cognac, Marius went and got

another bottle, and I continued to ask him questions, but he repeated the same thing. I think I kissed him and kept shouting, "We won't give in!" Apparently, I threatened to fix things. Apparently, I threatened to punish all those who had dug their claws into that mean business. Apparently, I fantasised about establishing an "Avenue of the Drowned" in the cemetery, so that people would always be reminded of where lies can lead.

"Wait. Hold on," said Marius suddenly, stopping me from continuing, sobering up out of the blue. "What graves? What avenue? What victims? There won't be any drowned. That's what's most important. None! There will be only those who died from a virulent outbreak of pneumonia."

"But you didn't sign!" I shouted. "You were the doctor on duty. Everything's in your hands."

"I'm not the doctor on duty any longer," Marius answered even more soberly. "They kicked me out and called in someone else. Maybe the hospital's chief, as if that were important in the long run. What's important is for him to have signed. Understand this – the most important thing is that nobody drowned. I didn't sign, but someone else will have. That's the worst thing. I didn't sign and they'll point the finger at me, they'll be so far up my ass like an enema for sure, but whatever happens, there won't be any victims! That's what's most important! If I remained a hero and I suffered for the truth, then all would be great. But I achieved nothing, that's the worst thing. My conscience stayed clean, but someone else will have signed. And nothing will change because of it – that's the worst thing. I stayed true, I will suffer for that, and that's the only comfort. But I didn't achieve anything else!"

And then I made a mistake. I suddenly remembered Father-in-Law. I quickly realised whom we needed to turn to. "I'll call up Father-in-Law," I told him quite loftily. "He'll take care of it." Yes, you could wake Father-in-Law up for this kind of thing.

"Idiot!" he shouted. "Moron! Who do you think called me? Who, in your opinion, ordered me to sign those death certificates? Some decrepit major, perhaps? Who gives those kinds of orders? Who do you think? Who?"

I wanted to barge into Father-in-Law's office the very next morning, but I was in very bad shape. I wasn't used to heavy drinking and so the next morning I felt like I was dying. I lapped up boiled water, ran to the toilet and retched. I didn't care about any of the victims or Fathers-in-Law. Sometime later, I stopped by his office. It often happens that we arrive somewhere too late because we had a terrible hangover at the critical moment.

"Nobody drowned, kid," said Father-in-Law, staring at me. "Nobody. Got some documents, by any chance?"

"People will testify," I grumbled sullenly. "I'll find them."

"You won't find anybody," said Father-in-Law firmly.

"Marius will testify."

"And what will he say?" asked Father-in-Law, raising his eyebrows in innocent surprise. "That he wasn't at work that night because he was drunk? He was taken to hospital at four in the morning. He was given a blood test. That Marius of yours was completely drunk."

Father-in-Law nonchalantly waved around a copy of the specialists' report. He stared at me like a boa constrictor, like an octopus, like a monster. Why am I bothering to tell you? You experienced that look of his not too long ago yourself. I didn't understand why he explained everything to me. He could have shown me the door and that would have been it. But he explained his secret ratiocinations very thoroughly. I still don't get it. Why did he talk to me? And why did he talk to you, not all that long ago, for God's sake? Was he showing off? Was he teaching us a lesson? I don't understand.

"Marius can't testify to anything," continued Father-in-Law calmly. "No rumours, no slander. By the way, he could easily lose his position as head of the department for being drunk on the job."

"So nobody drowned?" I inquired gloomily.

"Nobody drowned."

"But the pontoon bridge existed, right?" I said, trying to be ironic, but there was little joy in saying it.

"If need be," Father-in-Law said calmly, "we would do it in such a way that it was as if the dilapidated bridge had never been there at all – it's just that there's no sense in going to so much trouble."

He didn't speak in a triumphant way or with a clever smile. He spoke drily and matter-of-factly.

Marius and I never discussed it again. He never engaged me in conversation first. And I was afraid to even go near him.

I was afraid that he too would say that nobody had drowned, that he had not barged into my place with a partly drunk bottle of cognac, or that we hadn't shouted "We won't give in!" at three o'clock in the morning.

Anything you wanted could have happened in that world. Nothing was real. I hadn't been sure for a long time. I lived well, loved my wife and son. I ate well and didn't have to work hard. I knew how to write fantastic Komsomol reports – the best in the city of Vilnius.

I could leave my son the Volga with tinted windows, with the radiophone – if I ended up deserving one, of course.

At the time I was still totally green. I was devastated by those corpses which were not corpses. I empathised enormously with that story. As a true bookish Lithuanian, I relied solely on my feelings.

I started to think about it all somewhat later. And this is what I quickly came up with: the drowned or not drowned by no means had any significance on Father-in-Law's path. He just covered them up and deftly erased them from our paper reality. He eliminated many others himself. The post-war corpses, which he disposed of without rhyme or reason, also weren't the most important ones. The most important ones were the others – who died and are still dying in our days.

Think about it: no chemical colossus, choking absolutely everything around it, no poisoning of the land or water could get by without Father-in-Law's blessing. So Father-in-Law willingly let the dragon into Lithuania that's killing us all. Once he wanted to save some minister from another Soviet republic, his friend. Another time, he wanted to receive a medal without waiting in line. The third time… Who knows what other kinds of impulses, what kind of logic works in Father-in-Law's twisted world. In one way or another, he took care of everything, just not us. He quietly poisoned us. Some moronic bureaucrat may have not quite understood what he was doing, but Father-in-Law did. He always knew what he was doing.

Half of Lithuania was eating and drinking that chemical abomination, so that even the most sacred of natural miracles, mother's milk, was poisoning newborns – and all that was Father-in-Law's doing. That was his greatest sin, because he really did know what he was doing. He poisoned (and is still poisoning) people gradually, not killing anyone suddenly, you won't catch him red-handed. But it's impossible to count how many people have perished because of him, how many people he has made invalids and how many children he has caused to be born mentally retarded – that's what I gradually started to realise. A few tortured partisans, signallers or scores of people who had drowned suddenly became a small incident. Father-in-Law killed people wholesale, a few here or there didn't mean anything to him.

He can never be forgiven for this, because he knew full well what he was doing.

Crippled children and a fatally poisoned organism – that's what I could leave to my son by marching at Father-in-Law's side.

That autumn I was co-opted as the district Komsomol secretary for the city. Father-in-Law's tailor made me a wonderful grey suit from French material for the occasion.

The material suited me very well, the tailor's work even better. I had to enter my new dominion with that suit. My first crusade was to be the Komsomol work report for the entire Vilnius District. I had to read a speech about the wonderful successes of the Komsomol at the city's plenary session. That speech was written for me by at least five instructors, and the secretary who had to evaluate the report afterwards read it perhaps three times. The text of the speech was long and very dull.

I prepared long and very thoroughly for that session. I had to match the accessories to my divine new suit with precision. I put on a bright, wide tie. Wide ties in floral patterns were the fashion at the time.

I remember that I stepped up on the platform and surveyed the hall. As always, people were bored. Some read magazines, some were dozing, some of the girls in the back rows were trying to knit. I had yet to give a talk from such a podium, and can reveal that surprisingly everything can be seen perfectly well from it. Before I had thought that the speakers couldn't see how everyone was flipping through magazines or sleeping. But in reality everything was as plain as day. Before uttering anything, I was still thinking that in spite of everything I was perhaps going to wake them up.

I woke some of them up, but not all of them. Some slept all the way to the end of my first and last major speech. They didn't even notice that something unbelievable was happening.

It's of no interest to tell you what I said, although the speech was not asinine. I had prepared a long time for it. Today I'd receive an award for that speech, if it were published in a newspaper, or perhaps *The Homeland* newspaper would choose me as their journalist on perestroika affairs. I spoke coherently, I tried not to miss or forget anything. The content of my speech was more or less the following: why the Komsomol was deteriorating, who was to blame for it and how could we make at least some changes to it? I was doubtful myself as to whether it was possible to change anything at all. Nevertheless I suggested a few genuine ideas. I…

It's definitely not interesting to talk about the speech. So much is said about it today that talk of it is losing all meaning.

However, at the time that bomb left a bit of a mark. The secretary of the nearby Vilnius District, biting nervously on a cigarette, continued to pat me on the shoulder in a remote part of the hallway and repeated, "Hey, man, you said too much. Oh, you said too much! Imagine if you were the national secretary and gave a speech like that in Moscow!"

What could I say in reply? Perhaps just that if I were the national secretary, I certainly wouldn't be giving speeches like that any more. He continued to pat me on the shoulder and while coughing took drags from that crumpled, moist cigarette of his. I was very worried that someone would see us together. He was the first one to suggest I be thrown out of the Komsomol. I didn't need to be thrown out as secretary – I hadn't even been officially appointed yet.

Nevertheless I wasn't expelled from the Komsomol. I was rescued by Father-in-Law. He could have saved anybody from anything if he wanted. He invited me for a serious talk, and at once I asked about the drowned people. And I found out that there weren't any drowned people.

Then he calmed me down just so I didn't think I had given a scandalous speech at the Komsomol plenary session. It seems that the speech also hadn't happened.

"In my dominions," Father-in-Law explained dryly, "there are no such scandals."

The previously prepared speech was attached to the reports – the speech I had prepared myself. And no one had recorded that speech on a tape recorder.

There's no way I can forgive myself for that. Why didn't I think to record that speech? It would have been possible to compare it with what they're saying now when the red tape-recorder button that says "Permission Granted" is on. I wonder whether I was ahead of everyone back then, or whether the clever speakers of today would wipe the floor with me with their concepts and their ideas in general.

In any case, it's not important. Here, on the other side, there are a lot of things that aren't important to me. I'm once again dangling between heaven and earth, I'm neither here nor there, and I often wish to live in Vilnius again, especially now, in the spring of '88, when everything is changing every single day. Now, when I could proclaim my ideas, when I could openly gather my own community together. I'm a little jealous of you. Yes, we have many possibilities here, which you couldn't even dream of, but everything is endlessly stable and boring. Where you are, it's more interesting, which is why I'm a little bit jealous of you. And I do hold you heavily to blame: why didn't you take me with you, why didn't you take up my aims, why didn't you take on a role as an independent expert or intellectual advisor? We could have accomplished a lot together – your brain, and my hands and heart.

However it was easier for you to do nothing. Sometimes I think that perhaps you're already ruined, you don't believe in anything at all and don't want to believe, that you wrote your *Perestroika in Albania* just because you wanted to demonstrate your endless scepticism, just to show off and ridicule other people's efforts.

There are people that build homes, and there's always someone who turns up and sits on the sidelines, smoking, making wisecracks, and teaching others the art of building, though they themselves wouldn't be able to build anything, even if you threatened them with a shotgun.

And you, Tomas, could you still build something?

I know, I know how you secretly wrote *Perestroika in Albania*, how you hid the manuscript in parts in several places, and how you shook and woke up suddenly at night, but you overcame your fear. I also saw how you smiled bitterly leafing through the newspapers, reading the names of people you knew and didn't know, how you felt wounded, infinitely wounded when they didn't invite you to any informal communities, to any legalised movements, how you smiled more and more bitterly, always correcting and correcting again your manuscript, how conceptually you decided that you would never become part of any community or movement, how you wrote your opus all alone, without joining anyone, proving at least to yourself that you could build something.

But are you certain that it's a real structure?

The Eleventh: about my amateurish dissidence and Father-in-Law's secret space, the investigation into myself through the eyes of others and the appearance of the Great Li

Don't live in a country which is ruled by no one, ruled by many, ruled by a woman or ruled by a child.

When a person's vessel of life pot is broken, there's no point in picking up the pieces to glue them back together. It's best to mould a new one.

Everything became completely mixed up in my life after that fateful speech. I sat in front of a pile of shards and sadly picked them up, understanding perhaps for the first time what the vessel of my life was made of. All of my communities had shattered into pieces, all of them turned out to be fake. My desperate attack hadn't stirred anyone. A former classmate of mine I met probably spoke for everyone: "I heard you got involved in some Komsomol scandal."

He didn't know anything specific. He had simply heard people talking. In his voice, I sensed a bit of surprise, perhaps a bit more curiosity, however mostly I heard spiteful satisfaction. It was like he was saying: that's what you deserve, you fucking careerist. I didn't explain anything to him, didn't start proving that I had never been a careerist or plain trash. He wouldn't have understood anything, and he wouldn't have listened. He'd sized me up long ago. And it seems that everyone else had too.

During my relatively short life I looked for my community, and suddenly I was left as alone as anyone can be. It was horrible. It wasn't right. It was most certainly God's Grand Injustice. I've already written to you that I wasn't capable of being alone. And for all my searching, I didn't find even one friend. The word "even" here isn't of course quite right: to find a friend is hard, perhaps the hardest thing of all.

My family life also went downhill. Perhaps that time comes for every man when suddenly you see your wife through totally different eyes. However, it came too quickly for me. Virginija, my other half, my hand or heart, my irreplaceable part, seemed like she wasn't the Virginija I knew. Suddenly I saw who I was living with. Don't expect some sort of tumultuous tragedy, masks torn off, jealously or hopelessly. I simply saw whom I had been living with the whole time. My wife with the name of Virginija. She was a smart, particularly independent and not very sensitive woman. She liked her linguistics, she studied Eastern languages, and in the evenings she even learned ancient Japanese hieroglyphs. She didn't become a stranger to me, God help me, but it turned out that she wasn't a miraculous part of me, but simply another, a different person; I hindered her more than I helped her, and she couldn't help me. She didn't get angry at me for that horrible slap in the face, she even consoled me in her own way, but she didn't understand what that loss meant to me. She didn't understand that the vessel of my life had been shattered. It most likely seemed to her that I acted in a coherent and logical way, that the harmony I had once had was still inside me. But it wasn't there any more. I was a guy with a degree in physics, who didn't like either physics or physicists. I was a totally non-functioning Komsomol functionary. I was a prophet that had yet to be born, from the very beginning having forgotten that in this world it wasn't the prophecy that was the most important, but only those who listened to it – unfortunately I never had such people. I had to start everything from the beginning, but I didn't know where that beginning was. I didn't know where I had got lost, I didn't know who had set me on the wrong path.

Father-in-Law didn't pull anything on me, he didn't pit his daughter against me, he even annulled the document that kicked me out of work at the technical institute for my horrendous political mistake. Our director was in too much of a rush to draw up the document, in which he vehemently asserted that someone like me didn't have the right to teach the next generation. Father-in-Law didn't even bother to call him, he just sent his assistant, who modestly inquired if the director was tired of having his post. On that occasion I didn't even lift a finger, it didn't matter to me. I couldn't have cared less. It seemed to me that I would feel like that for a long long time.

I very quickly confronted the fact that my feelings had not become so dulled after all. I was compelled to be upset by a very simple thing: Virginija started to disappear more and more often in the evening. She would come home later and later, and she didn't think of explaining to me what she'd been doing. No, we didn't have rows, I didn't cause any scenes and I suffered quietly and hopelessly. I didn't even have the gumption to question her. I could almost understand her. We suddenly had nothing left to talk about. Having come home a bit earlier, she would make dinner, we would both eat in silence and we would then sit down in front of the TV without saying a word. If she stayed out longer – and she stayed out longer more and more often – she would definitely call and explain what I was to eat, and what to give to little Levas. I could almost understand her. The threads that inexplicably bound us broke quite unexpectedly and we didn't make love any more. Even if we did, we did it lazily. Almost without wanting to we lay down together, it wasn't any sort of lovemaking, the mysterious act of the merging of two bodies together. It was a dry, businesslike satisfaction of bodily needs, after it was over you just wanted to wash yourself as quickly as possible. I can admit – from the other side, I can admit everything without blushing – that

I didn't even want to make love. I didn't want anything any more – not even a woman.

The sad, lonely evenings weighed upon me, and drove me out of my mind. Without knowing where Virginija was and what she was doing, I imagined all sorts of things. Perhaps every man in such a bizarre situation becomes like that legendary dog in the manger: you don't desire your own wife any more, but even the smallest thought about her possible infidelity can cause inner rage. That's how I felt too. When I couldn't bear it any longer, I would go into the living room and with all my strength throw at the wall a cup from the dinner service Father-in-Law had given us as a present. Nevertheless I quickly found a universal tranquilliser. Don't have any expectations that it's anything special: I simply started to drink by myself. I'd down exactly enough to calm myself down, and then I'd talk out loud – with Virginija, with you, with Camus, with Jesus Christ. Hell, I started to go a little crazy. I'd sit at little Levas's bedside and tell him about my topsy-turvy life. I taught him to never follow my path, and argued with him, though he, understandably, didn't reply.

"Boo!" little Levas would shout at me. "Da-da! Pap-sa!"

I would nod my head very seriously, down another half a glass and respond miserably, "You're right. Most likely my main mistake was that I didn't want to join anything, but nevertheless I desired my own community. If I had joined some sort of distinct group – starting from childhood or at least from my teenage years – I'd be going along with them now. Devil knows where I'd go, but at least I wouldn't be alone. My most horrible misfortune is that no one has considered me one of them. No one has considered me to be a real friend.

And so on and so forth. I was briefly off my rocker, though after sobering up I would justify my behaviour: I was the one who had put myself into such a corner that I could start talking not only with a baby, but with the flies on the ceiling.

Occasionally, after emptying the bar, I wouldn't buy any alcohol on purpose, wandering the main avenue, trying to meet someone for whom I'd done something good. I was probably looking for sympathy or support. It's doubtful if a person can fall lower – it was purely spiritual begging. But I didn't receive anything from my begging: most of those I met didn't know about my fall at all, and I still wasn't ready to complain myself. One rocker that used to get my support sadly nodded his head and offered me a needle. At that time drugs were just beginning to spread, but the rocker had always been part of the avant-garde. Thank God I turned him away point-blank. I was always horribly afraid of injections into my veins. I would almost faint at the sight of a syringe.

I saw you a couple times, you greeted me without hard feelings, even without being casual, but I ended up not having the courage to talk to you, all I did was to start up writing letters to you at night, only to tear them up in the morning. I knew that you had changed your topic and defended your PhD thesis: if I'm not mistaken, it was something about Adam and music.

Having gone down the main avenue, I most often would go by Marius's place. We'd close ourselves up in the kitchen and gloomily down a bottle. We would talk very little, and not a word about the drowned people – that was taboo. Marius wasn't the department head any more, though he performed surgery just as masterfully. Now he was extracting three hundred roubles per operation. He gave the money to his family as a payment so they wouldn't bother him when he behaved as he saw fit. Unfortunately, he wasn't able to come up with anything clever: he drank the most expensive cognacs, fucked the nurses at the clinics and railed against Brezhnevism. He was the first to give me forbidden books. I think the first was *The Yawning Heights*. Or maybe *1984*. Keeping such books at home was a little scary but fun. If someone had found one in my house, I was supposed to say that I found it left on the trolleybus, that I flipped through it out of curiosity, and never ever change this story.

Do you find that funny? It was a little funny for me too. I read those books out loud, until little Levas began to whimper. If a child's subconscious records anything at all, then my son got a rather harrowing upbringing. I don't want to write anything about my son, at least in this letter. He's fifteen now, his hairstyle is post-punk, he knows Šapoka's history of Lithuania by heart. It's hard to say very much about him. He didn't inherit anything from me, except for his big head and droopy ears. He almost doesn't remember me. It's my fault entirely. I was the one who betrayed and abandoned him.

You, of course, knew long ago that I had started disseminating forbidden literature. It was a natural psychological reaction. It was personal revenge. A few copies of 1984 were copied by a guy who would copy whatever you wanted for a litre of spirits. I brought them home and with horror realised that I couldn't disseminate them. I didn't have anyone to give them to. Good God, I even thought that it would be worth leaving them on the trolleybus. Then I decided to take them to my former district communist committee house and leave them on the windowsill somewhere, then...

These were despondent ravings. I don't know what I would have cooked up, but one late afternoon when I returned home, I found Father-in-Law at my writing desk. He waited for me calmly, having piled all of my dissident output on the table. Father-in-Law was always as smart as the devil. He had foreseen this too, or perhaps it was out of habit that he had me followed – in the end, does it really matter?

"You haven't written anything yet," he inquired as calmly as could be. "You're not establishing a party? You haven't joined the Helsinki Group?"

He didn't lecture me, didn't make a fool out of me, and

didn't ask anything more. He annihilated me with his cold contempt.

"If you want something to read, read it by yourself!" he emphasised sternly. "Come by. You'll get the rarer stuff, not that popular crap. Milovan Djilas or Avtorkhanov. Clever men, though they're intellectual bandits. As far as I gather, you're interested in the structure of government?"

He was ridiculing me by expounding his own point of view. He knew all the works of Sovietologists and local freethinkers better than any professional dissident.

"And what else is there to read?" he explained calmly. "Leodead's speeches perhaps? His assistants give his speeches."

He was not afraid of any committee or group. I couldn't conquer him that way; I couldn't harm him at all. I couldn't take revenge on anyone at all like that.

"My little Virginija is walking around all pale," Father-in-Law said. "For God's sake, are you a man or not? You screwed up, so at least rise above it."

"How? How should I rise above it?"

"However you want. I'm not hindering you. Just if you do something stupid again, ask me first. I will stop you. So it wouldn't be like that speech of yours or these books here."

"My speech was heartfelt," I declared dejectedly.

"And totally foolish. Even if everything were to suddenly change according to your wishes – and that's not possible! – you'd be left behind. No one remembers the first ones, it's other people entirely that take the top positions. Everything has to be done at the right time!"

I took great care and made note of these words. You can see for yourself that Father-in-Law was on top of it here too. Nevertheless he did make one mistake, a crucial one.

"Nothing can change here in the next three hundred years, my child!" he said firmly.

That's what he really thought. He fatally counted on the unconquerable power of the phantasmagorical spores. He himself was hypnotised by those spores. That's exactly what he said: three hundred years!

Now, as I waste away on the other side, at least I can rejoice about that one: in one respect Father-in-Law turned out to be dumber than dumb. Hah – three hundred years! Ten years was enough!

I stopped disseminating dissident literature as suddenly as I had started. I was blown away by Father-in-Law's indifference to my determination and courage. Nevertheless Father-in-Law had an enormous impact on me: having seen that he wasn't afraid of it, I decided at once that it wasn't worth it.

And it wasn't worth it. I couldn't gather my community together like that, I could only hurt a community I didn't like.

Can you imagine me as a professional dissident? Dwelling in the zone, and if not dwelling – full of rage and fanaticism, buried in banned books, collecting everything sinister and horrible that is around, in general not understanding the real world any more, just the other one – the world of forbidden texts, of evil and of horror. Even now, when everything has changed so suddenly, I view new events with a crooked smile, spitefully look for flaws in the changes, and deride all public movements and groups.

I'm not convinced of it, perhaps it wouldn't be like that, but it seems to me that secretly, in the depths of my heart, I would be sad that our life became a bit easier and freer, I'd secretly wish for those dark old times.

Can you imagine me like that?

It was only somewhat later that I began to wonder what caused Father-in-Law to take an interest in me, and even look after me. At the time it seemed to me that the entire world should feel for me and comfort me. Perhaps that's a sign of misery, but I really did want that. However, no one – not even Virginija – was concerned about me. It just so happened that the person who was most interested in my issues was Father-in-Law.

But why?

Most likely it was all very simple: he wasn't concerned about me, but about his daughter. In Father-in-Law's big head there were incompatible things trying to become compatible: fatherly love and spiritual sadism, a sharp mind and heinous indecencies. He had enough common sense to not choose a special husband for his daughter. I'd say that he couldn't stand the offspring of the elite. He must have understood that Virginija wouldn't leave me, so he tried to help me in order to make it easier for her.

Though that's a far too simple explanation. It seems to me that for Father-in-Law I was like an interesting bug, like a little animal, which was fun to examine. Living in his unreal world with special hunting grounds, with a strictly defined circle of friends, and a special buffet, which even his closest aides that worked alongside him did not have the right to visit, Father-in-Law must have realised that such a life provided him with a highly distorted view of the world. He was curious, he must have cared about the different lives of normal people as well. By no means because he wanted to improve or correct something here – he had to care out of a childlike curiosity, like an exotic novel or a strange film which you could not only watch, but also re-film a bit of it. For him, I was most likely yet another tentacle exploring the world, a strange, independent tentacle. Perhaps that's why he wasn't preparing to stifle, change or deform me. I was useful to him as I was – an exotic little animal in his caste's monotonous zoo.

I tried to understand Father-in-Law more fully many times, but it was always in vain. I knew nothing about his origin, or about his parents. His wife, my mother-in-law, was an unseen, non-existent person, who didn't fit the stereotype of a high society lady. She didn't waste her free time or collect jewels, and nor was she some other sort of nonentity. She was a non-existent person. Mother-in-law worked somewhere, but I never paid attention to where it was. She dressed elegantly and appropriately, but never paid attention as to how. She spoke reservedly and almost wisely, but I never heard what about. Virginija said that – as much as she still remembers – Father-in-Law, even when he held the lowest of duties, didn't have any worries whatsoever. Everything was prepared, given, washed and ironed for him. He never knew how much bread cost and what people were standing in line for in the shops. His wife set him apart from the real world carefully and unfailingly, before the government got round to it. She had dissolved into her husband's being long ago and as a result didn't exist. She understood her life's purpose as such. Most likely she was happy.

I had been living with Father-in-Law's daughter for six years already, but she couldn't explain anything about her father.

He was always like that – that's all that she would say to me.

But what was he like exactly? What was he like still?

If it were possible to grasp this, then perhaps it would be possible to grasp the very structure of government. Perhaps we'd find out why it was precisely him, and not someone else, who had climbed so high.

Unfortunately, even I don't comprehend him. He exists in another kind of space than you and I do, than all of us. In that space, other laws of physics apply. In that space, time passes by differently. And I'm not talking about such details as morality or something like that.

The one thing I really did understand is that he dealt with and deals with all of his, and most importantly, all of our issues according to rules of that space which is alien to us. I don't think that he wanted to do bad things to us on purpose or tried to cruelly smother us. I don't think he killed us with chemicals on purpose. He simply operated according to the rules of his space, and its rules are foreign and incomprehensible to us. He did what was useful and right in that space, but the repercussions in our world were of all kinds – occasionally it worked out pretty well, but most often it was horrible. That's the whole secret.

Though no, of course, that's not all of it. I can babble on about all sorts of spaces and similar things as much as you want, but I still don't comprehend Father-in-Law as a person. For God's sake, he's a person after all – just as you and I are.

It would be very naive and ridiculous to proclaim that he is simply a monster.

That year we had a very cold autumn, or else a wet, damp winter. I wandered Vilnius like a lost soul, just like in my teenage years, feeling contempt as well as hatred for myself. I felt I was a total doormat, a banal and lame excuse for a human being. Everything in my life was banal. There were no miracles, no tragedies, no burning passions. Did that Komsomol pseudo-tragedy of mine mean anything? It wasn't a tragedy, it was a tragic farce. A circus. I could no longer accomplish anything decent in my life.

Even my love could not have been more banal. When writing you letters, I kept wanting to describe my love for Virginija but I couldn't find any special words. My love was exactly the same as that of thousands – millions – of others. I didn't need any special, unique words to describe it.

That's the way I was thinking that cold autumn (or damp, wet winter). I felt terrible. Even my carbon copy, my own reflection, my little Levas, didn't stand out from the other children – unless you counted his big head and stuck-out ears.

And then I had a strange idea: I urgently needed to find out how others see me. Suddenly I thought perhaps I had imagined myself, perhaps I wasn't really the person about whom I was so agitated, whose life I lay out for you here, not even for a second. Suddenly I thought perhaps I had imagined everything: Virginija, my goals, you, my little tragedies. I began to doubt whether a person could understand himself at all. Perhaps a person, at least a Lithuanian, is not destined to reflect. Perhaps all he can do is feel – this is pretty much what Lithuanian literature told me over and over again.

I couldn't and didn't want to believe it. A human, I thought, stands apart from lower animals because he is able to reflect. That's another topic, by the way, on which I'll write to you later.

That harsh autumn or damp winter I was overcome by a true mania: I had to find out, as quickly as possible, how others saw me. Only at first glance does this appear simple, but people are so used to hiding the truth that in the end even they themselves no longer know what they really think. It's almost impossible to ask a person their true opinion; he will lie to you without realising it and retouch his true thoughts, or make them more scathing. In our muddled world, it's absurd to ask a person directly: what do you really think of me? In the best case he will think you're an idiot. Or perhaps not, and he'll begin to wonder what your hidden intentions are. It wouldn't occur to anyone that you really want to know the truth. Each person immediately starts to guess at why you're asking such provocative questions, what answer you want to hear, and what use you're going to make of it. People have long forgotten the Socratic oath, "Know thyself", and any person who follows it appears very suspect indeed. I found this out myself when I started asking every person I met what he or she really thought about me. My behaviour was totally absurd.

"Listen, in your opinion, what kind of person am I?" I'd bluntly ask a former classmate. "What do I appear like to you? Don't lie. The truth is important to me."

It was only later that I thought to myself: what would I reply if I was asked the same kind of question? With some people, you wouldn't want to hurt them, and with others you'd be afraid of flattering them too much, and to others you'd lie on purpose, just for the spiteful satisfaction of deceiving them. I even had this thought: in order to tell someone the truth, first of all you cannot fear the truth they might speak about you. Those fearless people are rare. One of them is you, Tomas. And in that harsh autumn (or damp winter) I was one of them too. Well, to be more precise, I was briefly, until I extracted my first responses.

The first person I persuaded to respond was Robertas, who had graduated from the Faculty of Physics maybe a few years before me. He sarcastically turned his sour little face to me and rather scornfully sneered, "Maybe you think you're Jesus Christ? To me it always seemed that you secretly think that. Those speeches of yours at those meetings... Unbelievable! They were so naive, you sermonised like... I don't even know. It seemed like it wasn't the Komsomol, but some sort of sect... A very naive sect... No one listened to those speeches of yours, you know, that's the secret. The people who understood your desires couldn't care less. They understood the world in a more realistic and smarter way than you did... And the others... The others didn't even hear you... No one heard you, kid. If you wanted to be Jesus, you needed to make miracles happen. There's no other way to move the masses. No, you weren't Jesus Christ, you were... you were such a... naive little fool. Sorry, of course, but you asked for the truth."

While listening I blushed and then turned pale, my handicapped heart beat like crazy. I looked at the sneering mug of that sly fox, obscenely moving his lips, and I fumed. Little Robertas – bridge player, businessman, speculator and a bit of a playboy – was ridiculing me. A person whose soul had never hurt, who drank on my dime, had kindly agreed to shit on my head. At that moment I could have strangled him.

He was like a crooked mirror. After listening to him my

first thought was that no one could be my true mirror – each person is distorted in some way. You won't find out anything about yourself from others. They can give you different pictures of yourself, but not a single one of them will be the real one.

My desire to find the truth about myself from others cooled after the very first reply. Maybe I was just unlucky and listened to an unscrupulous person. No matter, I immediately became disappointed in them all. Listlessly, I asked a few more people but paid less and less attention to their words. Each shared their version of things.

Kazys, a former weightlifter, sighed at length and grumbled, pouring cocktail after cocktail down his throat, until he finally snapped and laid out his entire truth before me.

"You're a bastard! A bastard!" he snarled in a hoarse bass voice. "You betrayed the nation and gave it to the Russkies. What does your Komsomol have to do with the Lithuanian nation? What? What did you do the whole time, you bastard? Who needs it? What were you trying to do? You wanted bread with a lot of butter? A black Volga?"

And so on and so forth. Kazys spit it all out quite sincerely and at one point I thought he was going to hit me. He castigated me, belittled me, but he didn't explain one thing: what, in his view, was I supposed to do in order to be a true Lithuanian and an upstanding person? He was overcome with fury. He was a little older than me and in the old days his father had been taken to Siberia, though he was not guilty of anything, and killed there.

Linukas spoke the most calmly and with the most mercy. He was the only one who knew the details of my grand collapse. He kept smacking his lips and shrugging his shoulders. Simply put, his heart hurt. Not for me, but for the opportunities I had squandered of my own free will.

"What a chance you ruined, what a chance!" he lamented sadly. "You could have climbed really high. You could have climbed even higher than your father-in-law. You're very well suited for it. To me you always looked... innocent or something. It seemed to me that you could have risen through the ranks and not lost your human qualities. And then you upped and ruined it all. Well, you snapped, I mean, you talked. And what changed? No one knows anything about it. You should have behaved quite differently. You should have risen and kept rising. You should have stepped into the clouds, you understand? And only afterwards... Only then..."

"Taken off my mask?"

"You could put it that way. That was your chance. Having risen, you could have changed a lot of things. But you can't do anything now. And why did you try to fight it?"

Though Linukas spoke the most intelligently, he spoke so crudely. Everyone spoke crudely. Not a single one spoke about the spirit, the soul, or man's goal in life. Not a single one tried to paint my spiritual portrait. Everyone talked about facts, real life, or to be more precise, about what we usually call life.

I often think that what we call life is not life at all. Life is something totally different.

In the evenings I would sit with my son, and I began to read quite a lot. I began to stop understanding certain basic things. I looked around and searched for a person, a real person, but there were none to be found. I secretly hoped that perhaps you were that person, but you weren't around. And all the others left me hopelessly disappointed. I couldn't understand what there was left for me to do in such a world. Save money? I never had any, I didn't feel its power, which is perhaps why it didn't tempt me. Besides, I didn't have even the slightest bit of commercial talent. I had ruined my political career myself. I could no longer become a physicist. What was I supposed to do? I couldn't live like this, spend my days without purpose, raising children. It wasn't enough for me. I couldn't live like this. I needed something more. But I no longer understood what I was supposed to search for in this despicable world.

That's the way I was when Nijolė met me. She was Robertas's wife, the beauty of our class, who at least ten physicists had once fought over. Perhaps she wasn't so strikingly beautiful, but then there were only about ten girls studying in our year. Nijolė, without a doubt, stood out markedly. She took a long time to choose a partner, but she couldn't hold herself back when Robertas started to drive his own car to university. At the time it was a rarity.

Now she was raising two children and saw Robertas rarely: he was either playing bridge or had business dealings.

At that time Nijolė was causing a bit of a ruckus, she had at least two hundred roubles in her purse and, it seemed, that she was ready to spend it all right there and then. She pushed me into the Erfurt Bar, which she lived nearby. She was drunk and extremely sad. Her mother-in-law had taken the kids for the weekend, and her husband had left for Chelyabinsk. At the time he was reselling cars; in the Vilnius market they cost two to three thousand more than they did in the depths of Russia.

"Friends of misfortune we are," Nijolė waxed longingly. "Both of us live without love. Love is everything. Absolutely everything."

I wasn't even arguing, I was just listening. It turned out she had known Virginija for a long time already, she'd known her before we got married.

"Even back then, she said she wasn't sure that she loved you," Nijolė explained, looking directly at me with her big, beautiful, somewhat tipsy eyes. "She was only sure that you loved her. Her – not the daughter of an important father, but her. That sickly little *kikimora* Virginija."

Nijolė was probably behaving badly by talking that way, but her words hardly hurt me. Beautiful girls are always merciless to girls who don't look as good. God knows, those words didn't hurt me. I calmly looked at Nijolė's golden hair, her breasts quickly rising and falling. Her little snub nose became damp with tiny drops of sweat. I marvelled at how much she could drink. I was quite plastered, but she talked on and on without stopping, her tongue didn't get tied up. Only when she tiptoed off to the toilet did I see that she was walking rather unsteadily. We both talked and smoked, smoked and kissed right there in the bar. We kissed in a friendly way, out of drunk longing, like two people who are in the same boat. We both lived without love. That was what we finally and decisively agreed upon.

Of course I went to her place, and of course we slept together. You won't choose another word for it – we slept together, you can't say it in any other way. We were utterly wasted, I couldn't get her panties off, and in the morning she woke up completely naked, but with her bra still on. I don't remember anything else. We probably made love or at least tried to. As strange as it sounds, in the morning I didn't feel either disgust with myself or sadness. I was empty and light. Nijolė was wonderful: she jumped out of bed before I could even look at her, and half an hour later she returned good as new, bringing fresh beer. She was amazingly open.

"It's quite a lot of fun while it's new," she said with an enchanting smile. "No one is bored yet, there isn't a normal routine for such mornings, and it's not horrible to look at your partner."

She assured me that in the night everything had been very good. It had sobered her up, but afterwards she'd quickly fallen asleep. She laughed sincerely at us being pickled and readily said what she thought about me.

"Levas," she opened her beautiful eyes wide. "You were always wonderful. The girls in our class were divided into two groups over you. The stupid ones looked for handsome guys with muscles of iron, and scorned you, but the wise girls wanted to seduce you, as did I. Yet you were as straight as an arrow, you were an angel, you didn't even notice that a trap was being set for you. You were amazingly, stunningly naive."

"And in what way could I have been attractive?" I asked sincerely stunned.

"There was a trustworthiness that emanated from you. You could see at once that you're a serious guy. That if you love, then it's real love. That if you marry, then it'll be a real family. Not some societal unit, but a family! People could totally rely on you. What's more, you could achieve a lot, but needed proper guidance. You liked to blather, you needed to be looked after, and turned in the right direction."

"To blather?"

"Yes, you really liked to talk beautifully. It was nice to listen to you, when you spoke about a young person's aims and goals, and about all sorts of other things. You should have been writing books. In short, you were wonderful, just someone needed to take you firmly in hand. Intelligent girls dream about a man like that."

After being lauded like that, I said goodbye to Nijolė and hardly saw her again. That night was just a dream, and I didn't feel that I had hurt Virginija. I wouldn't have admitted that I'd betrayed her even if pushed up against a wall and threatened with a shotgun. I didn't feel that I had betrayed her, but instead felt that the night had never happened.

But at the same time that night and that evening impacted my life in a strange way. It was like I had broken out of a net of secret spells, I suddenly felt a taste for life. I'd even say this – I felt that I was still alive, that there was much in my life I had not experienced, that I didn't even know and couldn't even imagine how much I could still find in it. The whole time I had lived closed in a labyrinth of my aims, my rules, my morals, and not seeing what was beyond them.

After that night I felt freer, somewhat freer. I felt that I could do more. I just didn't know in what direction to direct my powers.

I walked around slightly dazed. In addition, I felt a spiteful glee that I was able to get one over on that damnably sly fox Robertas. I didn't want anyone to know it, or him to know it either. It was just fun to know that you could find weapons against people like that, even though it was deceitful. I couldn't tell you why I disliked him so much, I could barely tolerate his presence. We hardly ever met, and he never caused me any trouble. Perhaps what irritated me so much was the manner of his existence. He was my class enemy. Robertas was a talented physicist, but he focused all his efforts on illegal business. He prospered financially, but he had to give up his soul in exchange. He didn't have a soul, but the worst thing was that he looked down upon those who had protected theirs, those who still wanted to catch their soul as it wandered the world. Back then he drew wonderfully those who still wanted to catch their soul as it wandered, but now he mocked all artists. Back then he was one of my most active helpers at the faculty, and it was no coincidence that his opinion of me was the one I sought. But now his behaviour had pushed me into a fling with his wife and what's more, forced me to feel a secret joy for that despicable thing. He forced me to change. I was no longer as pure and honest as before.

By the way, Robertas very recently ended up behind bars, and I found out about it here, on the other side. He got mixed up in the production of illegal spirits in massive quantities. He was caught with a truck of stolen grain. He got five years and his assets were all confiscated, leaving Nijolė with four kids. He made children just as well as he did money. If I could, I'd certainly help Nijolė. Unfortunately, I can't. There's a lot that I can't do any more.

Remembering those years, I still want to write a letter to Albert Camus, the great expert on absurd man. A hazy letter, that is ultimately not clear even to myself. Camus crashed too soon in that car accident, he still had to add to the thoughts of his youth – with the wise lips of an old man and without a fire in his belly.

Dear Albert,

One of your thoughts really got stuck in my head – that we most often live for tomorrow: we essentially rely on the words "tomorrow", "later" and "when I get things done". I agree that "now" is somewhat more important: you have it right now or you will never have it at all, you do it now or you will never do it at all. You shouldn't think about "tomorrow", because "tomorrow" essentially means death. You see, death was always very real to me because of my lame heart. It forced me to hurry and take responsibility for every one of my actions, but it didn't solve any of the grand problems.

You said that there isn't a tomorrow at all, there is just death, which is why man is free. I had ended up in a situation where there wasn't any tomorrow left for me, but I didn't feel free at all. I had outer freedom – I could act as I saw fit. But I didn't feel any inner freedom, which was the worst thing. Religious people have one of two anchors to their being – unawareness or hope. I became aware and I didn't have any hope. Thus I remained confined: I knew that regardless of what I did, everything would stay the same. You see – it was as though I could do what I saw fit, but all of my actions would unavoidably change nothing; in other words, it became meaningless to do anything. All I could do was look for sensations and passions, sleep with a hundred Nijolės or one Nijolė a hundred times, all I could do was disseminate a hundred banned books or one book in a hundred copies, convince a hundred people of my views or write a hundred unsent letters to Tomas Kelertas. And it all was senseless, because a hundred is essentially just one.

You offered everyone an inevitable freedom as the torment of choice, but you didn't say what to do when each choice is meaningless. You constructed a system of thinking and said stoically, but now, when you know all of this, you need to live on and choose freely. And you made a crucial mistake: such a choice is valid only in your system of thinking, only in that constructed world of yours. You didn't think that one

174

could choose a different kind of world, and that choice is by no means torment. You were too rational, because you could only believe in God rationally.

You refused to recognise the world as a metaphor – I don't know what and whose metaphor it was. You didn't even consider that one could understand the world with a higher power, when logic becomes helpless, when you can't either prove or refute anything.

You didn't love yourself, but I, it seems, did love myself.

I don't even know what Camus has to do with this. Perhaps I remembered him because I always suspected that he died in that accident on purpose. He didn't consciously kill himself, that's true, but at the fateful moment he thought of something unimaginable and turned the steering wheel off to the side.

By the way, I don't even know the details of that accident. I'm just rambling.

At that time I was without question a man of the absurd, until after that night with Nijolė when I began to feel somewhat freer. Virginija's returning late didn't hurt me any more. Earlier, suffocated by horrible suspicions, I first of all felt pain, later perhaps the rage of a mate or a master. Afterwards everything suddenly changed. First of all, I stopped imagining that she was being unfaithful. To me, it began to seem too low and unimportant. My Virginija couldn't be so earthly, she had to be troubled by more weighty, mysterious things. I felt once again that she really was close to me. She was all the more close to me by having become distant. I began to wait for her until the wee hours, I would meet her, feed her and try to talk to her. She didn't want to talk, she just looked at me with those deep, hurtful eyes. Her gaze had changed, there was an indecipherable secret hiding in it. Even her body had changed – I once again felt desire for her. I examined her at night. It seemed to me that her body shined in the dark.

Well, you understand, it didn't really shine, but when you looked at it, touched it with your fingers, you would swear that it shone. She was hopelessly distant and unreal. I even thought that she had fallen deeply in love.

But she hadn't fallen in love. She didn't give off the scent of love. In our most intimate moments she caressed my hair like before and repeated my name only. She had been infected by an entirely different spirit. Pretty soon I experienced the spells of that spirit.

The first manifestation of that ill-starred spirit was run-of-the-mill, too tangible even. Returning home, I dropped by a bar called Žarija to have a few. I wasn't into drinking out of frustration, as had been the case until recently, but I knew that Virginija wouldn't be back anytime soon, and I deliberately didn't keep alcohol at home any more. I remember well that I made up a screwdriver – at the time they had Crystal vodka and Greek grapefruit juice in Žarija. At once I focused my attention on a guy with an Oriental face and magnetic eyes. I thought that he might have been Chinese. But he could also have been Uzbek. I thought about how we can't differentiate between nationalities, but we get angry if someone confuses us with Latvians. I decided that Virginija could tell at once who he was, perhaps even know how to talk with him in his mother tongue. Then I sank into lazy and absurd daydreams. I imagined I was the member of a great and important community. I had given meaningful lectures that touched upon the very essence of things the entire day – it was clear that they weren't stupid lectures on physics. Now I went to relax a little after an inspired day of work. I knew that an even more inspired day awaited me tomorrow. The screwdriver was really good, it helped me to calm down, but I couldn't fully relax, thoughts and ideas kept bubbling up in my head, I knew that people were waiting for my words, my works, I even became ashamed of allowing myself to relax with such abandon.

My daydreams were disturbed by a few drunk guys.

They weren't regulars, but were loud and clearly looking for trouble. At the beginning they threw a few offensive remarks in the direction of the Oriental, but he sat as calm as a rock. Then they started in on me.

I had always been frightfully afraid of violence. At that time no one had beaten me up badly, which made me more fearful of it. Upon seeing a loud pack of teenagers, I always beat it to the other side of the street. If the atmosphere in a bar heated up, I always tried to disappear quietly. When I had started to copy those banned books, I often imagined that I had ended up in prison. In my imagination I replied to my interrogators fearlessly, I mocked them and was as unbreakable as the greatest of revolutionaries, but having found myself in a shared cell, among criminals, my imagination suddenly petered out. I couldn't even think about violence. I was afraid of it. And I was afraid of those loud guys in Žarija picking on people.

They say that dogs immediately recognise a person that fears them by their scent. Perhaps those guys had something doglike about them, because they understood in a second that I was afraid of them. And yet, my pride didn't allow me to leave without finishing my drink. I was still proud. They began to harass me because of it.

"So what is such a droopy-eared stuck-up bloke doing here?" they said, or something similar to that.

I swallowed "droopy-eared" in silence, and acted like I hadn't heard anything at all. I pretended I was deaf and dumb, I signalled the barman for the bill. Fear suddenly permeated me down to my bones. It seems that is why I became so brave. I got up agitated and, suddenly having acquired the gift of speech, I clearly said while passing those two jerks, "Better a man with droopy ears than two girlish-looking swine."

That was stupid, pointless and physically perilous. I couldn't even come up with a wittier comeback, and what I'd said was nonsense. Those guys were by no means girlish, and having heard my words they were not exactly amiable.

I managed to run to the gate, but they caught up to me. I tried to defend myself, but I didn't know how to punch, and just like some mummy's boy I hysterically kicked the closest one in his crotch. The Asian from the bar ran up to the gate entrance, and my immediate thought was that they were all in cahoots. In my terror, I felt that something Asiatically refined and excruciating was in store for me. God knows, I wanted to say a prayer and goodbye to life. The guys had become unhinged, but the approaching Asian face was not human at all. He caught my glance, and I stopped kicking around senselessly.

The Asian landed both of them on the ground with two professional kicks, and managed to make an intricate ballet pirouette between them. Then he slapped the edge of his palm against one of them who was trying to get up. I wasn't able to grasp a thing that had happened.

"They acted uncouthly," the Oriental said calmly in an unexpectedly high-pitched voice, then he added in a throatier and lower tone. "Let's go, I will treat you."

"I should treat you…" I said, barely able to articulate the words.

"That is precisely why I will treat you. You need to break the rules," the Oriental replied.

At the bar he looked me up and down with his hypnotic eyes and said firmly, "You'll die of pneumonia. You should take care not to catch cold."

That was how Li Chin Chao appeared in my life, known better as the Great Li, a full-blooded Korean, who held my Lithuanian soul captive for a long time.

The Twelfth: about the non-existent Lithuanian spirit and God's forsaken corner syndrome, about Father-in-Law's Lituanica and your complexes, also about life and non-life

You will not leave your homeland –
wherever you run, it will follow you.

I don't know if my soul, which Li enslaved, was Lithuanian. I am not sure that a Lithuanian soul even exists. Even now I don't know what a Lithuanian is.

Those are simply answers to a question that I've asked myself many times: so why didn't I give all my efforts, all my soul to Lithuanian-ness?

Even now I don't know if I was a true Lithuanian. Logic demands that, in spite of everything, I was. I even immersed myself in all of the histories of the East just like a Lithuanian. That's probably what you thought – I remember your saying: Unfortunately, we're Lithuanians, whether you like it or not. Even if we refute our Lithuanian-ness, you said, we do it in a purely Lithuanian way. I always knew that I was a pure-blooded Lithuanian, but I didn't give it any thought for a very long time. It was the first time during those happy times in the dormitory that I felt a strange ambivalence when you proudly proclaimed,

"My task is to forge the non-existent Lithuanian soul!"

It was only much later that I found out you were imitating Joyce, though you probably had a reason for saying it like that. And what you said astonished me.

It was the first time a doubt fluttered through my chest

as to whether I really was a member of a nationwide community or if such a community even existed.

I remember very well another one of your ideas, and it seemed you weren't imitating anyone in saying it: "You need to create the nation's soul, even if that soul is not necessary for the nation itself, even if no one cares about it."

Grand ambitions, hopeless ambitions, laughable ambitions!

It is crushingly demoralising to create things that no one needs. When I was a student, I would look around our faculty closely, but I didn't see either Lithuanian-ness or a longing for it. We were all people without a nation – like earthworms exist without a gender. It was forbidden to talk openly about Lithuanian-ness, whereas the confidential conversations didn't explain anything. I don't want to say that the level of our Lithuanian-ness had plummeted to that of a prosthetic substitute such as the dance and music ensemble, Lithuania, but we were all sinking somewhere nearby. Our only advantage was that we were perfectly aware that the Lithuania ensemble was an unacceptable substitute for Lithuania.

But despite it all, even now I don't know what a Lithuanian is. No one has yet forged that non-existent Lithuanian soul. Stop a young person madly waving around the Lithuanian tricolour and ask him what his assertion, "I am a Lithuanian", means. All he might say is the following: I, my father, my grandfather and my ancestors lived in the lands of the Lithuanians and spoke Lithuanian. That's all that he can logically say. Of course, he'll talk a lot, especially if you've encountered a chatterbox.

He'll tell you that Vytautas the Great expanded Lithuania from the Baltic to the Black Sea.

So what? Where's the Lithuanian-ness there? And let alone the Lithuanian-ness of people today? Perhaps what is particularly Lithuanian is that we still remember this?

That nationally minded young kid will explain to you

that Lithuanians always fed themselves and also fed other peoples – unlike some of the nations close by.

So what? All nations in all times fed themselves or thrashed other nations, otherwise they would have simply disappeared. What's particularly Lithuanian in all this?

That youngster will also tell you...

You know very well what that youngster will say; he won't explain anything to you, regardless of how sincerely he tries. Mainly because you need to know something well yourself, if you want to explain it to someone else. Waving the national flag around won't inspire appreciation of it.

We are not metaphysical genderless earthworms, having eschewed our sex by choice. We are poor, misled patients, our limbs were secretly replaced with prostheses while we were sleeping. The only thing we might be guilty of is that we were sleeping. We were raised like that, we were moulded long and meticulously into people who didn't have roots or at least didn't feel that they had them. We only know that we should have them, so we declare that we do.

Our roots were chopped off, chemicals were used to shrivel them up. In that phantasmagorical institution we call a school, we were not taught in Lithuanian at all. The Lithuanian language did teach us though, it taught us non-Lithuanian subjects. I understood long ago that if you are a Lithuanian, you even understand the sun and moon, wind and rain in a Lithuanian way. It couldn't be otherwise, because you see with Lithuanian eyes, hear with Lithuanian ears, you smell only Lithuanian smells. In school we were taught to look at all of that with the genderless eyes of metaphysical earthworms.

Even Lithuanian books were explained to us in a non-Lithuanian way, and they taught us to think the way a non-Lithuanian brain thought. Yes, yes, that's the most important thing: it wasn't just our limbs that were supplanted by prostheses, but also our brains. We were plunged into a twisted world, and it was recorded by our brain prostheses.

They say that Gorky or someone else came up with the idea of publishing a grand library of world literature, the works were to be selected meticulously – not the full texts, but works that had been meticulously censored, corrected a bit, even supplemented here and there. Upon publishing that library, no other world literature was to be published any more. That castrated, repainted library, with this and that appended to it, was to serve as the world literature of all times for the people.

They say that they weren't able to publish such a library, or to be more precise, they weren't able to ban all other books.

But at the end of the day something more was achieved. The phantasmagorical school curricula – it wasn't just literature, it was a library or museum of the whole world, edited according to that principle.

Upon completing your school years, you couldn't be a member of the Lithuanian nation, you couldn't be a member of any nation, you could only be a genderless metaphysical earthworm.

No informal agreement, family, school, grandparents or other person could save us any more. Maybe they could have, but they didn't. At most they thrust sketchy scraps at us: about Vytautas and Gediminas, about Darius and Girėnas. We resembled a potato with pieces of bacon stuck into it: it's true that it contained bacon, nevertheless it was still mainly potato.

I searched, I searched long and hard for my nation in that nation of mine, but I didn't find it. I would really like to know when and who invented this Lithuanian, who is written about in numerous books, who is talked about constantly. The worst thing is that he's talked about constantly, even in an intimate circle of friends, having a cup of coffee or a drink. Who invented that fatal "nation of tillers of the soil"? All I know is that they were spouting nonsense that a Lithuanian in the city is an émigré, whose real motherland is the village. And who invented "a feeling and not the mind" and all of those other horrendous things? Tomas, you know everything – maybe you know who, when, and for what reason they thought all of that up? Who decided that a Lithuanian has to be like this, and not like that, and who and in what way did they examine every Lithuanian down to the very last one, categorise their traits and characteristics, and determine which of them were dominant? And what's worse – how could they declare that these were the real Lithuanians, and the others weren't. With what miraculous tool was it determined what a Lithuanian HAS TO BE? Tomas, explain to me, at least explain it to me now! I don't understand it.

I read and heard about those supposedly Lithuanian traits, but I never came across them in myself. I was horrified to find myself contemplating who I might be – a Swede, Zulu or Belarusian?

Neither my father nor my grandfather worked the land – they were artisans. My great-grandparents also didn't work the land – they made gods. Does this disqualify me from being a Lithuanian?

No one from my family was particularly emotional, nor did they sigh while looking up at the starry sky, but they all liked to spout on about things – the more general the topic, the better. Would that have been too un-Lithuanian?

I really wanted to belong to a nation, to our great community, but I never found out how I should belong to it. There couldn't be any theoretical philosophising about national ethnicity, and in my naivety I tried to set up a club for Lithuanian history at my faculty. The dean didn't scold me, he just put his head in his hands and mumbled, "Do you want me to lose my job?" All that was left was openly available Lithuanian literature, and I read a great deal of it. I doubt there was a person in Vilnius who read it as attentively, who caught each hint about the Lithuanian soul as studiously as I did.

You're smiling, you're even doubled over with laughter?

So what was I supposed to read? Even when I turned to banned books, all of them were Russian, there couldn't be anything about the Lithuanian soul there.

I read what I could get. I looked for answers, but the more I read the more I began to fail to understand something essential. I found one and the same thing in those books: either genderless metaphysical earthworms, or an agricultural nation, emotion without intellect and all of the horrors of helplessness: restraint, submission, caution. I didn't want to believe it, I couldn't agree that that really describes a Lithuanian's soul. The Lithuanian of books was indeed a worker of the land, passive as the land itself. All of his traits were too akin to spiritual impotency.

But what blew me away the most was the universal lack of thinking. The Lithuanian of books lived some sort of pre-intellectual life, he wasn't able and didn't want to think, all he did was feel – the sadder and more helpless the better. You could read between the lines that thinking was very un-Lithuanian.

Almost all of this literature convinced me that sensual cognition was the deepest, most human and most spiritual thing, while the intellect was more or less an invention of the devil, a seriously anti-Lithuanian thing. I was invited to only feel – in other words, surrender myself to the activity of my glands – and not dare to think.

You're laughing again? Well I'm not joking at all. I read precisely the following in an essay from one critic about a pretty good book: you see, author N's book is very intelligent, but that was supposedly bad, the book of a Lithuanian writer should be emotional throughout. It wasn't hard for you to read between the lines: "emotional throughout and pleasantly idiotic". You're still laughing, but I didn't tell you the punchline: that essay was published in none other than the monthly literary journal *Victory*.

I couldn't belong to a community which demanded such characteristics from its members.

But I'm a Lithuanian. That's simply a fact, and that's

that. But throughout my life I've had a particularly hard time in showing restraint and being submissive or cautious. Most importantly, I always tried to reflect. Whatever the outcome, I've tried to reflect. I avoided giving free reign to my feelings, let alone getting to know the world only through feelings.

So there was no way I could blend in with people who seemed to love Lithuania, who talked a lot about it. I couldn't blend in with them or the things I would hear.

"We peck at the grasses like little birds, and then sing sad little songs…" someone would say.

"God, how beautiful! God, how sad!" another would sigh.

"A Lithuanian does his work, carries his cross, doesn't wander under the sky aimlessly…" yet another would interject.

"God, how right! God, how beautiful!" the reply would come from somewhere.

If I tried to mention GGI, ecological niches, community, the feeling of security, phantasmagorical spores or something else which tormented me, I was called a modernist, a snob or altogether crazy.

Then they would all eat potato pancakes, along with oatmeal *kissel*, or occasionally potato dumplings.

I always preferred roast beef rubbed with spices, and a dry red wine.

Perhaps my ironic viewpoints and culinary comparisons weren't particularly well received, but you'll understand what I'm talking about. You're no dummy, you understand everything, you just don't do anything. You announced that you were forging the non-existent Lithuanian soul, but if you think that you created it while writing metaphysical diaries, studying the reflections of the world inside you – then you are very wrong. You should have done something. I was expecting that for a long time, and had so much faith in it. Soon, soon, I told myself, Tomas Kelertas's book about the real Lithuanian will start to be passed around from hand to hand, there's not long to wait. The longer I waited, the more clearly I understood that I was just fooling myself, but in the depths of my heart I still hoped.

Why did you abandon us all, Tomas? After all I certainly wasn't the only one. There were plenty of us – young and intelligent people (somewhat more intelligent than me), who didn't want to acquiesce to what was called the Lithuanian soul. Those people didn't want to be a nation of farmers without a mind, they didn't want to show restraint, be submissive and cautious. However, that supposed Lithuanian-ness couldn't offer them anything else. So they dived head first into Buddhisms, Krishnaisms, rock 'n' rollisms and who knows what else. Those things were nevertheless closer to them than sad songs and birds pecking at grass. But those were the best, most intelligent young people, Tomas! Unfortunately, Lithuanian culture, the seizing of the non-existent soul was left primarily to others – those who do their work, carry their cross, don't fly to the stars, just sigh and don't dare to think.

Now, living here on the other side, it seems to me that all characteristics that are typically Lithuanian are promulgated by people whose aim is to quietly stamp out and do away with the Lithuanian people. A very precise method: the most intelligent, most ingenious and loudest are pushed away from Lithuanian-ness, and so that this place isn't emptied, the most submissive and those who sigh the most are sheltered in it.

If you want to bring a people to ruin, first take away their minds. I wrote a letter to Kafka:

Dear Franz,
One of your works is forever stuck in my head. No, I won't elucidate upon either The Trial or The Castle, what stuck in my head were a few lines from your diaries, it seems they were from The Blue Octavo Notebooks.

You wrote that you are a typical Western Jew, and that means that you don't have a moment of peace, you don't have anything, you have to acquire everything – not just the present and the future, but even the past. Forgive me if I'm not quoting you very accurately, but that was the essence of that entry after all.

I want to tell You that for us Lithuanians, it's even worse. We also don't have anything, we also have to acquire everything – not just the present, future and past. We need to acquire a soul, so in other words ourselves. You, Western Jews, didn't have a homeland, however, you had the Promised Land. You were persecuted and driven away. But you could expect the Messiah. Don't downplay that, Franz, you all had a lot – you all had an idea.

We have a homeland and a language. They tried to expel us, exile us from our land, but we defended ourselves by the skin of our teeth. Our language was banned, but we preserved it by the skin of our teeth. We have a land and a language, that's a lot. However, we don't have our own idea, Franz, that's what weighs on us. We walk around without an aim, we live without an aim and talk without an aim, we're not expecting any sort of Messiah for ourselves, and that is horrible.

If we don't find our very own unique idea, we won't stand out from others for something, and if we don't stand out for something, then what good is a separate name for us? Let's either just call ourselves what everyone else calls themselves or not give ourselves a name at all. Do you understand what our great fear is, Franz? If you don't find your own idea, you also slowly start to lose your name. It's just our ideas that name us. You shouldn't complain, Franz, Jews always were and will remain Jews.

There are those who are unluckier than you, there are those who know very well what they are called, but don't know why they are called precisely that, what their name means or what it should mean. There are those, the names of whom are just a faint label, a formal sign. We, Lithuanians, are such a people.

I should write things in my notebooks that are even sadder

*than yours: I am a typical Lithuanian, and that means that
I don't have a moment's peace, I don't have anything, I have
to acquire everything – even my non-existent soul. The only
thought that gives me comfort on the gloomy nights of non-
existence – that I still understand that I am a Lithuanian, I
still understand that I have to have my own soul. That means
I still exist, it's not just a name that is left of me as it is for
many other peoples.*

Activists for Lithuanian-ness would most likely kill me
for such a letter. Thank God, I can't be killed any more. I
am floating around on the other side, which their hands
can't reach, where, on the whole, there are no hands. I am
very bored here, which is why I think about life even more
than the living do.

I think that there is a secret conspiracy that exists,
which tries to belittle the Lithuanian people, declaring
that Lithuania is a godforsaken corner of the earth, and
Lithuanians – God's pawns. Flip through one of our
weeklies – it's easier for you to do that – and you will
certainly find such philosophising. Why should we, a
nation of peasants, bother to aspire to the passions and
depths of Strindberg or O'Neill, we're better off doing it
quietly under a Lithuanian linden tree with feelings, and
not with the mind... People who write like that, who are
willingly published, they are even right in their own way –
with respect to themselves. This is the sacred truth: why
should those peasants even bother!

But who allows them to talk in the name of everyone
and why? Why do the incapable and the soulless speak
courageously in the name of the nation, and the capable
and intelligent stay silent? Why have you stayed silent until
now, Tomas?

It can't really be because you are Lithuanian, being
cautious and keeping an eye on things, can it? The incapable
and soulless apologetics of this godforsaken corner are a real

force, but you and those similar to you are only nameless ghosts, which don't even appear to anyone.

Hey you, those who I never got to know, forge that non-existent Lithuanian spirit as fast as you can before it's too late!

I remember, as though it were a bad dream, the fierce attacks on every person who tried to come out from under that Lithuanian linden tree and look around for broader horizons. He's following foreign paths, they would say with animosity, he's pretending to know more than the others and trying to shock everyone with his exaggerated imaginings. And that vitriolic, fake compassion was used when explaining away each cultural emigrant: good God, how could he, a poor inept Lithuanian, accomplish anything in the wider world; he won't accomplish anything – poof and he'll disappear! The eyes of that sighing person would light up wickedly, clearly saying that he would strangle that emigrant just so that, God forbid, he wouldn't achieve anything. Even those who had left for Moscow to at least fight for a decent place for themselves in the Soviet hierarchy were castigated both behind their backs and publicly: see, he gave in to the desire to get laurels from strangers, and one could say, he betrayed us. You see, he should have sat at home and not even stuck his nose out of our godforsaken corner.

Some unnamed person invited us to boil in our own juices the whole time and not stick our noses anywhere. All we should care about are our things, that person taught, and let others take care of their own things. We carried out this programme perfectly: not one Lithuanian made his way into the world's spiritual elite, and if someone naively tried, the nation would not only not help him – they would hinder him all the way.

All the world has heard about are Lithuanian athletes: about Gerulaitis and Sabonis. How terrible. All that'll be left in the world's greatest books is something hastily written in the margins: Lithuanians are sometimes able to manipulate a tennis ball or basketball well. And that's all. A great nation, a powerful nation!

I quickly shot off a short letter to Mykolaitis-Putinas:

Dear Professor,
I learned that you were offered the chance to publish In the Shadow of the Altars in England and France, and you refused. According to your philosophy, it was unseemly to disseminate your writings in the outside world. You supposedly write for the Lithuanian nation about the Lithuanian nation; others don't need to know all of those things. And you have no interest in literary glory.

I don't even know if this was true, but if it was, then I cannot forgive you. Every Lithuanian line of prose, every Lithuanian painting that goes out into the wider world is a victory for all of us. We need to achieve such small victories with all our strength, all the time and through our joint efforts. Only in this way can the nation acquire its name and its soul.

If you did refuse, I cannot forgive you!

Once again I've forgotten myself a little, I've started to pity all Lithuanians. Almost all of them – after all, Father-in-Law is a pure Lithuanian. At one point I had asked myself: could Father-in-Law be some sort of mouthpiece for Moscow? After thinking for a short time I had to admit it: no, no way, the environment that he got his sustenance from was right here, in his homeland.

I had the opportunity to see him up close, and that's why I argue that such a person couldn't live anywhere else, Lithuania was necessary for someone like him. Father-in-Law is essentially two-faced, one of his faces is turned towards the centre, while the other is turned towards his own people. I used to be amazed to hear how he spoke Russian with his eminent guests: without the slightest accent, mixing in subtle Muscovite slang (he had studied at a Communist Party school). But I was even more amazed listening to how he gave a speech in Russian, when his own people heard him: with a horrendous accent, twisting his words and pausing to sigh. He did everything deliberately, to him there was no such thing as an insignificant detail.

Restrained, submissive and cautious people who judged the world with their feelings and not their minds suited him very well. He appealed to feelings masterfully, if it served his purpose – this included national feelings. He liked to boast that he shaped national poets with his hands.

"They are needed," Father-in-Law would say thoughtfully. "They are needed like a safety valve, though Lithuania isn't a steam generator."

"But what is it then?" I once enquired cautiously.

"A swamp," Father-in-Law replied without getting angry, without malice. "However, even that swamp is by no means hampered by a safety valve. Swamp gases can also cause an explosion."

I wanted to chide him: if that was the case, then he was nothing more than the little devil of the swamp, but I kept my peace. I remembered your lesson well: it's better to keep it to yourself and reflect on it. It's not too late to say an intelligent thought the next day, but putting yourself out there like a fool is always harmful. Think three times, and only then say something.

The problem was that after thinking about it three times, I wouldn't say anything at all – my grand speech being the exception.

"The only important thing is that we're the ones regulating that safety valve," Father-in-Law once candidly explained. "As long as the national poet in question comes to us in advance to discuss his nationally infused masterpieces – everything is fine."

"And what if he doesn't return?" I inquired combatively.

Father-in-Law smiled at me pleasantly and told me his

grand secret: "You need to train him in such a way that he would write what we need without asking beforehand."

But perhaps what stuck most in my mind were the views on Lithuanians he confessed to, which I heard that time, that one time I found him at home totally drunk. He was lying flat on the sofa totally naked, as big as a mountain, nodding his head and moaning. I thought that he had something wrong with his heart. He had a hard time making me out, even after covering one eye, but having recognised me, he calmed down and just sighed heavily:

"And what more do they want?" he asked sadly. "They were supposed to be deported to hell, like the Tatars from Crimea. They weren't deported. They live on their land, gorge themselves till they're full. They live somewhat better than all those Russkies do. What else do they need?"

It seems to me now that it was after the Kaunas events, though I may be mistaken. I never did understand that man. I couldn't understand why he so cynically explained his methods to me, and revealed his real views. He was certainly neither stupid nor vain. What's more, there was no glory in boasting to a pup like me.

Perhaps I am greatly mistaken, but it seems to me that he wished to find some heirs. Father-in-Law wished to leave his spiritual seed to the world. I couldn't understand that until I listened to the monumental conversation between you both. Yes, Tomas, I heard it from the other side, I participated in it, I was granted such powers. I was a fly, buzzing around in Father-in-Law's office, I was a sunbeam pushing the office's weighty dust around. I could be there because Father-in-Law remembered me, he thought long and hard about me. That was my only experience of the new times. I took note of every word, from the very first ones:

"What the hell!" Father-in-Law murmured somewhere to his moustache, not even to you. "Time and again we choose people who aren't worth taking on for anything at all. They're incompetent morons. And the real men with balls pass right on by. Like you – you're not even a party member, are you?"

"No," you replied in a doubtful voice.

It seems to me that you didn't hear everything during that monumental conversation you both had. You turned red, and became pale and extremely nervous. At first you were frightened, later you became enraged, and finally you felt an all-encompassing hopelessness. You focused attention only on yourself, Tomas, you did that far too often. But I focused my attention only on Father-in-Law. He had never talked so openly even with me. In fact he flipped over a card or two for you, and that was enough for you to freeze up. He very much wanted to turn me and you (especially you) into his people, not into ourselves. Without even knowing my class theory, he hit where it hurt.

"Judging from this very work, you consider me a class enemy," he said by no means gloomily, but rather craftily. "You won't find a stupider theory. There aren't any classes. There are smart people, not very smart people and morons. We both belong to the first category. And you want to harm me. It's not logical."

You replied that you didn't want to harm anyone, you just wrote down some of your ideas, by no means everything. And you thought that he nevertheless was afraid of you. You were pretty terrified, when your manuscript ended up on Father-in-Law's desk so quickly, but you felt a delight that he nevertheless did fear you a little bit. Father-in-Law glanced at you, smiled, and for some reason you thought that he was able to read the thoughts of others.

"No, no one is afraid of you," said Father-in-Law pleasantly, "you yourself are interesting. Interesting, because you're unexpected. I'm already fed up with those newish movements, they're pointless. They won't say and won't do anything unexpected. They're easy to control and suppress. A lone wolf is somewhat more dangerous. You never know what will pop into such a person's head."

You said that perhaps nothing would pop into your head, and that you wouldn't pop anything into anyone else's head, that was an old joke of yours, but you mumbled it like a robot, and then realised that some kind of miracle was occurring: Father-in-Law wasn't castigating you or threatening you, he had even relinquished his official tone. He spoke to you as an equal, as if you were an old acquaintance, though you were meeting for the first time.

Father-in-Law once again read your thoughts: "I know you from my son-in-law's stories. I always thought that he made you up. There wasn't any Kelertas that figured in my lists. Now I see that he not only didn't make you up, but described you rather accurately. Thanks to Leonas, may he rest in peace."

You didn't say anything, you just thought like you did back then, in your youth: that freshman again, can't I have any peace!

Am I telling it just as it was? Just as it was? Now do you believe that it's really me who's writing these letters? I'm also writing them to you because you're probably the only person who could believe them.

You sat in that huge office unconsciously cringing, because you were in fear of Father-in-Law. You thought about your entire life, in which you'd feared so much. It began to seem to you that there was hardly anything in it – except fear. You inherited it genetically from your parents and grandparents. However, that wasn't enough – you were inoculated with it in early childhood like smallpox. Now you sat in fear of Father-in-Law, he could do anything he saw fit with you, and at that very instant it suddenly dawned on you (though you had proved it very logically in your work) that nothing had changed in the world around you, that you were still as lonely and helpless as you had always been, while Father-in-Law was still just as powerful and cynical. He could crush you with his little finger, and no one would help you. You suddenly regretted that you'd chosen the lot of a lonely thinker of your own volition, you suddenly desired (you finally desired) to belong to a harmonious, united community, which would protect you. But Father-in-Law stood across from you, smiling pleasantly and reading your thoughts.

"You won't join any of those newfangled movements," he said sternly. "Your pride won't let you. You value only the power of personality and the mind. And the crowd doesn't like such men. The crowd doesn't need a mind. All the crowd needs is to get its fill of shouting. You wrote that work yourself, *Perestroika in Albania* – it's rather witty, rather interesting to read. You probably thought that everyone would pay attention to it and start snapping up copies one after another? That everyone would value your thoughts? But who valued them? I was the only one. I have been the only attentive reader of your masterpiece. I can even quote from it: 'In Albania neither the structure nor the nucleus of that structure have changed – only specific people are able to make decisions and govern. In other words the decorations of the opera and the words of the arias have changed, but everyone is still singing the same Albanian bel canto, and the orchestra is playing in the same Albanian mode with the same Albanian harmony.' You didn't really think that we would let this be printed for public consumption, did you?"

"In addition to Lithuania, there's still Moscow," you said despondently.

"And what are you going to achieve there? Do you really think the Russkies will care about your wounds? By the way, we won't let it get printed in Moscow either."

"Your hands don't reach everywhere."

"Will you send it to Chicago? You think the Chicagoans will be very interested in it? Send it, send it, that's all we need."

"Who exactly do you mean by 'we'?"

"Us!" Father-in-Law's voice suddenly became stern and

angry. "We who established and maintained this order. We who forged and fortified the structure, making it unconquerable. No, we're not those weaklings who only cared about stuffing their purses, showering their family with gold. We are working men, we are giants. We did work that your little mind doesn't understand and won't understand. And we did it our way. We're unconquerable. Who, do you think, ruled the country, while that asylum of decrepit old men gave out stars and divided up diamonds amongst themselves? Who ruled the country? We did! And we still rule it!"

"That asylum of decrepit old men doesn't exist any more..." you said, trying to get a word in edgewise.

"...And the new people will rule? No, my boy, they took over the government from that asylum, but not from us. Single people can be vanquished perhaps, but our structure is indestructible, millions of people work in our interest, without even realising it. You're a smart man after all, you even grasped the structure's nuclei, you just didn't understand what kind of structure it was. No one has fathomed us out yet. Not dumb writers with their naive magic words 'bureaucracy' or 'nomenklatura'. All that means nothing, they are chasing ghosts, but not us... I will be the first to throw a rock at that idiotic bureaucracy, we don't need people like that, all they are is ballast, their place can be occupied by anyone, by any kind of ballast... You can convene a hundred conferences or summits, you can declare that we don't exist any more, but we're still here, we're definitely still here."

As Father-in-Law talked, he grew and expanded, flooding the entire space of the enormous office, his body became transparent, you saw an endless amount of strange, totally inhuman veins and nerves inside him. It wasn't blood that was flowing through them, but the phantasmagorical spores, now very visible, even seemingly alive. Your fear had disappeared long ago, all you felt was rage and helplessness.

I felt sorry for you. In that instant you wanted to grab all of the copies of your work and simply hand them out to passers-by in the street and implore, People, here's the truth, here everything people fear is covered. People, read it and remember it!

But all you saw around you were empty eyes and sweating faces. You didn't believe in those people. You didn't believe any more that they were even alive. You felt that you were too late for a train which, it was true, was going who knows where, but nevertheless it was going, and you'd stayed on the platform, where a smiling Father-in-Law was waiting for you, having crossed his arms on his wide chest, immoveable and unconquerable. He winks at you like you're a fellow conspirator and silently, with only his lips, says, That train won't be going anywhere, we ripped up the rails long ago.

The real Father-in-Law in his office had already come back down, and once again resumed his normal shape, but you already knew that it was just a mask, that his true shape was the other one, that you had never come up against such an enemy before, that throughout your life you'd been as naive as an infant: you'd thought all you had to do was name everything, and it would be possible to defeat it. Now you understood that there are things that can't be put into words.

"And the people?" you said loudly to yourself.

"There aren't any people here," Father-in-Law said curtly. "There's a crowd. Some of our people were frightened by that new movement, perhaps you heard – there was one that made itself known a week ago. The namby-pambies were scared. But I tell you, they're nothing. It's a crowd. They're Lithuanians after all. Did you ever see a mad dog chained up by his doghouse? He's angry, simply horrible, and it seems that if you unchained him – he would tear you to pieces then and there. But what happens when he breaks the chain? He runs around like crazy, barks at the air and rolls around in the grass until you catch him again and chain him up. And then… Most important is what happens next. Does he furiously start to bite on the chain? Does he become mortally dangerous? No, my dear, he goes into his doghouse and falls asleep, tired and happy. We will once again tie up the dog with a chain – and that's it. Let him run around, roll in the grass, and catch air for the time being. As one of my neighbours, a veteran, says, Let them make a noise, that's really good – it'll be clear who you have to shoot. He's a plain-spoken old man, all he knows is one medicine for all illnesses – shooting. I think it won't come to that."

"Thank you. Thank you very much," you murmured.

Your head was empty. You awaited threats or demagogy, but heard what you heard. No, Father-in-Law wasn't afraid of you, he disregarded you entirely, you were an empty space to him.

"Gorbachev will crush you all," you spit out, barely able to control yourself.

"If we let him to do that," Father-in-Law said calmly. "But we won't. We already didn't let him do a lot of things. Gorbachev isn't eternal either. We will take care that someone else like him doesn't emerge."

"But he's still there."

Father-in-Law nodded his head in agreement; his eyes were fierce, but his facial expression was gentle and humble.

"Listen, did you notice how sad his eyes are sometimes," he asked longingly. "It's more and more often. Doesn't it seem to you that he senses what awaits him?"

You almost couldn't hear that any more. You began to feel that everything here was unreal. Having calmed down, you took a seat. Your rage subsided and disappeared, you thought logically why all of this just couldn't be. Father-in-Law could have invited you, let's say as a former friend of his son-in-law, but he couldn't have talked with you in such a tone, even more so about such things. You always liked to repeat Kant's observation that only beauty does not strive for benefit, and maybe you really believed it.

Which is why you now wondered what benefit Father-in-Law would have gained by talking like that. There couldn't have been any benefit, ergo, he couldn't have talked like that. You must have been imagining it. It seemed to you that he was reading your mind, but he couldn't have been. You were just imagining it. You glanced at him, he was already sitting at the table, to you he seemed as enormous as a cliff, austere and stark as a cliff, fighting with him was as pointless as beating your fists against a cliff. He said what he had to say and at once stopped taking an interest in you.

"You're free!" he declared dryly. "I'll keep the manuscript, it will go well with the other samizdat literature on my shelf. At last something Lithuanian has turned up there."

You slowly walked to the street, still solving the riddle, putting things together logically. Logic offered the only solution. It was absurd, but that day you resolved to follow Tertullian and believe it precisely because it was absurd.

Father-in-Law wanted you to immortalise him. He deliberately explained this and that to you, and simply pushed you to write a new work slowly, meticulously, attentively. There was even a title that flashed into your mind: A Song about a Monster. You even smiled to yourself: you would try, and he would follow you every moment, see how you were doing, and the moment you'd finished it, he would take all the copies of the manuscript. So others would read about it publicly? He couldn't possibly want that. So what did he want?

A rally had just finished on the main avenue, national flags and the Gediminas columns were flapping all around. They irritated you. Everything irritated you. Something had not really quite panned out in your life. When things were banned, you were more radical than anyone, and now, when this and that became legal, everyone rumbled on by in crowds, and you were left unneeded. You wanted to be a loner, and when you became one, you suddenly felt an unfathomable bitterness, that no one was clapping for you, and they were clapping for other people. Those other people didn't complain about their life too much earlier, and they were doing fine now as well. You understood all too well that this was the only way it could be, and that it's a common, universal rule. You remembered Camus and his *L'Homme révolté*, and you understood it all. Suddenly you stopped dead as though you'd been paralysed and angrily spat right on the pavement.

You suddenly understood, why Father-in-Law spoke like that with you, you understood that he had achieved his aim at least partially: a strange, implausible thought stirred deep inside. Perhaps it was worth spitting on all those invented principles and non-existent gods, use the confusion and jump up, not a step or two, but maybe ten? Father-in-Law would help you – goddammit, you'd jump and then you'd see. You see everything better from above.

I don't blame you. I myself have thought the same more than a few times.

Are you interested in how I got to know your thoughts so well? I know a lot, but I don't have any use for it. You perhaps won't agree conceptually that it's "me" that's writing, but it really is me. Yes, I don't have a body, and I am just a soul, but I think, therefore I exist. Ha ha, that's a joke.

I don't exist. I just think.

It seems to me that only a dead person finally coincides with his soul that's wandering around the world.

My non-life is infinitely boring. I am jealous of you all. You are all doing something, and you all suffer and lose. I can only remember.

Who am I? A nothing who can write a memoir. An unreal memory, which cannot only remember, but also see what came afterwards. A soul, which wants to understand everything and is unable of changing anything.

I can still add many more descriptions. Here, on the other side, we're very partial to vivid descriptions.

The Thirteenth: An unhappy
number and unhappy content

*So what have I figured out? There's
misfortune – I've figured that out. There's
a source for misfortune – I've figured that
out. There's a way to stop misfortune – I've
figured that out. There's a path for stopping
misfortune – I've figured that out too.*

*The dreams that visit the ill, the sad, the cruel, the passionately
in love and the drunk do not come true.*

The Great Li said right away what was most important:
"You need to break the rules. You need to reject all habits
at once. People become used to only living wrongly, but
then expect that having changed a single wrong, they will
achieve happiness."

The Great Li said resolutely, "Incorrect thinking states
that happiness isn't a state, but just an aspiration. That
happiness can be only somewhere and sometime, but in
no way here and now. Incorrect thinking is dictated by bad
people. Their goal is to hide happiness from people, which is
always here and now, you just need to find and recognise it."

The Great Li threw a smelly rag in my face and asked,
"Do you understand?"

Just as I tried to open my mouth, the Great Li began to
hit me in the face with the rag.

"Bad! Bad!" he repeated. "You are trying to reason, but
you should be happy. Those who reason aren't happy."

The Great Li showed me a tree in my courtyard. "Did you
see it earlier?"

"No," I admitted honestly. "I never used to notice it."

"You never used to notice anything," the Great Li said sadly. "Incorrect thinking had blinded you."

We came back from the Žarija bar to my place on that occasion. To my surprise, Virginija had already returned home. The Great Li shook her hand tenderly. For a moment I thought that he held it in his too long, while Virginija looked straight into his eyes far too tenderly. I quickly found out that they had been acquaintances for a long time already, and even something more. I found out where she disappeared to during my long alcohol-infused evenings.

"Li helped me to understand a thing or two," Virginija explained sincerely. "I didn't understand anything myself any more. You on one side: downcast, hopeless, searching for something – who knows what. And on the other side, mother, a silent shadow, giving you everything, but unable to really give anything. Father with his mafia-like ambitions and global narcissism, always boasting of vile deeds with delight. Work with all of the bickering, fights for positions, wages and flats. Right after I was appointed head of the group, there was an explosion: your dad's behind this, your dad's behind this! I didn't understand anything any more, all I did was swallow pills by the handful. But the worst thing is that when it's indescribably hard going for a person, they are all alone. All alone! Li showed me that it can be different."

"What incorrect thinking calls life is nothing but fiction," the Great Li explained. "I will speak plainly: a government minister is almost always unhappy, while a beggar in a dump in the Fabijoniškės neighbourhood can be happy. You lack for money – you are unhappy. If you are demoted or not promoted – you are unhappy. People, where are you looking, what are you doing? You need to break those rules, you need to disobey them, though along with that you should disobey yourself."

"Disobey yourself," the Great Li taught. "Disobey your first thought, your second thought, your third thought. And then breathe in deeply and obey your first impulse. If another person, your big brother, accepts your impulse, then there is happiness for both of you. And if he does not accept this, always blame yourself, not the other, but just yourself."

Afterwards it was said that when we gathered together, all we did was get drunk. That's a lie. It was only those who specifically wanted to drink on that particular occasion. It was strictly forbidden to offer a glass to someone else, and still more to convince them to drink. It was strictly forbidden to provoke others: drink to my health, today's a celebration for me. Li also taught us to break the rules in this case: an occasion to drink is searched for, in other words, one can drink only when there is no occasion: celebrations are watered down by alcohol, in other words, one can only celebrate soberly.

We gathered almost every day, each time in a different place, in a different flat, often outdoors as well. Li spoke quietly, but very clearly. His voice was smooth like flowing water, like a gentle ruffling of the wind. He didn't convince you of anything, you could opt to not listen to what he was speaking about and we often didn't listen, because he would say the most important things only face-to-face.

Afterwards it was said and written that Li was an unattractive and rather stupid guy, that they didn't understand how educated adults could gather around him. If that was true, then it really was incomprehensible. But Li was not like that, everyone noticed at once, just as I did when I first saw him at the Žarija bar. His gaze had a magnetic force, which you couldn't resist. His manner of speaking was slow and calm, sometimes he would repeat the same thing numerous times, and then he would let you think everything over, believe it or challenge it.

He didn't command anyone. He didn't force you to believe in him, we believed in him ourselves, of our own free will. He offered us mutual breathing, he opened our eyes: we didn't need to create or invent that mutual breathing at all, it had existed long ago, all you needed was to get into its rhythm. He clearly demonstrated that we (at least I) live covered with gas masks and respirators. You could say we deliberately avoided breathing in fully on purpose, we deliberately sprayed smelly chemicals on ourselves so we couldn't breathe in deeply.

The first time when he, without any warning, got naked as can be, everyone was stunned, with a few girls even bolting from our gathering. Li didn't explain anything, he just smiled and went to get dressed. When he undressed the second time, the third time, the fifth time, without explaining anything to anyone, we began to slowly grasp what he wanted to express with this, but we weren't able to conquer the strange barrier. Li didn't hurry us. The turning point occurred on a muggy, damp day, when Laima, shaking her bewitching curly locks, also got undressed. The Great Li suddenly became downcast, went up to her and symbolically slapped her in the face.

"You're lying!" he said rather more sadly than angrily. "You undressed because you wanted to show your beautiful body. You wanted to enchant and captivate. I cannot be naked any more. You awakened shame in me."

After that event the strange barrier suddenly fell. Each of us could undress calmly in view of everyone else, if we wanted to. But anyone could also sit next to a small, secluded lake in the company of naked people, that person alone being clothed, if he or she wanted to.

It certainly wasn't easy for us to conquer our feeling of shame; it even makes me feel sorry for myself, when I think how mired in lies and hypocrisy I was. After all I, like everyone else, avoided my nakedness not out of some sense of morality, but only because I was frightened of appearing weak, ugly or altogether defective. I was afraid of appearing the way I am. I was afraid of being myself.

That was the Great Li's first important lesson, and it was very similar to your lessons – just in a totally different form. Even then I understood why the Great Li had so many followers, why his lessons were so understandable. They were exceedingly real, simply tangible. Your lessons were always purely intellectual, far too abstract.

"From childhood you are taught to occupy the highest place in the structure that you can," the Great Li declared. "You are judged by your place in that structure. But it wasn't you that invented it. What's more, you weren't even asked when they concocted that structure. Moreover, you are strictly forbidden to change it. Just try doubting the rationality of that structure, and you'll end up in a madhouse. I don't invite you to break it, that is not within our power. All we can do is spit on that structure, and free ourselves from it. All we can do is relax, and escape from its shackles."

The Great Li revealed colours to me. Until then I hadn't seen that the world was so colourful. Everyone in our community, as I did, experienced an abundance of colours, their flavour, coolness or warmth, even their sound. I, being a fool, always thought that a colour was just a colour, I didn't even suspect that each colour resounded with its own tone, was coarser or smoother on touching, became salty or sour to the taste.

Li gave me the gift of scents. Until then I hadn't even suspected that there were so many aromas in the world. In our community everyone, including me, experienced the gamut of scents, their hues, weight and music. Even my dreams began to be infused with scents.

Li even gave the gift of scents to poor Linukas, who smoked and snuffled with his allergic nose persistently. Linukas had never experienced scents in his life. He couldn't smell flowers, he ate food without aromas and he loved women without a scent. Li gave him the gift of an entirely new world. It did not come easily. Even Li couldn't simply wave a magic wand and cast a spell on Linukas. He toiled for a long time, after each session he would be pale, his entire being shaking due to weakness, but a day or two later he would once again sit in a corner with Linukas and suffer persistently, patiently. At the beginning Linukas's runny nose let up just a little bit, then it began to diminish considerably, and finally it disappeared. At first you could say we were scared, because Linukas began to run riot. He couldn't take in this new world that had suddenly opened up to him all at once, the scents didn't let him fall asleep, he couldn't concentrate, all he did was loudly sniff up scents and breathe them in incessantly. But gradually everything fell into place. When Linukas would begin to smell something particularly strongly, he would close his eyes and begin to lay out melodies from the scents, he would hear scents particularly clearly, he could instantaneously hum the scent of a room, which others could barely hear. He not only regained what had been taken away from him, you could say the world repaid its debt to him for all of those scentless years, at once endowing him with a twofold, threefold, tenfold sense of smell. But it did not surrender this willingly; it had to be forced by the Great Li.

Li knew how to transform a person's world, sacrificing his own life force for it. It was like he squeezed vital juices out of himself and fed them to others. He did something essentially the opposite of Father-in-Law: he didn't infect people with phantasmagorical spores, but healed others with himself.

Now I myself find it strange that I surrendered so quickly and thoughtlessly to the Great Li's teachings. I didn't inquire at all as to who he was, why it was he came to Vilnius of all places. I didn't try to ascertain where and how Virginija found him. I wasn't interested in knowing. I didn't even get angry when Virginija spoke Korean with him. Perhaps he had cast a spell on me, hypnotised me with his eyes that worked like magnets. His gaze really was magical, it sufficed for him to look at your hand a little longer, for instance, and your hand would suddenly go numb, it would start to be poked by small invisible needles. I'm not even mentioning the fact that he could see a person's aura and cure illnesses with his biocurrents.

The Great Li truly was a miracle maker, which makes the person he eventually turned into all the more terrible.

He gave us the gift of the world, different than the world of other people, but one common for all of us. I began to inhabit two separate worlds equally. The first world was old and feeble. In it I would get up in the morning and leave for my damnable technical institute. In that world I was done for. My naive and grand aspirations couldn't materialise in it. I had wanted to be a prophet, almost like Prometheus, but I'd turned into a grey weakling, a spiritual masturbator. In that world nothing interested me, except for books. You needed to endure that world, exhaust yourself, so you could finally dive into an entirely different one as quickly as possible.

The second world was brand new, alluring and mysterious. I would step into it cautiously, not daring to hurry, in it I was needed. In it, what was important was my soul – the way it was. In it, the soul of each one was important, regardless of what it was like. Our community comprised very different people, and we would never have met each other in the first world, still less would we have got along. In the first world we were just the masticated by-products chewed up and spat out by circumstances and angry people. In the second world we were a robust community, having experienced an implacable, life-giving mutual breathing. In the first world perverted morals as well as a phantasmal nightmare dominated. In the second, love and intrapersonal harmony reigned. In the first you had to trample and lay waste to something – people, morals or ideals – in order to achieve things valued in that world. In the second you could feel safe. You didn't need to trample anything there.

Most likely a vein of the physicist still beat within me, I didn't give up logic and I liked to arrange things symmetrically and rationally. There were four assessors that inhabited me: one evaluated the first world from positions of the first world, the second evaluated the second world from the second world's positions. The third evaluated the first world from the positions of the second world, while the fourth evaluated the second world from the first's positions. That fourth one greatly concerned me. He called our holy community a pathetic sect, useless and even dangerous to society. He was like a mini Father-in-Law, a feeble-minded little Father-in-Law, he would always repeat his threatening little phrase: such a sect is dangerous for us, it teaches people to obey not us, but someone else. That is not allowed, and we have to destroy that sect.

I was the first to address Li, I told him about that fourth assessor.

"We will be judged like that," I warned him. "We are a very harmonious community, but just among ourselves. We wouldn't know how to defend ourselves, if we were attacked. We only have an internal feeling of security, but we are totally unprotected against external enemies."

Li just nodded his head. He had thought much about this.

"You are right, Leo," he replied to me. "We must engage with the outside, poisoned by insidious thinking, according to its rules, not according to our own. We will not imitate Mahatma, we will not proclaim non-resistance to evil, because we are too few. We cannot send tens or hundreds of thousands against the barrels of their guns, as he did. Our fist must be ironlike, but directed only at the outside."

I understood at once what he was talking about, I

remembered well his shiver-inducing ballet, which he performed in our archway, when we met for the first time. Li looked me in the eye intently and smiled: "Don't worry, you will not have to learn taekwondo. There are special people for that."

At the time it seemed natural and necessary, I wanted security after all. At the time it didn't seem to me that something was wrong. Ju-jitsu and kung fu fighters began to swarm around us, they were silent as ghosts, however, they provided peace and a feeling of security, which my entire life I had so desired. All you had to do was throw them a little money.

Money is what oppressed us most. But we couldn't get around it at all. We couldn't completely shut ourselves off from the first world. It was painful, but unavoidable.

I remembered my own spiritual mountains less and less, I tried to remember them, but I couldn't see them with my inner vision, however hard I tried. They were shrouded by an intoxicating mist, in which the slopes' contours, precipices and cliffs dissolved. I didn't know if I was still climbing somewhere or just walking through a foggy valley, having simply invented the mountains in my head. That wasn't important to me. A peaceful bliss rocked me and put me to sleep, I breathed in rhythm to the much dreamt-of mutual breathing and I couldn't have wished for anything better. Around me were people, whom I loved, whose affairs I cared about, just as they cared about mine. Only in the morning would I still have to get up and go on a sluggish excursion through the first world: the technical institute, lectures and colleagues who didn't understand anything about anything.

Though not all of my co-workers were like that. I had already noticed Birutė before. She had huge eyes, and hair the colour of grain ripened for harvest. She was tall, almost my height, and perhaps a little unhappy because of it: it was the rare man who decided to court her. At the technical institute I was the only one like that, though even for me it was a little uncomfortable: I was used to women's heads being more or less up to my chin. Birutė would look me right in the eye, not raising her head in the least. Her eyes were big, brown, and a little dewy. She smelled of a field in the heat of August. I wanted to invite her to our place. My secret world also influenced my everyday: I very much wanted to invite each agreeable individual into our community. If the face of a good person became enveloped by the fog of concern, I wanted to help that person at once. But I could only help them in one way: by bringing the Great Li into their world. Birutė entered our place in an entirely simple way, her brown eyes were not surprised at all upon seeing our colourful community: some were naked, while others were clothed, some were slurping down cocktails, while others were drawing something on big sheets, though they didn't know how to draw, still others simply rested with their eyes closed, sometimes breathing in air and trying to taste it.

"God, how simple everything is," she said at once. "Even when alone, I don't know how to relax like that."

Birutė was the last person whom the Great Li allowed to enter our place.

"We all go together, and together we carry our world," the Great Li taught. "We've gone far, and each time it is harder to return even temporarily to the world of incorrect thinking. But it is not possible any more for people from that world to enter ours. Upon seeing us, they would be frightened and become angry. They would trample us, out of fear and jealousy. Incorrect thinking encourages intolerance."

At times I felt uncomfortable that we were so separate, that mutual breathing was only possible in such a small community as ours. There were barely two dozen of us who gathered together, and in most cases I only saw their second world, while never hearing anything about their first one, and I didn't want to, as I already knew what had driven us there.

We were all children of our time. We were all like twins, although with different goals, different minds, different souls. We were all united by the loss of the great belief. Earlier we believed or at least really really wanted to believe, but the world had destroyed that belief of ours. Those who had never believed or never wanted to believe didn't join our community. They were fine with living in the first world. It's very easy to live without believing in anything, though it is dreary. But dreariness can be tamed, filled with intoxicating substances, and more or less endured until one's death. It's worse when on top of that, the dreariness is shrouded by a feeling of loss. Then it's only the Great Li who can save you.

We were all wilted flowers. Some of us wanted too much, while some of us could do too little. Some of us didn't agree to keep to the rules of incorrect thinking, while some of us tried to keep to them, but our natures wouldn't allow it. We all had experienced God's Grand Injustice.

"There is no such thing as God's Grand Injustice," the Great Li taught me patiently. "God is neither right, nor wrong. A person is not good, bad, weak or great. A person is who he is, and should be proud of that. You lament that you didn't find a place in the world of incorrect thinking. That's nonsense. After all, you don't hang yourself because you don't know how to play chess, while others do. Why do you lament that you don't know how to play the chess of incorrect thinking? Why do you blame poor God? In the world, there is not only chess – you see that yourself now, you feel that yourself, you smell that yourself. There is no God's Grand Injustice. You are just you, and you are right."

That was the first time that – very very briefly – a thought popped into my head, that the second teacher of my life categorically contradicted the first, and I didn't want to lose either of them, even though their ideas were incompatible.

Laima's beauty was her God's Grand Injustice. Already at fourteen or fifteen she felt that she was particularly beautiful. At the beginning, like every beautiful girl, she was very proud of it, but then – as a rare beauty – she wanted to be judged for things other than her beauty. Laima was disgusted by all the varieties of careers for professional beauties: from the actress who couldn't act at all, to the wife of some famous person – not to mention the oldest profession in the world. She wanted to be judged not for her beauty, but for her soul, that her person would be respected. She didn't want to be considered a living doll. She didn't understand who had placed this desire in her brain. She tried to write poems, she tried to become a famous psychologist, but each time she experienced with horror that all of her achievements were worthless, that the most important thing was her beauty. Men went wild over her, but Laima shoved them all away, until one clever guy appeared, who understood her secret. She would have lived happily with him, unfortunately the clever guy apparently ended up not being so clever: during an inconsequential quarrel he, in his anger, revealed to his wife that he'd deceived her, his respect for her soul and talents was all a pretence. After her divorce she had contemplated burning her face with sulphuric acid, but thankfully she met the Great Li just in time. Laima's case was of course specific: she had a gift from God, but not of the kind she desired. Crying and sobbing she explained to me that she would agree to be lame, bow-legged, a hunchback, if only she could be a famous artist or poet, or a scholar of some sort. Of course, she was lying without knowing it, but not out of malice – she simply had no idea of what it meant to live as a cripple.

I loved her in a refined way, as you love a work of art. Her body was like that – a warm, tender work of art. Sometimes I would ask her to take her clothes off – just to admire her. Really. All I did was admire her. In our community that was possible, we broke flawed rules: a man could admire a beautiful naked woman, and no one thought twice about being surprised or teasing, that they'd jump her right then and there. Laima's body was a work of art. It would have been perverse to up and make love to her. You could only make love to her in the dark, without seeing her body.

A somewhat more usual, though sadder, story was that of chain-smoking Linukas. He surrendered to his unconquerable fear of violence, and despised himself for it, but there was nothing he could do about it. The fear was stronger than he was. He felt it for the first time while serving in the army. The veteran soldiers in his company didn't torment him, beat him or torture him too much, nevertheless he had to pass one exam of submission. A simple but unmistakable one. It was late autumn when, the entire company had colds and coughs after marching all night, the older soldiers smilingly invited him into the sergeants' room. There was a big polished table in the room. The old soldiers had spat all over it with white, yellow and green phlegm, and suggested Linukas clean it all up and make it shine, but only with his fingers, with his fingers! They didn't threaten him, didn't frighten him with anything, they just told him to clean the table, and that's all. Linukas said afterwards that he had dreamt of that task they gave him a hundred times, and cursed himself a thousand times. And yet he cleaned the table quite nicely, all the while cracking jokes.

That story, which anyone else would have forgotten as quickly as possible, tormented him his whole life. Linukas became a journalist. He wrote poignant, fearless, denunciatory articles – understandably adhering to what was possible to write at the time. He was persecuted and wronged, forever lacking money, walking around half-starved, but he didn't give in. If his resolve ever weakened, he would remember that story in the army and once again gain strength. Eventually he outdid himself and became a problem for the Kaunas mafia, no less. It seems he became a problem in a rather painful way: he was threatened by telephone, with letters, he was beaten up on the street twice, and had his little bachelor room set on fire.

The wise and agreeable public prosecutor even assigned security to him. It was then that Linukas started having hush money offered to him, with each week another ten thousand roubles being added to the sum. Linukas withstood it all, he even began to respect himself again, but one fine day he was called in by the wise and agreeable public prosecutor. At first he stunned Linukas by admitting nonchalantly that he belonged to the mafia. And then he started to paint the everyday life of prison and work camps for him vividly and minutely. With fine detail and black humour. Finally he declared that he was giving Linukas three weeks to think it over, and if he wouldn't stop after those three weeks, he would be put away.

Not only did Linukas drop his investigations, but within those three weeks he moved from Kaunas to Vilnius. He got out alive, walked around free, no one threatened him either by telephone or letters any more. Some unknown kind-hearted people even threw a pile of money into his letter box – almost half the sum that had been promised. You see, in their eyes he had shrunk to only half the man he had been. In Linukas's own eyes, he had dropped to zero; he had become a nameless man. He ritually burned the money, but it didn't help. He could no longer respect himself. Millions of people lived perfectly well, even prospered, without possessing any self-respect. Linukas couldn't live without it. As a result he didn't live, he existed or vegetated, until he met the Great Li.

I loved Linukas with a tender love, like a younger brother. I understood him – I too feared physical violence greatly. I feared it right up to the time of my death.

Our number also included Rimvydas, who couldn't recover after his thirty-year-old wife died slowly and torturously. There was Stasys, who at first tried to become a writer, then devoted himself to making obscene amounts of money, then became a skirt-chaser, and finally said to hell with everything in the world, except for the Great Li. There was Margarita, the old maid with horrible make-up and an incredibly pure soul, who just wanted to take care of us all. There were three professional female musicians, who in unison confirmed that our community was closer to music than anything else in the world. I didn't know the stories of most of the members of our community, but I saw in all of their eyes the same sign, the mark of hopelessness, loss and spiritual hunger. I even saw it while looking in the mirror. We were all children of our time. The first world spit white, yellow and green phlegm over us all and mockingly made faces at us. In it a single person was nothing but empty space, worse than an empty space – at least nothing was demanded of such a space.

In the second world we were all close, we were all important, each person knew that the wheel of the world would stop without him or her.

"Without each of you the wheel of the world would stop," the Great Li taught. "Each person is indispensable, each is the most important. Incorrect thinking often forces you to feel remorse that you are worthless, insignificant, unwanted. Incorrect thinking lies. Each person is worthy, great and indispensable. Everyone needs him. He has to share his wealth, his health, his very being with others."

Li would validate all of his statements by his living example. He truly didn't begrudge us his health: his extrasensory efforts would totally drain him, but he still assisted each person who needed help.

In this way he also differed from you. You always taught abstractly, often failing to apply your lessons to yourself.

Do you at least remember what you taught me? Sometimes I think that you knew an endless amount of intelligent things, but you didn't believe in them yourself.

Perhaps all teachers in our world can only teach what they don't believe in themselves?

That year I felt at ease and was happy. The only thing that proved difficult was to communicate with the first world on a daily basis. All of the community's members were being pulled more and more to Madagascar or some such place, or even better – to some totally uninhabited island.

We began to entirely lose touch with the everyday world, which we increasingly dropped out of. This concerned me, and concerned the Great Li too.

"Of course, one can establish communes or kibbutzim," he reasoned casually, "but that's not my style. It's far too simple to run away. It's precisely here that we need to create more of these kinds of circles – in the cities, in the bustle. We need to set up branches of paradise in the middle of hell. Of course, it's necessary to unwind, to relax a little bit. We'll arrange that as well."

Back then you taught me that the inner changes of a person or community of people are first of all revealed by language. All you have to do is carefully follow what new words, sayings, grammatical constructions, and comparisons appear in the language, and you'll figure out at once how people's way of thinking has changed or what the new government's ambitions are. You examined the classic example of bureaucratic newspeak with relish. At that time this made a big impression on me, I followed the speech of all of my acquaintances for a few weeks and joyfully reached some conclusions, some of which were too sweeping.

I was compelled to, I was forced to notice how the Great Li's manner of speaking gradually changed. He began to travel more and more to other cities of the Union, though he still considered Vilnius to be the centre of his activities. From every trip he brought back new words, new comparisons, new phrases. Some sort of half-military, half-aristocratic sayings appeared in his speech. I was forced to notice this, but I had probably been blinded. I had looked for meaning for far too long, I had worked too hard to earn it to analyse calmly and retain the faculty of doubt. I had worked too hard to tap into the mutual breathing, I didn't have the strength to distance myself from myself and look at everything as an outside observer. And then I didn't want to have my eyes opened any further.

That's how man is made. His sense of self-preservation doesn't allow him to start seeing clearly, it forces him to fool himself, to see reflections of heaven in places where they haven't existed for a long time.

And the Great Li changed markedly, he became smaller and smaller. Now I understand this well. There's a lot in my life I understood too late. Sometimes it seems to me that in my life I understood everything too late. I would always fail to see the most obvious warning signs.

"Man must refuse his sense of property," the Great Li taught. "You're not allowed to feel that your things belong only to you, that your wife belongs only to you, that your body belongs to you alone. You need to share absolutely everything generously. Otherwise you will remain alone – just as you are in the world of incorrect thinking. You can't perceive your generosity as some sort of tax or tribute. As long as you think that, don't share anything. Only when you feel that sharing absolutely everything is just as natural for you as breathing is, will you know that you've stepped into the kingdom of freedom."

Later it was said that our community spent all our time carrying out immoral and depraved acts, and did things bordering on sodomy. It was all rumour and hearsay. Those relaxation camps did happen, but I barely took note of them. We were essentially the same at those as we were in Vilnius, but we no longer had to leave for the mundane first world every day. That was all. During those two weeks we experienced as much freedom and naturalness as we were able to collect in half a year or so in Vilnius. Li was able to rip off almost all of our armour. I myself have sat in a bed of moss and watched how a couple drunk on freedom made love next to me naturally and beautifully. That did happen at times. But it wasn't a rule or our aim. And what's more, it wasn't immoral as most people understand it. We didn't belong to that majority, we didn't have that concept in our heads at all. We rejected numerous conventions of our own free will. Even when I saw Virginija in someone's embrace, I wouldn't have felt either jealousy or mortification, or even a feeling that that was immoral or forbidden. She belonged just as much to me as she did to all the other members of the community. She loved me just as much as all the other members of the community.

That mutual love didn't need to express itself physically, but if it did express itself in precisely that way – that would be natural. If you'd felt shame, mortification or anger because of it, you would simply have needed to leave the community. But not one of the community's members experienced such feelings. We had truly come far. We were very proud of that. We felt that there aren't horrible things in and of themselves, that they are only made horrible by people's views and judgements. Life, unfortunately, once again confirmed this: some suspicious characters found out about our second camp, they crammed into two cars and showed up with quite clear intentions. Their faces were distorted with lust and a sense of their power. Then for the first time I saw how much we needed ju-jitsu and kung fu masters. They finally carried out their mission. The camp was hopelessly ruined, nausea and bitterness was left inside each of us, but did that make us guilty? Were we guilty because our natural existence caused dirty thoughts for those men who turned up? I think that those people and people similar to them spread indecent rumours about us. I swear that we never did anything indecent; we did only what was beautiful, pure and natural.

Now I indulge in hopeless speculations about what would have happened later, if the rumours and hearsay about us hadn't spread. Would we have been able to maintain our mutual breathing? Would the Great Li have become what he became? Or perhaps after driving him out, would we have maintained our mutual breathing without him?

After those camps we would once again return to the first world and slave away from morning to night. That's how it was, because in the evening we hurried to the community. I know that I won't be able to express the feeling of that community, that feeling of mutual breathing, but I will try to. I think that it worked like drugs.

It was enough to open the door of the meeting room, see familiar faces, hear familiar voices – and bliss would slowly overtake me. It would first overtake my toes, then my ankles and knees. That was the feeling, really it was: it seemed you were slowly wading into the waters of bliss, until you immersed yourself entirely. Sometimes you weren't able to make yourself relax, you were too tired or irritated. Then you would have to call for the Great Li's help. However, you would certainly plunge into bliss. That was the only reason you went to the community and you were never disappointed. You could pay a lot of money for it. God knows, it acted like a drug.

However, all drugs cause a horrendous withdrawal syndrome. Nothing is given for free in this world. You have to pay for everything. It was enough to briefly leave the community – and horrendous chaos would befall you.

I am mixing things up, I am totally mixed up, Tomas. I can't remember the details any more, I can't judge anything, everything's all confused inside me. I didn't sense when the Great Li became a crook. I didn't sense when I started to love Birutė. I didn't even notice how my son disappeared from my life, that big-headed, droopy-eared Levukas.

Most likely it was only after seeing that Levukas barely lit up, when I visited him (he had been living at my mother-in-law's place for a long time already), he hardly found anything to ask me, anything to talk to me about, and for the first time after those years of sweetness, I felt terrible. I was beset by withdrawal symptoms.

There was no place for children in the Great Li's teaching. The world he created could only stand in one place, hover in a sweetish mist. Our community could only exist in itself, enjoy itself, but couldn't give birth to anything more. It's easy to philosophise about it now, it's easy to feel omniscient, but at the time I simply freaked out; I felt I had lost something very important. I looked at Levukas's big head, his accusing eyes, I tried to get into his good graces in every way, but he sat on the sofa in the pose of a wrathful little god and refused to forgive me. What surprised me even more is that even Father-in-Law unexpectedly appeared to be more humane than I was.

"You totally abandoned your son," he sighed as he stepped into the room. "Why did you have him? My God, if I had a son…"

That time I slipped away from Father-in-Law's home, and didn't get involved in a conversation, but a seed of anxiety was sown in my heart. I understood that once again I was doing something wrong. I tried to meditate on it, reason incoherently, but everything ultimately had got all mixed up my head. I didn't know any more which direction to go in, I couldn't think of where to go.

And I dropped by your place, I dropped by suffering from those withdrawal symptoms.

I knew the whole time where you lived, I had stumbled around by your home dozens of times, but I had never even stepped through the entry door. That time I would have stepped in, I would have come up the stairs, pressed the doorbell bravely. I would have told you everything, I would have asked your advice...

It's very easy to philosophise about things that didn't happen. I met you by chance as you were coming home. You came in rather miserable and angry. You greeted me barely nodding your head, and looked at me with such indifferent, meaningless eyes that I froze on the spot. Not only didn't you look happy to see me, you didn't take an interest in me, not the slightest spark of feeling or thought flashed in your eyes. You looked at me like I was an empty space and in the same moment you forgot me.

That late afternoon you killed me.

You were the only person who could have weaned me off those despicable spiritual drugs. However, you pushed me away. I suffered for another day or two, but then... What can a drug addict do? I once again hurried to the community, I felt once again how that bliss overtook me gradually: from my toes – and higher, and higher, and higher...

My son didn't end up saving me. The effects of those horrendous drugs of the spirit were too strong and suffocating. I was on the verge of becoming cognisant for just one moment. Then everything at once plunged again into the mist, because I was visited by my nightmarish love.

I left my son alone against the entire world. History repeated itself: I also had had to figure everything out myself. I was elated when he was born, I planned a miraculous future for him, I strove to create a world for him in which it would be worth living, but in the end I abandoned him like some sort of soulless object.

That was perhaps the greatest misdeed of my life.

I shouldn't have had children at all. Failures and the damned have no right to reproduce their image in this world.

The Fourteenth: about love and
death – with melancholic well-wishing

*Let a thousand arrows be shot at man, he
will not die, if his hour has not arrived. But
if his hour has arrived, he can die from a
grain of dust.*

At first true love seems like a joke, but it ends far too
seriously, tragically even. It breaks out during a time of
inner turmoil, hatches like a wet little bird, it's unexpected
and inexplicable, because the time of turmoil itself is
inexplicable, it is itself like an unfunny and stupid joke.

I fell in love with Birutė, whom I had known for three
years, whom I myself had brought to the community and
whom I had almost forgotten; she became the same as all
the others, I would discern her pure smile among the crowd
of concentrated faces only on some rare occasions.

There isn't another smile like Birutė's in the entire world.

My sudden love was boundless, its traits were far too
noble, far too intangible for it to be possible to fully describe
them. At the time I wouldn't have been able to fully recount
them, because that love was my hands and feet, my body
and blood, my thoughts and dreams. My entire being was
made up purely of love. I can't fully describe it now either,
because it's far away now, it seems like a sequence from a
shocking and gruesome film even to me.

Only one thing will I tell you, but it will reveal the depth
of that love of mine: it dispelled all of the narcotic charms.
In an instant it conquered those horrendous withdrawal
symptoms. My love was stronger than everything in the

world. For a whole two years I had slowly dissolved in the narcotic smoke of our community, it seemed like no one would dispel it any more, but love dispersed that fog at once. It pushed out the stupid and imagined bliss, because it was itself an even greater bliss – suffering diluted by sweetness. I began to look around at my surroundings, unable to understand much of anything. I taught at the technical institute and made enough to feed myself. Virginija, who was already a PhD candidate and group leader, earned a bit more than me, but all the rest went to the Great Li. She had given herself up to him body and soul. But for me the Great Li and the entire community suddenly became a part of the routine. The first, everyday world slowly, but unavoidably swallowed up the second. I saw that Li imperceptibly turned into the president of some grand corporation. And Father-in-Law became my best friend. He would come to visit and shoot the breeze (he would come of his own accord!), I would answer his questions, laugh at his jokes and unwittingly thought that this kind of friendship was possible only in our world: the friendship of the executioner with his victim, the friendship of a mouse with a cat. It broke all the rules of nature and ethics, but it really did exist: I talked with him sincerely, I didn't fear him in the least any more, I no longer felt hatred or contempt towards him. He was just a handsome man getting older, looking frustratedly for a non-existent son in me, though he knew well that I would never be one. Sometimes Father-in-Law would turn into a kind-hearted uncle who had been through a lot. "God, why did I make such an effort, what was I fighting for," he would say then. "I did a lot, I achieved a lot, but what was it all for? You're right – you need to eat, drink and make love. Everything else is just nonsense and vanity."

When he said this, he had our community in mind. That was how he understood it. He knew about it long before. Father-in-Law always knew about everything. He seemed quite pleasant, I would think that he was simply tired, that he'd like to relax. Sometimes I even thought that before retiring he would suddenly start doing a lot of good works.

But I would only think like that for a moment. The feeling of power would once again prevail inside Father-in-Law.

"One day I'm going to give that Chinaman of yours a good beating!" he would declare ominously. "He has gone way too far!"

And he would have beaten him up, beaten him up badly, if Virginija hadn't threatened to commit suicide. She said that she would kill herself so calmly that even Father-in-Law himself was rattled. He threatened and foamed at the mouth, but he secretly protected Li from trouble. And it was occurring more and more often – the shadow-like ju-jitsu and kung fu fighters were punishing wrongdoers in one place, and then another. Those wrongdoers were from our own fold. I couldn't understand that at all. I tried asking Li, and I tried to wring information out of the victims of these beatings, but they refused to speak. I was enveloped in a stifling silence, and it was only Father-in-Law who would speak to me.

What world had I ended up in? Was it possible to understand it?

It wasn't even possible to understand my love, just as it's impossible to understand any true love. Yes, I had loved Virginija once. She remained a familiar person to me even now. But that other love was natural and healthy. This new love of mine was stifling, sickly and forbidden. Having started to fall in love with Birutė, I stood against our entire community. I suddenly felt that I didn't love everyone the same any more, because I loved her. I couldn't feel like we did earlier, when we all loved Birutė. One day I realised that I alone loved her, that this love of mine was mine alone, and not the community's, not everyone's, but mine, mine alone.

In an instant even the community disappeared. My gaze

followed only her. All of my speeches were imperceptibly directed towards her. I became excited each time I saw her, I even became excited while hearing someone talk about her. I even loved whatever she'd touched. I loved the glass she'd drunk from. I wasn't surprised in the least that I had found her so suddenly, though she had always been nearby. It could only be like that, because she was precisely like that.

Her eyes were the tenderest and most spiritual in the whole world.

She walked pure as an angel among us, the unclean and the imperfect. Even when she undressed at our meetings or camps, no one suddenly yearned to touch her, or to sully her in the least. Nor did they want to touch Laima, because she was like a sculpture, like a work of art. Nevertheless it was possible to make love to her at night, in total darkness. But it wasn't even possible to graze Birutė, as she was like a vestal virgin, everyone understood that. She didn't walk, but glided, raised slightly above the earth's surface. She was protected by Li himself.

On those days of desperate love I could envision people's faces very well. In the everyday bustle, people surround you like ghosts, like indistinct signs. You neither take note of them, nor remember their faces. But on those days I was surrounded by expressive faces that weren't similar to one another. You could say an original, totally different way of seeing things had opened up within me. I saw Virginija's face: thin, exhausted, with fearful eyes, with a wandering, preoccupied gaze. I saw Father-in-Law's face: angular, with protruding cheekbones, his eyes teeming with phantasmagorical spores. But what frightened me the most was Li's face. I remember him well just as I saw him the first time: expressive, almost noble, with hypnotic eyes. Now he had changed unrecognisably. Over two years Li had put on a little weight, his expressive facial muscles, dimples, sharp features had smoothed out. It was as though his face had dimmed, lost its impact. His strange nobility had been supplanted by a boundless belief in himself. His eyes didn't give off the same hypnotic radiance any more. His glance became controlling, dictatorial, no longer enchanting, but only stifling.

The Great Li's eyes became similar to Father-in-Law's eyes.

All I could have done in the throes of love was to perhaps vaguely sense it, since that wasn't what was in my head and heart at all – but suddenly I realized that the Great Li was slowly turning into a small Father-in-Law. I was totally stunned by the though. I had freed myself from a suffocating spell, and I had slowly started to think again. I was unexpectedly able to view our community from the outside and I saw a grim picture. In a grey, rocky desert under a low, heavy sky a cocksure Korean, plagued by a mania for greatness, led a small group of people – without any goal, without any direction, in crooked zigzags. And those people followed him from behind like a herd of sheep. To be honest, I didn't care at all, I didn't care about any of them in the least, but in that herd, raised a bit above the earth's surface, Birutė was also hovering.

That image tormented me day and night. I couldn't see any mountains with that inner gaze any more, and didn't want to climb anywhere any more. I first of all had to escape from that grey rocky desert, and then... I didn't even try to think about what was going to happen next. But I didn't need to think, I had to wrest Birutė from them, I had to kidnap her, she was the only one I cared about. I had a concrete, clear goal, that was my salvation. I knew full well what I had to do. I talked to Birutė with my shaking voice, I caressed her hands with my trembling fingers. I didn't even know if she had managed to really fall in love with me. She was enchanted and spellbound by the Great Li, she was getting a high from spiritual narcotics, which had until recently been having the same effect on me. We would meet at the technical institute every day, I besieged her like a demon, I talked constantly to her, I simply didn't let go of her hand, I tried to pour my inner waves into her. My technical institute colleagues would throw us contemptuous glances, but I didn't care, all I saw was her. It was only occasionally that I thought about how I must have looked to them: Father-in-Law's son-in-law, the member of some sort of sect, who was messing around in the most open of ways with a melting Birutė. We would kiss in the stairwell of the technical institute. My colleagues were kind and simple people. They most likely called Virginija anonymously, and if they were able to get through the assistants and other hounds of Hades, they may even have reached Father-in-Law himself. However, it was all the same to me. All I cared about was Birutė. Birutė was my whole world. Until then I hadn't experienced a true, all-encompassing and all-consuming love, but now I was revelling in and suffering from it. My first love for Virginija seemed as bland and trivial as a potato pancake. It was an ordinary, biologically natural passion. But now I had experienced Love. Like every true love, it couldn't be happy. Birutė pressed herself up to me, caressed me with her heavenly smile, but evening would inevitably approach, her eyes would gradually become glassy, she would start to sigh wistfully – and all my efforts would fail to save her, she would slowly be seized by the pernicious sorcery of the Great Li. I didn't have the power to say to her: don't go there, let's stay together. I didn't have the power to force her, inside her the power to make herself stay was no longer there. She wanted to stay with me, but she couldn't. She had stayed with me numerous times, but it was just her body that stayed. Birutė's eyes would glaze over, she wouldn't hear anything I was saying, she was plagued by a horrible hunger for those spiritual narcotics. She would want to overcome it, but she couldn't. I was going out of my mind. A fierce, invisible battle was taking place between me and the Great Li. We didn't say a word about it to one another. We didn't throw evil glances at each other, but the tension between us continued to grow, I would barely approach him, and the shadowy ju-jitsu and kung fu masters would become anxious, as they moved like his tentacles. Now the Great Li was barely distinguishable from them, and they truly became his extensions, powerful and menacing slithering tentacles. I wanted to tell him directly to hand Birutė over to me. But I was afraid of him. Love blinds and intoxicates you, but it did leave me my mind. It seemed to me that he would rather stab her than give her to me.

Perhaps such a thought seems silly and neurotic to you. All I can do is say one thing: you didn't know the Great Li, you didn't see his slithering shadowy tentacles up close. He could have committed any sort of monstrosity. The only thing that surprised me was that he didn't do anything to me. It was only later that I understood why he didn't dare touch me, though he desired to very much. The Great Li had not been great for a long time, and for a long time he hadn't been any sort of guru. He had become a mini-tyrant, a tiny dictator. At the beginning he treated and took care of all of us, he had a sacred aim, but gradually even he was infected by the horrible phantasmagorical spores. I was horrified by this discovery. Even a semi-underground sect wasn't able to avoid those spores. They infiltrated everything, they could even destroy a community whose goal was to fight against those spores! I became alarmed: most likely even my love could be beaten by them. The Great Li was undermined by them in a very simple way. He felt a thirst for power, and that defeats everything in a man.

Now I know full well: people can be divided up the most accurately by whether they have the desire for power or they don't. That's the most important distinction. If all a person desires is to become leader of the pack, then a beastly biological instinct is dominant in him. And you have to guard yourself against such a person as you would a wild beast.

But you will never fully defend yourself against such a

person, such beasts wait in ambush, stab you in the back or bite your throat. Let it be a lesson for you, Tomas: never feel safe, never let your guard down, keep one eye open even while you're sleeping.

I almost felt a real threat, but I continued to calm myself down. I didn't have to calm myself down that much: as soon as I saw Birutė, the whole world disappeared. I would see only her. I couldn't compare her to anything, there was only her, nothing more. She was tall, almost as tall as I was. When we met, our faces touched, I could kiss her on the lips without bending over at all. We didn't need to talk, as we understood each other from our eyes. We both knew that we couldn't survive without one another. We both knew that we were like a living future for one another. Without her I would have fallen to pieces, I didn't have any sort of future, there were just dead ends everywhere. Frozen corpses walked around me, I myself was as cold as a corpse, if I pressed a cup of tea in my palm, it would cool in an instant, because an icy cold emanated from me. But Birutė was alive. Unsullied blood pulsated in her, she would bring me back to life, hold me in her embrace, until my breath became warm again.

"I already thought that there couldn't be anything more in my life," she would say quietly, "later it seemed to me that our community could still exist there. Only now do I see why I have lived: so I could meet you. Don't leave me, I will suffocate without you. I will wilt like a flower without water. Don't leave me!"

That's how she talked! How could a family or the Great Li, Father-in-Law or even big-headed, droopy-eared Levukas compare in this situation?

He kidnapped Birutė in an ambush, I was expecting it, I was almost waiting for it. One day I didn't find her at the technical institute, and at the personnel department I found out: she had asked for unpaid leave because of a pressing family matter.

A family matter! She didn't have a mother, a father, a husband or children. She only had me, and she didn't say a word to me! When Great Li disappeared from Vilnius as well, it was all clear, but I couldn't understand how she was taken away: had he drugged her? Put her under a spell? Tied her up? Yesterday, just yesterday we had dreamt about a future that no one could take away from us. And the next day she'd gone.

I ran through Vilnius like a madman, I ran around to all the members of the community, but they just looked at me sullenly and glumly shrugged their shoulders. It was only the next morning I saw that Virginija wasn't at home either. I once again ran around to the flats of acquaintances, I begged on my knees for help, but all their eyes looked at me strangely and indifferently. I had already lost hope, but I was saved by a rather tipsy Linukas. He was rolling around on the carpet in his flat with the door unlocked. He'd been drinking for a week, hadn't gone to work, and in general had it in for the entire world.

"I can't detect any smells again!" he declared sombrely, barely able to move his tongue. "I figured out that Korean rat long ago, but I was afraid of saying something. You're fine – he's afraid of you or to be more precise, he's afraid of that father-in-law of yours. But what about me? Before bolting, he collected money, and those who didn't give anything were roughed up by his rangers. They pulverised them until each of them gave up what they had."

Linukas definitely wasn't a dumb guy, he even put together a rather coherent thought while being quite tipsy. While seeing me out, he told me what I most likely already knew myself.

"That Korean rat doesn't give a shit about Birutė. And he doesn't give a shit about you. But he can't lose. He can't imagine that he could lose. And he will win, you'll see. Take care, Levas, he will definitely win. If there's anything that he does have, it's strength."

That same day I hightailed it to Leningrad, assisted by a fervent and zealous ally. In a flash Father-in-Law took care of the tickets, a room in a hotel for high-ranking officials, wrote down an entire page of important telephone numbers, which were to save me in any situations that might arise. I didn't understand right away what drove Father-in-Law to do all this. Of course, I told him I was looking for Virginija – but who was I trying to fool? Father-in-Law knew everything, he must have known everything. In all of that confusion he didn't even mention Virginija, he just cursed the Great Li. Suddenly I understood what was driving him forward, what caused his vehement rage. He saw a threat to his power. He saw that a different ruler was emerging – though he wasn't prominent, he was nevertheless still able to exhibit stronger control over a group of a dozen or so people than even Father-in-Law could himself. Li had to be trounced and destroyed. Father-in-Law armed me in royal fashion. I could have even called Romanov himself. I could have called some general or other and, if I needed it, got a company of soldiers. Father-in-Law sent me off to storm Leningrad.

For the second time I found myself in that mysterious city. My sister Stanislova lived there. Now somewhere in its depths were both loves of my life. Through the fog I saw streets and people, I got a luxury suite in an old-style hotel, hopelessly thumbing through Linukas's sheets of barely decipherable addresses and not wanting anything more in my life. I remained there only because I couldn't imagine what I was supposed to do if I returned to Vilnius. I no longer had strength or desire. My defective invalid heart pulsated irregularly, the autumnal chill penetrated me even in that warm hotel room. I don't know why, but I felt that it was all over. I still loved Birutė, but I felt that she didn't exist any more, that she had been swallowed up by a terrifying dragon. It had swallowed up her big watery eyes, her heavenly smile, it had swallowed up my love, my boundless human will. I felt old and powerless, though I was only twenty-seven years old. I couldn't dive headlong into battle any more, and didn't even know who I was supposed to fight against. I sat in that two-room luxury suite and ate crab salad, washing it down with pineapple juice: hotel standards decided my menu for me. There was even a red state telephone next to my bed. I very well could have called Romanov or even Brezhnev himself. I could have explained what I thought about them and about that entire system of theirs. But I didn't want to. I didn't even want to write letters to anyone any more. I was already dead.

It turns out that even the dead still have willpower. Or at least they don't lose their logic. I had six addresses that were written down by Linukas, but I had to hit the target on the first shot. If I started to wander blindly, Li would be able to hide from me. I contemplated for a good while how to guess where his lair was, until I found a simple but genius solution. Li liked to have absolutely everything within easy reach. In Vilnius he based himself in our flat and slept there, because it was in the very centre. I chose the address on Nevsky Prospekt and hit the nail right on the head. The street number didn't mean anything to me, but as I approached the grey building with moulded cornicing and decorative balconies, I understood that I had been here before. My sister had lived here, right up on the third floor, just in a different stairwell. The door was opened by one of Li's tentacles. His pupils became constricted at once, his face however remained stone-like.

"Traitors!" he growled through his teeth. "And I had hoped to turn them into true people!"

For him, true people were those that obeyed him blindly. He'd torn us from the grasp of the everyday, but he did that only so he could enslave us, so he could rule over us. Now he ruled in an old and elegant flat. The flat was enormous, just like my sister's flat had been. A wall clock in an engraved encasement struck nine. It counted the last hours of my life. Birutė sat on the couch, she glanced at me with fear and hope, but said nothing. Virginija was also there, continually making and bringing everyone tea. She hurried around here and there like some sort of robot.

"What do you want?" Li asked me mockingly. "Do you want the vestal maiden shared by us all? Is that any way to act, Leo? And in full view of the woman who is still your wife?"

I felt only emptiness inside, a cosmic vacuum expanded inside me. What wife, I thought doubtfully, I haven't had a wife for a long time already. I thought I had found love, but I soon wouldn't have that any more either. So what do I have? Myself? Just myself. It would have been better not to think that.

Most likely even an amoeba, even a virus, even a dying patient desires to live for as long as possible, to not lose themselves for as long as possible. Alas, you are the biggest virtue for yourself. The instinct of self-preservation rules each of us. I suddenly became scared. Li's smile didn't bode well for me, his kung fu tentacles were only waiting for a signal from him. I was paralysed by a horrific, hopeless fear. I was alone without any protection. Li thought that Father-in-Law's hand couldn't reach him here. Father-in-Law's hand did extend here as well, but he didn't know that, which is why he felt all-powerful. I suddenly understood that it would have been wise to come here with a company of soldiers. Naively I tried to escape, but a second later I was already on my knees in front of Li with my hands forced behind my back.

"Everyone obeyed," he said calmly and tenderly, "everyone understood the way things are in this world. But you became a rebel. So rebel! Fight! Rage! Let's agree to the following: fight as much as you are able. It will be difficult for you, but fight, fight until the end. If I see that you are fighting to the very last, if I see that your life isn't even important to you, if I see that – I will give your vestal virgin over to you. On the word of the Great Li! Fight! Show what you have!"

God knows, this is not easy for me to remember – partly because everything that was left was shrouded in a fog of boundless pain. I could write an epic poem about pain, terrible physical pain, but I'm not writing you a letter in order to cry floods of tears and look for solace. I simply want to tell my story.

Li turned to Birutė, bent down and said something to her. She shuddered, and Li looked at me, gave a crooked grin and bared those beastly teeth of his. He was checking to see whether I saw everything. Then he once again leaned towards her – Birutė had frozen where she sat, so he lazily got up and slapped her across the face lightly – in a symbolic and humiliating manner. He slapped her again, and again. I tried to free myself from his iron tentacles, I tried to kick him, I tried to bite the hands that were holding me back. They beat me in response. They kicked me calmly, in a professional manner, endlessly on target, striking the places where true Pain shot through me the most. I resisted. And they beat me once again. They were also like robots: they kicked me without anger, without passion, monotonously and indifferently. As soon as I stopped resisting, they would calm down. However, I continued to resist. I would rest and resist again.

Birutė saw everything, though probably the scene was not ghastly, what had to have been ghastly was just my face. What must have been apparent was Pain. Li continued smiling, while suddenly Birutė started undressing, undressing herself, no one was forcing her to, no one was tearing her clothes off, she was going naked slowly as in a dream, throwing her clothes casually to the floor, finally she was entirely naked and glanced at Li inquiringly – not at me, only at Li. He once again bent down to her saying something, Birutė froze, and he once again struck her across the face, this time harder, then again, and once again. I dived into Pain, I was drowning in it, and I may have yelled out, but then again maybe not. I didn't lose consciousness, my eyes didn't go dark, I saw everything even too vividly. Li's soulless tentacles didn't overwhelm me, they just rigorously and uniformly caused me Pain. But I still continued to resist. We spoke a strange language of Pain: as soon as I tried to escape, I was permeated by Pain, but as soon as I calmed down, Pain subsided. They struck me in the very same places, kicked right at Pain, it assumed different levels, it wasn't pain that it had turned into any more – I don't know what it had turned into. The longer I resisted, the slower Pain would recede upon calming down, it receded in cascades, in waterfalls, in tsunami waves. But I still continued to resist.

Li had already undressed. Pain bound me, froze my will, I saw everything, I saw everything very vividly: Li lay down on Birutė, she turned her head indifferently and finally looked at me, straight at me, silently yelling, shrieking, that she was being held by a power stronger than physical force, she called for my help, I struggled with all my might. Pain struck me in those very same places for the thousandth time, Li also looked at me, he had not yet started, astonishment and hesitation had started to slowly emerge in his eyes, he looked right into my soul, as only he was able to do, perhaps all I needed to do was to fight one last time, Birutė's eyes looked at me beseechingly, I felt that Li was hesitating, perhaps all I needed to do was try a few more times. But suddenly I thought what will happen if Pain never goes away. Li continued to be apprehensive. He looked right at me, observing my soul, waiting for it to totally disappear, probably that's what happened, I still had to continue struggling again and again, but wasn't able to. I could only think about Pain, which would never end, and I suddenly gave up. I froze to see whether Pain would subside, and that traitorous pause was my downfall: Li understood everything at once and read the signs of loss in my eyes. He had already started, and I was supposed to lunge forward, bite him in the throat; I commanded my muscles, but they didn't obey, they just revelled in the fact that Pain had subsided – in waterfalls, tsunami waves, a moment or two more, and it would recede entirely.

I wasn't being restrained any more, but it was already too late. Even having realised it, I kneeled humbly and with horror looked at the greatest shame of my life. Having already been released from the tentacles I was afraid to even move, just so Pain wouldn't return, which appeared to be stronger than my spirit, than my soul – than absolutely everything. And thus I remained kneeling humbly until the end, until it was all over, until Li rolled off Birutė's helpless body and glanced at me victoriously. I understood that I myself had lost, and Li understood that I understood that, which is why he said nothing, he just gawked at me contemptuously and began getting dressed.

And that entire time Virginija was making and bringing tea for everyone, she moved like an Egyptian mummy, inside of which someone had installed a wind-up device. The entire time she continued to make tea and just bring it around.

No one stopped me from leaving. I stopped in the archway and howled with the voice of a wild animal. I can't lie to you, here, on the other side, we can't lie or hide anything. I didn't resist to the very end. Li was depraved, but I wasn't much better – I didn't resist to the very end, I didn't attempt to resist, though no one killed me, there was a long way to go until then, I was simply beaten, faultlessly and monotonously kicked in the very same most painful and most sensitive places. I was the one who gave up, I understood this while still standing in the gateway. After all, while being kicked I didn't even lose consciousness. I was the perfectly gutless weakling, and I would have been broken on the very first night in Beria's basement. But Li was more refined than Beria: he didn't demand that I sign anything, he just demanded that I didn't move, that I do nothing.

It was a late chilly evening. I sat down on the stone pavement and was determined to wait. Perhaps at the time it seemed that Li would release Birutė, that I would wait for her and attempt to explain something to her. Perhaps that's what it seemed like, or perhaps I simply wanted to kill myself that way: sitting on those stones, until I turned into stone myself. Somewhere very close by my sister Stanislova was sleeping. I could have gone to her place, but I didn't want to. At one point I had genuinely been prepared to call in that company of soldiers, but the desire passed as well. I didn't want anything any more. I had already died, and all that was left to do was carry out the formalities.

In the morning I was taken by an ambulance that a kind-hearted old woman had called. I was still of a clear mind, though I already had a high fever. Those miraculous telephone numbers were in my pocket, I could have called Romanov himself, I could have lain down in the best ward in Leningrad, had the best medicine in the world pumped into me, but I didn't want to.

I was put in the corridor of an old crumbling hospital. At first I lay on the floor, then someone died, and I was brought a cot. Brown water flowed slowly and sadly through the cracked walls of the corridor. At the end of the corridor someone constantly moaned and shouted. My diagnosis was clear: pneumonia. I was given some sort of cloudy liquid from a dirty, poorly sterilised needle. I was feverish the whole time, but I wasn't delirious, I could still have called somebody, but I didn't want to. I didn't want to use any of Father-in-Law's telephone numbers. I didn't want to ask for any help from my sister. It seemed to me that I was finally the person that I really always had been: a droopy-eared kid from a semi-basement flat who was only destined for what he was destined for, nothing more.

On the second evening I started to wheeze severely. I

understood this in a hopelessly calm way. What could this minor suffering mean in comparison to the great suffering I had experienced a few days earlier. I saw in front of me not a wall washed away by muddy water, but a naked Birutė on a leather sofa, her screaming eyes, Li's ghostly smile. I most likely even wanted to die, I don't remember. I never would have tried to kill myself, but with a strange hope I calmly waited until death approached me itself.

Don't expect me to tell you something magnificent or horrible, Tomas. Death is simply a hideous thing, and that's that. When you die, don't expect any sort of lofty visions, pictures from your life or similar splendours: you'll experience how it all happens: it's very very hard, very very horrible, as you plunge into an abyss, and then are blinded by an endlessly bright, all-encompassing, unearthly light, while down below you already see a black and endless Valley of the Shadow of Death.

The Great Li was the last to say goodbye to me. His face shot out from that blinding, unearthly light and mumbled, "You will die of pneumonia."

He was right. My poor invalid heart ran out of oxygen. It would probably have been saved by the simplest of oxygen masks. But in that hospital there wasn't even a pillow to put under my head – just some sort of hard, dirty bundle. I died on the fourth of November, nineteen seventy-nine.

Amen.

I wrote a short letter to Emanuel Swedenborg. You'll find it of interest too.

Dear Maître!
Your writings are undoubtedly of great use simply because they reveal some of the rules of the afterlife. However, you lied ever so slightly, probably not out of ill will – perhaps the spirits that guided you through the afterlife gave you inaccurate information.

You state that fiery-faced angels appear in that blinding

unearthly light, that they talk with you, and ask if you are ready for death. There is nothing of the sort – in the best-case scenario some fucking Korean appears with his pseudo-prophecies, which were described to me a long time ago by a local therapist.

You write that man doesn't understand that he's already dead. That's also inaccurate. Of course, if they are waiting for their consciousness to shut off, then they will wait in vain. Even I, who had expected that I would be able to write these letters, understood at once that I had ended up on the other side.

I agree that on the other side feelings and thoughts crystallise and become cleansed. I agree entirely that your former life stands before your eyes in all its details, that you can't lie about it or hide anything.

However, I totally, categorically disagree that on the other side we are enlightened by the "divine light of understanding". That's a lie, a lie and once again a lie. After we die, we understand exactly the same amount as we understood while alive – in other words, we don't understand anything.

It's somewhat more interesting on earth than it is on the other side – even if you are fated to live in Vilnius. While living, you always have something in front of you, while on the other side everything is behind you. You can't change anything any more, you can only flip endlessly through the pages of the same book that's already been written.

Even with letters, all you can do is write them in your mind.

Even with epigraphs for your letters, all you can choose from are Hindu proverbs that are stuck in your head from the distant past.

I am jealous of you all, especially now, when you can do what I couldn't do back then. I bowed out, because I wasn't able to live any longer. I didn't kill myself, but I did give up.

And it would only be a non-life that would be left for one who has given up, even if he were to exist on earth.

I wasn't able to prevail, perhaps I wasn't able to concentrate properly.

I rely on you a lot, Tomas. You'll most probably understand me, if I tell you why: because you have a brain, but you don't have any desire for power.

Only people of this kind can do something good – even if they become government leaders.

Doing nothing but wasting your time and conserving your energy is not allowed. All I did was waste my time and conserve my energy. You saw what became of that.

I won't allow you to settle down. If you resign yourself to it, I will haunt you.

You can't trudge on calmly towards your death, certainly not because there's nothing at all on the other side, but because the thing or two that is here is so negligible that here on the other side, there's nothing left to do but to hopelessly long for your earthly life.

I hope to god that you never long for life as much as I am longing for it.

I hope to god that you don't despairingly understand that you're not going to live any more, that it'll get harder and harder for you to even witness the lives of others. You can't see a person when you want; for that to happen at the very least you need that person to think about you intensely. Later even that doesn't help, and then nothing helps: I lost sight of Virginija long ago, I don't know anything about her. I lost sight of Li Chin Chao long ago – I know that he apparently ended up in gaol or a madhouse, but that was long ago. Even you I see more indistinctly. I know that soon I won't see anything. Soon the entire world will disappear once and for all. You could say that I will die for the second time, all I will have is my past, my memories, my non-life. I'll no longer be able to write letters to anyone.

Think about me, remember me – even if it's just

sometimes. I don't ask anything more of you. Perhaps you'll be able to call me to you. Perhaps I will still be able to make you out at least once. I don't see you any more now, I don't see anything at all. I am unable to say anything more. Perhaps these are my last words.

The rest is silence.

1987–1988

Translator's Acknowledgements

As in most endeavours in life, there were numerous people that worked behind the scenes to make this translation a reality. I would like to thank Nijolė Gavelienė for entrusting me with the task of translating this monumental work, a novel that I had dreamed of translating for more than a decade. I would like to thank the Lithuanian Culture Institute for financial support, without which I would not have been able to finish the translation, and publisher Allan Cameron and everyone else at Vagabond Voices, who was willing to take on the task of bringing this novel out in English.

Several people were involved in the editing process. I would like to thank Inga Stirnaitė for looking through an initial draft of the first few chapters, Ernesta Kazekaitė and Tomas Mrazauskas for the many conversations over several months on various aspects of the book and the Soviet era. My biggest and heartfelt thanks go to Professor Violeta Kelertas, who went through the translation and supported me, and illuminated the text in a way that no other could.

Translator's Biography

Over the last fifteen years, Jayde Will has translated works on various aspects of Baltic history, culture, and society, along with its literatures. Recent or forthcoming translations include Latvian writer *Daina Tabūna's* short story collection *The Secret Box* (The Emma Press), Latvian poet *Inga Pizāne's* poetry collection *Having Never Met* (A Midsummer Night's Press), Latvian poet Eduards Aivars's collection *Phenomena* (Parthian Books), and Latvian poet Artis Ostups's collection *Gestures* (Ugly Duckling Presse). His articles, essays and short stories have been published or are forthcoming in *Words without Borders*, *In Other Words*, *Lituanus*, *satori.lv*, and *Kultūrzīmes*.

Remember the Translator!

Vagabond Voices continues to celebrate translations and its translators. It is proper that translators are occasionally invisible (particularly when the reader is busy suspending disbelief), as their task is to present the authors and not themselves to the reader. But the actual words are not the authors', but the translators', and it is also proper that the reader recalls the presence of this intricate and generous craft.

www.vagabondvoices.co.uk/think-in-translation